The Dimensions of Deceit

Divorced accountant Mark Markby's plans for a peaceful break by the sea in Aldeburgh are turned upside-down when by strange coincidence he meets his ex-wife Eve, who runs a local café. Markby stays on to help, and as the couple fall in love again even the jealousy of Eve's old school friend and business partner Moira cannot mar their happiness. Until the nasty anonymous telephone calls begin . . .

Then one night Markby hears that his London flat has been vandalized, so he rushes back to check on the damage. But when two policemen knock on the door it is not to investigate the break-in. Eve has been killed, and the police have arrived to arrest Markby for her murder.

In one savage blow, Markby's dreams of a happy future with Eve are shattered and he finds himself living every accused man's worst nightmare. Then the case of Regina versus Markby begins. And while the prosecuting counsel impresses the court with the evidence gathered against him, Markby fears that his heartfelt plea of 'not guilty' is doomed. As the rigorous verbal battles of the courtroom intensify Markby realizes that his only hope lies in finding out what really happened on the night Eve died. But how . . . ?

Both an ingenious murder mystery and compelling court-room drama, *The Dimensions of Deceit* is a crime thriller of the highest order.

The Dimensions of Deceit

Miles Tripp

MACMILLAN
LONDON

First published 1993 by Macmillan London Limited
a division of Pan Macmillan Publishers Limited
Cavaye Place London SW10 9PG
and Basingstoke

Associated companies throughout the world

ISBN 0–333–60064–9

9 8 7 6 5 4 3 2 1

A CIP catalogue for this book is available from
the British Library

Phototypeset by Intype, London
Printed by Mackays of Chatham, PLC

PART I

1

The town can be bleak in winter when a piercing wind whips down from the Arctic over the wastes of the North Sea, but there's a rugged defiance in the houses which huddle together like a small peasant army confronting eternal and unconquerable forces. If the wind veers to the north-east, and strengthens in force, residents put storm-boards outside houses on the sea-front before darting back to the warmth indoors. When the wind is in this direction the sea, pounding a narrow shingle beach, may among the millions of pebbles wash up one or two little pieces of the translucent fossil resin known as amber.

The sea encroaches year by year and has already swallowed half the town as it existed in the Middle Ages. Eventually, concrete defences or not, the town will lose its long battle and disappear from the map of East Anglia. I'm referring to Aldeburgh, renowned for its music festivals, but unknown as the place where one of the worst catastrophes – if not the very worst – which can crush a man, befell me.

I'd gone there to get away from things, as the saying goes, and to sort myself out. A bit of peaceful contemplation, even self-analysis, was required. I wanted a direction, a purpose. I badly needed a purpose. Aldeburgh was a town I'd known since childhood and apart from going to the music festivals I'd spent many holidays there. The air is pure and invigorating, and I've always left Aldeburgh feeling refreshed and more at peace. It was the obvious choice of venue for interior monologues about direction and purpose.

I booked in at a sea-front hotel on a night early in May. The following morning after breakfast I went for a stroll along the beach north of town, my eyes scanning the shingle for anything

3

unusual in the hope of finding something more interesting than common flint or milky quartz pebbles. I'd never been lucky enough to find amber but possessed a small collection of cornelians and banded agates.

Every so often I paused to look around. It was a fine morning and the sky was half-filled with clouds sailing very slowly out to sea like a fleet of stately galleons under the guidance of a navigator who couldn't make up his mind which direction to take.

I could identify with that imaginary navigator.

Apart from one on-shore fisherman there was nobody to be seen. A ship on the horizon looked like a black ant glued to a taut thread stretched across the placid grey-green sea. Small waves broke on the beach and then washed back in a softly sighing undertow.

During breaks from beachcombing I lapsed into reverie and let me say at once that I'm not about to indulge in self-pity. I don't pity myself, and I don't want anyone's pity, but for the purpose of what was to happen it is necessary to mention that three events had come together to shatter my life. All had occurred within the space of twenty-four hours. During this short span my four partners in a firm of chartered accountants practising in the City of London had been convicted of theft, false accounting and conspiracy to defraud; my wife had left a note to say she'd gone to Spain to be with her lover; and I had a telephone message from France informing me that our only child, Joanna, aged twenty, had been killed in a car crash on Autoroute Six. Stephen, her boyfriend, who was driving, had been badly injured but would survive.

Until the Fraud Squad began their investigation I was completely unaware of my partners' criminal behaviour and, because I believe that dishonesty is a stain on the reputation of my profession, I assisted the Squad by providing some vital evidence they needed. On conviction three partners accepted their sentences impassively but the fourth, Harry Feldman, sentenced to a longer term of imprisonment than the others because he had masterminded the operations, shouted at me from the dock, 'I'll fix you one day!' Not long afterwards I received a typewritten note: 'This is to warn you to watch your back. He who uses the knife will have the knife used on him. Any time, any place, anywhere.' The

4

note was unsigned. I showed it to my solicitor, Mr Frobisher, who said that if I received any more threats I should contact him again and he'd notify the police, but I heard no more from the anonymous writer.

Feldman hadn't been alone in condemning my honest conduct, my professional probity; there were others who felt I had shopped, grassed, been a Judas and a copper's nark. However, to a precious few I was a man of integrity, and it was for these loyal few that I still prepared accounts. Not surprisingly perhaps, I was unable to get another job in London. I was *persona non grata* in the City.

As for my wife's desertion, I knew the man my wife had run to. Saul Harris, a property developer, was one of my clients and had been a guest at our house. He owned villas in Spain and the south of France as well as a house in the upmarket part of Golders Green in north London. I sent my wife a cable addressed to Spain and told her of our daughter's tragic death and the date of the funeral. Joanna would be brought back to England and her body cremated. I received no reply. I cabled again and this time sent a duplicate to the French villa. I also telephoned the Golders Green address but there was no reply except for an answerphone. Saul was evidently not in residence.

It was two weeks after Joanna had been cremated that Eve gave me a phone call. She was distressed but explained that she and Saul had been on a cruising holiday in the Caribbean. No, she said, she wouldn't be coming back to England. It was a long call and at the end I said I would be instituting divorce proceedings on the grounds of unreasonable behaviour; I wanted to spare her the stigma of divorce for adultery. She said she wouldn't defend and wished me luck for the future. 'What will you do?' she asked.

'I'm looking around. The partnership's been dissolved. I'd like to find a new direction.'

Her voice became sharper. 'You used to get on at me when I said I wanted something fresh, a new start, now you might understand how I felt.'

I didn't want to quarrel and said so.

'Neither do I,' she replied in a more moderate tone. 'You go your way and I'll go mine.'

'Right. Goodbye then.' As I spoke I realized how sad this farewell is.

5

'Goodbye,' she replied, and in spite of all our differences, and her infidelity, I felt a sense of loss. I had loved Eve more than I realized and far more than she knew.

The divorce went through on a rubber stamp. Eve didn't claim maintenance or a share of any of my assets including our home. She had never been grasping and, to be fair, the marriage's failure was probably six of one and half a dozen of the other. Towards the end we were kept together by Joanna but once she left home and had a steady boyfriend in Stephen the differences became acute. I neglected Eve. I was too preoccupied with my work, almost a workaholic, and she, perhaps naturally enough, became a typically bored housewife. She wanted some outside interest like working in a dress boutique; she wore her clothes elegantly and would have made an excellent saleswoman. Moreover, she was physically attractive, had a persuasive charm, and belief in herself. But foolishly I discouraged her ambitions and denied her the capital she needed to start a small business. Her resulting boredom might have been predicted by anyone but me. She took a lover, a man who I only knew by his first name, Simon. The affair ended when his company posted him abroad to manage a subsidiary in Australia.

Eve was very contrite and for a few months our married life was fine. I had no idea that a creeping boredom would once again snare her with extramarital temptations and it was a dreadful shock when she ran away to be with Saul Harris. What could she see in a man who was constantly boasting of the money he made, whose belly bulged, and whose nose went ahead of him like a great curved scimitar?

But I mustn't digress . . .

After an hour of leisurely beachcombing I turned round and retraced my steps. It was about eleven thirty when I reached the Moot Hall at the northern end of Aldeburgh and I decided to complete my walk by strolling along the promenade on the front known as the Crag Path.

One of the joys of Aldeburgh is that nothing seems to alter. As if in a time-warp it stays the same year after year. But my pleasure at the town's static character was abruptly jolted when I noticed a change in a serried rank of villas set slightly back from the sea-front. The ground floor of one villa, close to the house where

6

Wilkie Collins wrote *No Name*, had been converted into a café serving morning coffee, light lunches and afternoon teas. A discreet board proclaimed that this was 'Fran's Pantry'. On impulse I entered.

The place was filled with customers and was evidently a rendez-vous for the matrons of Aldeburgh. I took the last vacant table. There were no waitresses visible but after about half a minute a woman emerged from the rear of the café. At the sight of her my heart missed a beat, or maybe two or three beats, before accelerating at alarming speed. The woman could have been Eve's identical twin.

Ideals in human looks vary widely which for the perpetuation of the species is just as well. Homer knew what he was doing when he never gave a physical description of Helen of Troy and I'll partly follow his example and simply say that in repose Eve's features had a cool aristocratic aloofness which would suddenly melt into the mischief of a come-and-get-it commoner when she smiled. With fair hair brushed back from her forehead, the perfect symmetry of her face, and her lissom walk, she possessed all the elegance and poise of the late Princess Grace of Monaco. No wonder she had attracted admirers.

It must have been at least twenty minutes before she came over. 'I'm sorry to have kept you waiting so long,' she said. 'What would you like?'

She was Eve! I knew it the moment she spoke. But why was she treating me as a stranger? My hair might be slightly greyer, and lines on my brow a shade deeper, but surely I hadn't altered beyond recognition.

'Hello, Eve,' I said. 'What are you doing here?'

A flicker of embarrassment crossed her face. 'Look, not now, please. I'm rushed off my feet. Let me take your order.'

'A coffee.'

'Cream? Milk?'

'Milk, please.'

'Nothing else? A doughnut, perhaps?'

She had remembered my fondness for soft sugared doughnuts with raspberry jam in the centre!

'Yes, a doughnut.'

She made a note on her pad and departed leaving me feeling

7

like someone who has stepped from humdrum reality into a strange dream.

She brought the coffee and doughnut during a lull in activity. 'It's been one of those days,' she said. 'How are you?'

'Fine. What about you?'

'I'm OK.'

'Is this place yours?'

She nodded.

'Why is it called "Fran's Pantry"?'

'The previous owner's name was Frances. She did her own baking and this was more a coffee shop than a café. It was all very gingham tablecloths and dainty petits-fours. I've lowered the tone of the place by providing lunches.'

'You look as though you could do with some help,' I observed.

'I should have two girls working for me but they've both gone sick today.'

'And you're doing the lot?'

'Not quite,' she replied. 'There's Mrs Andrews – Barbara to her friends, if she has any – in the kitchen. She does the cooking, but she only comes for three hours and won't lift a finger to do anything but cook light lunches. I think she disapproves of me. The other day she made a pointed comment about women who go to pubs.' She gave me a look I recognized and had always thought of as her defiant stare. 'But why shouldn't I go out sometimes at the weekend for a drink and a bit of company?'

The question wasn't rhetorical; it demanded an answer.

'No reason,' I said, and as I uttered the placatory reply I realized I was taking a habitual non-confrontational, line of least resistance, stance. It had been only when Eve had wanted to expand her horizons that I'd fought for dominance.

Three newcomers entered the café.

'I can't gossip now,' said Eve. 'Business calls.'

'Just a minute,' I said as she turned away. 'If you're the proprietress I've got something to suggest. If you need a hand, I'm here.'

She gave me a look of amazement. 'You aren't offering to help?'

'I am.'

Her amazement swelled into outright incredulity. 'You would?'

'Yes.'

'Are you serious? It would mean working in the kitchen.'

'A kitchen isn't the forbidden planet to me.'

'I badly need some dishes and cups washed up.'

'I'll do it when I've had my coffee. I'll wash up.'

The ghost of a smile softened her amazement. 'You always were keen at washing up,' she said. 'You found it relaxing after a day at the office.'

'It got things out of the way, tidied up.'

Her smile lingered. 'I know. I'd have left the dishes until the next day . . . I must go. See me when you're ready.'

She swung away and went to the new customers. I heard her say, 'Are you ready to order?'

When I'd finished the coffee and doughnut I went to the counter where she was standing. 'You'd better show me the way to the sink.'

Without demur she said, 'Through here.'

I followed like a man in a trance. To be honest, I was taken aback by my own behaviour. I don't normally make decisions without considering the long-term effect of my actions.

In the kitchen I was introduced to Mrs Andrews, a tall, skinny woman of about fifty with rounded shoulders and thin arms. Her dark hair, worn in a bun, was streaked with grey. Eve explained that I was an old friend, a former neighbour, who by chance had dropped in at Fran's Pantry and, noticing the staff shortage, had offered to help. Mrs Andrews gave me a sidelong look, cold as a glass of iced water, nodded and resumed wrestling with a chip-pan. Within a minute I was up to my elbows in detergent washing plates, cups, saucers, and cooking utensils.

I wondered what had happened to Saul. A seaside café in a small town was a come-down from continental villas and holidays in the Caribbean.

When Eve shut up shop after teas had been served, and Mrs Andrews had long since departed, she said, 'I'm very grateful. What can I give you?'

'I don't want anything. I've enjoyed myself.'

She looked me over, her gaze lingering on my old jacket and unpolished shoes. Eve had always been particular about shoes. One could tell a man's character from the way he was shod, she used to say. Perhaps Saul's shoes had been the attraction; they were hand-made from crocodile hide.

Lifting her gaze from my shoes she asked, 'Are you down on your luck?'

I had to laugh. I was staying at one of the best hotels in the area. I said, 'In some ways I'm down on my luck, but not financially.' And then I posed the question which had been hovering at the top of my mind. 'What happened between you and Saul? Why are you here?'

She sat down at the table and lighted a cigarette, and then pushed the packet towards me. 'Like one?'

'No, thanks. I gave it up a year ago. I'm now a pious killjoy who frowns when people light up.'

She got up, fetched an ash-tray, and sat down again.

'You asked about Saul,' she said, flicking a shred of ash into the tray. 'He died,' she said simply. 'A heart attack. We were on board the yacht of one of his friends, having an evening meal, when he suddenly clutched at his chest. By the time we reached port he was dead.'

'Had he provided for you?'

She shook her head. 'No. He had been married. I wasn't entitled.'

'Married? I thought he was single.'

'And so he was when he became your client, but he'd been married previously. His wife died in childbirth. It would have been their second child. The first, a son, is still alive and he inherited everything.'

'I didn't know anything about that.'

'Why should you? It was none of your business. You were just his accountant.'

'I thought I was also his friend.'

She gave me an oddly wry look in which there was a hint of compassion. 'Anyone but you would have seen ten miles away that it was me he was after, and you were the means to get me. Once he set his sights on something or someone he was quite ruthless. That's why he was so successful in business.'

'I see . . . But why weren't you entitled to anything?'

'I did see a lawyer, a chap in Cannes. He told me I didn't have a chance. French law is different from English and the laws of

10

inheritance are quite different. Even a remote blood relation had priority over a common-law wife. Not that I minded too much, but it was a bit of a disappointment.' She paused. 'He would have married me. I'm sure of that. He approved when I changed my name.'

'Changed your name?'

She looked me fully in the eyes. 'By deed poll,' she said. 'After the divorce I decided to drop your name. I'm not Eve Markby any more, I'm Eve Harris.'

I shouldn't have felt a pang of regret – or was it wounded self-esteem? – at her name change, but I did. However, I maintained a blankly impassive expression, a look cultivated over years of listening to clients' pleas to fiddle the books, and asked, 'What happened next?'

'I don't think you ever met Moira, did you?'

'No. Who's Moira?'

'We were close friends at school. Very close. Then she went with her family to Canada about the time I first met you. I didn't tell her at once about us; she was, well, always a bit jealous. Then just before we married I sent her a note saying I was marrying. I got a stinging letter back. Nothing for six months, and then another letter to say she too had got married, and he was very rich, and apologizing for her previous letter.'

Eve stubbed out her cigarette before continuing. 'One day when I'd got nothing to do, and shortly after I'd changed my name to Harris, I decided to write to Moira and ask how she was. I told her I was divorced and living with a man in the south of France. Luckily the letter reached her. She hadn't changed her address, but her husband had died and left her well off. She'd been thinking of coming back to England. To cut a long story short, that's what she did. She bought a house at Leiston, about four miles from here. It was a sort of homecoming; she'd been born there. Anyway, she came over from France partly to see me and partly to look around for a holiday home. It was good to see her again. She hadn't changed much. Anyway, she met Saul, but only once. They didn't hit it off. And then, within a week or so of her arrival, Saul died. After I'd seen the lawyer we met and I told her of the legal situation. She asked what I was going to do. I said I'd like to go back to England and maybe try to raise the wind to buy a

11

little shop. She said there was a seaside coffee shop for sale at Aldeburgh and she'd stake me if I took it on. I decided to, and here I am, thanks to Moira.'

'And so we meet again,' I said after a long pause.

'Are you here for long?'

'I haven't got any firm plans. There's a Mozart concert at the Barbican next week I'd like to go to.'

'Where are you living now?'

'London.'

'Have you sold our home?'

'Yes. It was too big for one. I rattled around in it, a pea in a pod of memories. I've got a flat in Kensington.'

'You didn't remarry?'

'No.'

Her eyes brightened as she asked, 'Any woman in your life?'

'Only someone who comes to tidy round and do my ironing.'

'What's she like?'

'She's a West Indian. Verity da Costa, by name.'

'Old?'

'Young, but married with three children and an unemployed husband.'

'Do you fancy her?'

'Eve!'

'Sorry. Mustn't be too personal, must we.'

I couldn't say that the only woman I had ever fancied was the woman sitting opposite me.

She looked at me as though weighing up whether to ask another question and then said, 'I'm just going to cook myself something. Nothing much. Cod fresh from the sea this morning, with parsley sauce, new potatoes and petits pois.'

'You always did like petits pois.'

'Still do. Why don't you join me? You've earned it.'

I hesitated, but not for long. 'Are you sure?'

She sighed. 'No, I'm not a bit sure. I'm just a silly woman who says the first thing that comes into her empty head.' And then she gave the smile which had once made my heart turn somersaults. 'I'm kidding,' she said. 'Of course I'm sure. But there's one stipulation.'

'Stipulation about what?' I asked.

12

Fixing me with an unwavering look she said, 'Stipulation about you and me. If, after you've had your meal, you walk out of here, and we never see each other again, fair enough. But if . . .'

'But if,' I prompted.

She reached for the cigarette packet. 'But if you come back . . . I mean, if you come here again, I don't want any references to our marriage when other people are around. So far as other people are concerned we were once just neighbours. OK?'

She took a cigarette from the packet, lighted it and blew out a plume of smoke. 'I know it's nobody's business but our own,' she said, 'but I don't want us to be regarded as a couple who were once married, either by other people or by ourselves.'

'That makes it a bit of a charade, doesn't it? A game of let's-pretend?'

She didn't answer at once but stubbed out the cigarette she'd just lighted, rose from the table and went to the sink to wash her hands. After taking a whole cod from the fridge she began cutting it into steaks.

'You're right,' she said at length, 'it will be a pretence. But I suppose it's part of my damn guilt complex.'

'Guilt complex?'

'About Joanna.'

She took a couple of thick steaks and sprinkled breadcrumbs on them before putting the remainder of the fish, wrapped in foil, into the freezer compartment. I waited for a further explanation. It wasn't forthcoming until she'd put the potatoes in a saucepan and lighted the gas.

'I broke up the family,' she said.

'Joanna had already left home. You didn't break up the family.'

'You don't know how I felt when I eventually got your cable. I cried for days. Saul was very good but in the end he was telling me to pull myself together. I felt so guilty!' She turned to look at me and I saw tears in her eyes. 'You wouldn't know this but just before Stephen and Joanna left for their French holiday I told her I was planning to leave you. I thought it only fair she should know in case I left while she was away. I tried to explain. I thought she was adult enough to understand that if two people didn't get on . . .' She broke off to dab her eyes with a tissue.

'I'm making a fool of myself,' she continued. 'What I'm trying to say is that Joanna and I had one hell of a quarrel. I hadn't realized she'd known about my affair with Simon. And now it was Saul. "How many others are there that Dad doesn't know about?" she asked. "I reckon you're nothing better than an amateur prostitute." This made me see red. I said, "Am I? Well, it takes one to know one. Will you and Stephen be having separate rooms? You're just a bloody little hypocrite." And that was the last thing I said to her. She walked out on me without another word. No goodbye. Nothing. That's my guilt complex.'

I sat silently while she finished preparing the meal. I couldn't think what to say. Some assumptions I'd made about Eve had been blown away. I hadn't appreciated that she'd felt Joanna's death so keenly or that she'd suffered feelings of guilt. I had always been the one with the conscience; she was the one who regretted nothing except being found out in a deceit.

Satisfied that the meal was on its way, Eve returned to the table. Her eyes were dry. 'You're quiet,' she said.

'I'm taken aback.'

'Don't be. I won't get all heavy again.' She gave a little smile. 'What are you doing these days? Still juggling with figures?'

I told her I still had a few clients but now I worked from my flat. The trial of my partners, and the part I'd played in it, hadn't advanced my career.

She gave me a quick, rather wry look. 'I suppose I owe you an apology.'

'What for?'

'Walking out on you at a time when you needed support. Believe me, I felt guilty about that too, but it was then or never. Saul was leaving England for good and either I went to him or it was all off.'

'All water under the bridge,' I said.

'You must have been angry with me.'

'I was angry at first but since then I've realized there were faults on both sides. I was a workaholic.'

'Aren't you still?'

'No, I've rather drifted since those days. I suppose I lack motivation. It's a great mistake to put all one's eggs in one basket. Luckily, there's still music.'

'For all our differences we did have music in common.'

14

'Yes.'

'Anyway, what do you do with yourself all day if you don't have a regular job?'

'I've built up a good collection of tapes, records, and CDs. I go to lots of concerts and operas. I keep in touch with one or two old friends. I read quite a bit, mostly biographies. The great thing in life is not to pursue happiness but to avoid unhappiness. I'm managing to do that. Music is a great ally. Last week I went to a performance of *Billy Budd*. It was one of the things that made me want to visit Aldeburgh again.'

She gave me a curious look. 'It's your safety valve, isn't it? Music, I mean. You can let it all hang out when you listen to music. You can laugh or cry. It's your outlet.'

I gave a noncommittal shrug.

'We all need outlets,' she went on. 'Mine is this business. I've become a workaholic.' She smiled. 'We've switched roles.'

Something had been nagging at the back of my mind. 'When you took on this business,' I said, 'you must have known there was a fair chance you might see me here one day. You know I love the place.'

She nodded. 'Yes, I did. But I didn't come here because of that. It was sheer chance that Moira happened to live where she did and knew about this place being for sale. If she'd been living at Bournemouth I'd be in Bournemouth now. I guessed that you and I would meet again one day and I'd even planned what I might say – don't worry, I've already said it. But when you walked in, even though I was expecting to see you one day, I felt as though the floor had shifted under my feet. You didn't see me at first. You were closing the door. I jumped back in here and collected my wits. I decided I'd pretend I hadn't seen you and I hoped, I actually hoped, that you'd get tired of waiting and leave. But you didn't, and every time I looked out of the corner of my eye I could see you staring at me. In the end I thought I'd better go through with it and I decided to be distant. But I couldn't keep it up . . . The meal should be ready. I must have known you were coming. I hope you're hungry.'

'I am.'

'You always did like fish.'

'I liked your meals,' I said, 'and your company.'

15

She opened her mouth to say something and then seemed to check herself. I think she was going to say, 'If you liked my company why were you always in a hurry to finish your meal and start work on the papers you'd brought home?' What she said aloud was, 'It's kind of you to say you liked my cooking. I hope you'll like this . . . What am I thinking of? This calls for some wine.'

It was shortly after we'd raised glasses to each other that she said, 'I've never been like you, good at figures, and it's caused complications.'

'What complications?'

'The tax man has asked for my accounts. I don't keep accounts. At the end of the week I pay my takings into the bank. But I don't keep any books.'

This was a story I'd heard before, but I said nothing.

'I don't suppose,' she began, and then stopped.

'You want me to give you a hand?'

'Would you?' she asked. 'I'd pay, of course.'

It was a critical moment.

'I wouldn't want payment,' I said, 'but . . .'

'But you don't want to get involved with my business affairs.'

I was in a quandary. Straightening out Eve's accounts would provide an occupation, if not exactly a purpose in life, but on the other hand I feared emotional involvement. She'd let me down more than once; I didn't want my emotions ravaged again.

She had stopped eating and was watching me intently.

I took the plunge. I said, 'I'll do it.'

She gave a dazzling smile. 'That's great!'

'I shall need your bank statements, details of any mortgage, and a statement of all your outgoings including payments to staff, National Insurance; all your annual income and expenditure. I shall need to know absolutely everything.'

With these words I sealed my fate.

2

When the meal was over we went upstairs to have coffee in the sitting room. It had a strangely lifeless atmosphere: it might have been the rest room of a small residential home for the elderly, randomly furnished with secondhand furniture. Eve said, 'I bought the place as it stood, lock, stock and barrel. One of these days when I've got time I'm going to refurnish it completely.'

I walked across the room to a wide window. Light was fading and dusk deepening. The darkening eastern sky merged into the flat darkening sea. Primitive man, gazing out at such a scene, must have thought he'd reached the end of the world.

Again, as if sensing my thoughts, Eve said, 'This room gets the early morning sun.' She put down the coffee tray and began switching on table lamps. 'Sometimes, if I can't sleep, I come in here and watch the sun creep over the horizon.'

She came and stood beside me. I'm a fairly tall man and Eve seemed shorter than I remembered; and then I realized she'd always worn high-heeled shoes during our marriage, even when relaxing, but now she was wearing flat sandals.

As she poured the coffee I glanced round the room looking for evidence of identity, personal touches which would alleviate the bland anonymity. The only artefacts I could associate with Eve were a reproduction of Vermeer's *A Lady and a Gentleman at the Virginals* hanging over the fireplace, a shelf featuring paperback editions of currently popular novels, and a silver-framed photograph showing a man in overalls standing by the nose of a Spitfire. It was a photo I'd seen before.

'I recognize the photo of your father,' I said.

'He'd like to have been a pilot,' she replied, 'but he failed the maths test for volunteer aircrew.' She laughed. 'I've inherited his innumeracy.'

17

'But those ginger china cats on top of the bookshelf, they weren't your choice, were they?'

'No fear! They're a present from Moira. I think they're quite valuable. I've had to put them on display. After all, without her help I'd never have been able to buy this place.' She gave a slight grimace. 'I've never been bothered with having many possessions of my own, and Saul wasn't overly generous with gifts, except for clothes. He liked to see me looking good and rather pampered my dress sense, but I left most of my stuff in France. Anyway, his son collared all the effects in the villas.'

'I can't understand why Saul didn't leave you anything.'

Without a trace of bitterness she replied, 'Oh, I can. He thought it was unlucky to make a will, and he thought he was immortal . . . But enough of that. Would you like a brandy?'

'If you'll join me.'

'I certainly will.' She went to a carved oak chest near the window and lifted the lid. 'This is where I keep my few treasures and the booze.' She took out a bottle and a couple of glasses. She poured the drinks and handed me a stiff measure of cognac. Lifting her glass she said, 'Here's to us. Both of us.'

'Here's to us,' I responded. 'Each of us.'

Her eyes narrowed slightly. 'Both? Each? . . . Did it upset you very much when I left?'

'Yes, it did.'

She winced. 'No one can accuse you of giving the soft answer. I'm sorry if I hurt or upset you, but I thought you'd probably be relieved to be shot of me. I wasn't the perfect wife by a long chalk. But that's enough of "old times" talk.'

For a while we talked of meteorology, global warming and the environment. And then of the Greens, political opportunism and social engineering.

I glanced at my watch. It was nearly ten thirty and I hadn't yet written up my diary. Since childhood I have kept a diary and written it up before retiring to bed. It is because of this diary or journal – it is really a *journal intime* – that I'm able to reproduce snatches of conversation.

When I said that I must be on my way she replied, 'Shall I see you tomorrow, or are you having second thoughts about doing my accounts?'

18

'You'll see me tomorrow. I'll do the washing-up and start work on the accounts.'

'I'm terribly grateful.'

I thanked her for the evening and said I'd enjoyed it.

Her face brightened. 'Have you? Have you really?'

'I have really.'

She led the way downstairs and at the front door she leaned forward to give my cheek a peck.

I could feel its imprint on my cheek as I walked back to the hotel, and this annoyed me. I wasn't a steer to be marked by the branding-iron of Eve's lips.

She was right about the rain. I heard it in the night. When morning came I drew the curtains and looked out: an opaque mesh of rain made it impossible to see where sea joined sky. With past experience of east coast weather I'd taken the precaution of bringing a book to read. But reading was to have been a fall-back occupation; my intention had been to go for long walks bird-spotting in the salt marshes, beachcombing, or wandering through gorse-lined tracks on the commons.

The café, when I arrived there shortly before midday, was almost deserted. Only two tables were taken and Eve was standing by the cash-register counter. I went over to her.

She gave a smile. 'I wasn't sure whether you'd come. You might have had second thoughts. And then I remembered how reliable you used to be.'

'I'd sooner be called reliable than predictable, although to some people they mean the same thing.'

Her smile faded and I realized she had remembered the times when, already into heavy boredom, she had accused me, 'You are so predictable!' Such is the treacherous ground of past memories.

'Maybe you're right,' she said, 'but we aren't going to be bogged down by semantics, are we?'

'No. I've come to help with the washing-up and to sort out your accounts. Have you got the bank statements?'

'Don't you want something to eat first?'

'No, thanks. I've had a good breakfast. I'll skip lunch.'

'You've had a gin,' she said sternly. 'I can smell it on your breath.'

19

I suppressed the desire to say, 'That's better than a smell of tobacco on the breath,' because at that moment I couldn't smell anything but a perfume created to entice the sleepiest male hormones out of hiding. Once again, showing that she was on my wavelength, she said, 'I haven't had a single cigarette today.'

'Why not?'

'Because you don't approve.'

I was amazed. Since when had she cared whether I approved? Her eyes sparkled and she laughed outright. 'Have I thrown you?'

With stupidly naïve honesty I replied, 'You've disconcerted me.'

'All right, then. I'll put you at ease and change it to something which doesn't disconcert you. Moira has been nagging for ages for me to give it up and I've decided that as I owe her so much it's the least I can do.'

This was the Eve I remembered, the woman who usually outsmarted me when the battlefield was emotional and with whom I could just about hold my own when warfare was waged on the field of reason and logic. But before this could become an issue a young man walked into the café. He had been in the rain and his shoulder-length hair hung in rat's tails. His black leather jacket looked as though he'd been swimming in it.

'Oh, no!' Eve exclaimed. 'Excuse me.' She went across to the new customer, said something to him, and he left. I went to the kitchen where dirty chinaware was stacked by the sink.

During the afternoon I asked, 'Who was that young fellow who left in a hurry?'

'Doesn't matter,' she replied.

The café was empty. 'I'll make a start on your accounts,' I said. 'Have you got the bank statements?'

'Look, I'm a busy woman. I was up at six this morning. Six! I'll bet you were still fast asleep.'

This unexpected hostility reminded me that anything which could remotely be construed as an attack was always met with a counterattack. As ever, in spite of experience, I tried to resist any counterattack with reason.

'I simply asked if you'd got the bank statements. You do want me to sort out your tax position, don't you?'

'Of course I do, and I'm very grateful. But don't pressurize me.

20

You, of all people, should know that pressurizing me is counter-productive.'

I felt resentful. She had acquired the free services of a professional accountant, someone who could get her off the hook of tax demands, and yet was snapping at the helping hand. But before I could voice my resentment she unexpectedly moderated her tone.

'Don't take any notice of me,' she said. 'It's the wrong time of the month. I'm truly grateful. I'll look out the statements when we've closed.'

Custom at seaside cafés can be random. Just as Eve was about to shut the rain stopped and people came from nowhere for cups of tea and cakes. It was almost seven before she cashed up and, as on the previous day, started to cook a meal: fish pie with new potatoes and petits pois.

We had hardly started eating when the telephone rang.

'Oh, damn,' said Eve. 'I wonder who this can be.' She went to the phone.

'Hello . . . Oh, Cat dear, I wondered if it might be you . . . Tomorrow? Why not? Hold on, I'll ask him.'

Putting a hand over the mouthpiece she said, 'It's Moira. She's invited us to her place tomorrow evening for a meal and to watch a video. It's Zeffirelli's production of *Carmen*. Care to come?'

Us? How did Moira know about us?

'Hurry up,' said Eve. 'Do you want to come?'

'Yes, I'd like to.'

'Yes, Cat, he'd love to come. But what about transport? . . . You will? . . . Lovely. See you any time after seven then. Bye.'

She returned to the table.

'How does she know about me?' I asked.

'I told her.'

'You told her how I'd dropped in here for a coffee and we'd met up again?'

'Something like that,' she replied evasively.

'Something like that? An approximation of what happened?'

She stopped eating and looked across the table at me. 'Explanation time, is it? Moira fusses about me. She's been on at me to get the accounts done. I rang her this morning and told her I'd found an accountant.'

'Found one?'

21

'I said you'd come in for a coffee and I recognized you as someone I'd known as a neighbour years ago when we were living in Ash Close. We'd got talking and you'd offered to help me out.'

'You didn't say I was your ex-husband?'

'No.'

'Why not?'

'I just didn't want her to know. That's why.'

'I can't think why not.'

Annoyance registered briefly on Eve's face. 'I didn't tell her because it's private. Moira's a great friend, and as I've told you I owe her a lot. But I don't want her to know every little detail about who I meet. So far as she's concerned you're an old friend who I met again by chance and that's the way I want to play it.' A defiant note entered her voice. 'Any objections?'

'No, not if it means so much to you.'

'Anyway, it's true. We are friends, aren't we?'

'I hope so . . . Why did you call her "Cat"?'

She dug her fork into the fish pie. 'It doesn't matter. I'll tell you sometime.'

I decided not to pursue the topic but I didn't much care for the deception. Why shouldn't Moira know that once Eve and I had been married?

For a while we ate in silence and then she asked, 'How's the pie?'

'Excellent.'

She smiled. 'You're an easy man to cater for. Do you cook a lot for yourself or do you go out for meals?'

The remainder of the meal was passed in talking about domesticity.

After the meal we went upstairs and she took a sheaf of bank statements out of the oak chest.

'Here are some,' she said.

'Only some?'

'I'm not sure whether I've kept them all.'

'Have you kept receipts or invoices for goods or food ordered?'

'No.'

This wasn't good news but I said, 'If you always pay by cheque we should be able to construct something from the counterfoils.'

She looked amused. 'You'll be lucky. I don't always bother to fill in the counterfoil, and anyway I sometimes pay with cash out of the till.'

I sighed. 'It's not going to be easy to draw up accurate accounts.'

'You'll manage it. You're good at that sort of thing. You like to get things tidy, get things straight.'

'Order out of chaos.'

'That's right. Order out of chaos, and boy, did you have chaos with me! But that was partly my way of protest.'

I ignored the temptation to resurrect old differences and leafed through the statements. 'These go up to January of this year. Can you get the ones for January to April?'

'I'll go to the bank tomorrow.'

'And try to get duplicate receipts from your suppliers.'

She shook her head. 'You're being difficult.'

'Do you want me to prepare accounts for you?'

It was her turn to sigh which she did very audibly . . . 'All right. I'll try.'

'One other thing. Where did you get the loan to buy this place? I shall need to have all the details.'

'I thought I'd already told you. Moira staked me. Does it matter?'

'I have to supply the name of the lender on your tax return and give details of the mortgage. Was a deed drawn up?'

'Oh, I had to sign some sort of a document,' she replied in an offhand manner, 'but Moira's very good. She hasn't asked for the interest.'

'So it's virtually an interest-free loan?'

'I suppose you could say that but' – she added hastily – 'don't tell the tax people that. Let them think I've been paying interest through the nose.'

'I shall just reproduce the terms of the mortgage.'

Eve seemed to hesitate for a moment as though unsure whether to raise a new issue, and then she said, 'There's something else.'

'What's that?'

'Moira also lent me a few thousand to install new equipment and decorate the eating area, but it's a personal loan. There aren't any documents but it makes her a sleeping partner. If requested I'm supposed to give her a quarter share of the profits, but she's never asked for anything. It's all very informal.'

We talked some more but there was nothing relevant to a future which was waiting in ambush like a guerrilla force prepared to slaughter anyone, however innocent, who comes its way.

3

The night was a furnace of dreams stoked with oddments of the day, symbolic puzzles and suppressed desires. But one dream was so disturbing that I recorded it later in my diary. Eve, wearing a diaphanous négligé, came towards me, and we were about to kiss when she turned away to embrace a vaguely defined figure. And then I was in a mortuary and one of my former partners wearing cassock and surplice was saying, 'You drove her to it,' and with dreadful misgiving I knew Eve had committed suicide.

The troubling dream made me face the reality that I still cared deeply for Eve and was physically attracted to her. I'm not a womanizer and my libido isn't as strong as some men's. Eve is the only woman who has ever moved me to tears through frustration and hypererotic insanity through sensual arousal. I felt the dream had been a warning and I resolved not to allow myself to be at the mercy of instincts and emotions lurking in the reptilian hindbrain like ageless, unreachable mini-dinosaurs. After breakfast I cleared my head of night phantasms by a beachcombing stroll to the south of town. On this part of the shore-line one can find peat from submerged forests and driftwood of all sorts, from bleached Scots fir to bamboo, as well as amber if one is lucky.

Shortly after midday I went to help Eve. The café was fairly busy and we didn't have much time for conversation. It was evening, and I had papers spread out over the kitchen table, when Moira arrived unexpectedly early. She walked into the kitchen saying, 'You are hopeless, Cat. Front door unlocked again.'

'Oh, hell! I popped out for a moment and forgot to lock up when I got back.'

My first impression of Moira was that she and Eve could have been related. Their hair-styles were different – Moira's was cut short like a boy's whereas Eve's was shoulder length – and Moira didn't possess Eve's classically perfect face. But she could have been an ugly sister or an imitation badly sculpted by a novice attempting to copy a master's work of art.

However, what made them completely different was their dress. Eve was wearing a pale lilac blouse with mauve skirt and matching top while Moira wore a sloppy grey sweater, secured at the waist with a scuffed leather belt. Her legs were covered by baggy blue trousers which had brown oil stains on the knees. In one hand she carried driving goggles and a pair of string-backed gloves. She could have been a rally driver who'd just called in at a checkpoint.

She came across to me and extended a hand. 'I'm Moira. You must be Mark. Same name as Eve's ex, but I suppose you know that.'

Eve quickly said, 'Moira's a very old friend and knows all my history. We were at school together.'

'You might not believe it when you look at us now,' said Moira, 'but as kids there was quite a close resemblance. The teachers sometimes got us mixed up. It was great fun. If I'd been naughty like pulling Jean Croft's hair . . . Do you remember that whingey little creep, Cat?'

'Sure do,' Eve replied, smiling broadly.

'And if a teacher spotted me,' Moira continued, 'and came over to tick me off, and called me "Moira", I'd say, "I'm Eve, miss." '

'Didn't your teachers catch on?' I asked.

'They did in the end but it was great while it lasted.' Moira laughed at the memory and then, in a more serious vein, said, 'I'm glad you're doing something to help Eve.' She glanced at the papers scattered across the table. 'It's naughty of me to be dragging you away from the good work but I was keen to meet Eve's friendly accountant. You were neighbours once upon a time, I believe.'

Eve's posture betrayed a sudden tension; she was willing me to play along with the deception. But was it such a deception? We had been very close neighbours, living in the same house and sharing the same food, and towards the end of the marriage we had neighbouring bedrooms.

I said, 'That's right. Eve and I were neighbours when we were both living in north London.'

Eve shot me a grateful look. She had been as tense as a drawn bow and the arrow she'd dispatched was feathered with relief. Quickly, and before Moira could follow up the neighbourhood line, she said, 'Come on, let's not waste time. I'm ready. How about you, Mark?'

'I'll get my jacket and then I'm ready.'

A long sleek metallic-silver car was parked outside the café.

'Do you enjoy cars, Mark?' Moira asked.

'Only as a means of getting from A to B.'

'Did you come here by car?'

'Yes.'

'What make?'

'BMW 316.'

'I'm a bit of a nut. This is an Aston-Martin four-seater tourer, the same model that won at Le Mans in 1935.' She opened the passenger door. 'Can you clamber into the back? I won't drive too fast. We don't want to blow you away.' As I climbed in she went on, 'In 1935 this model cost £640 and the annual tax was £9. Times have changed.'

Moira's house was a fairly large double-fronted detached building on the outskirts of the town. Its sitting room was furnished with items of value, all of which seemed to complement each other, even though sometimes out of period. While we sipped aperitifs most of the talk was between the two women with an explanatory crumb of information about a person or place being occasionally thrown in my direction. Anyone would have thought they hadn't seen each other for years and were catching up on news but I suspected that Moira was establishing for my benefit that her friendship with Eve had priority over mine; she was the favourite, I was an outsider.

Gradually I became besieged by boredom which was broken by an unexpected diversion. The door was pushed open and a fat tabby cat walked in. It regarded me, came to me, and jumped on to my lap.

'Well, look at that,' Moira exclaimed, and she didn't sound pleased. 'It's unlike Jessica to go to strangers.' She turned to Eve. 'Perhaps we should make your friendly accountant an honorary tom-cat, or do you think that'd break up the party? I'll go and dish up, Cat dear.' The cat followed her from the room, tail raised like a periscope.

Moira was an excellent cook. The main course was loin of pork Alsacienne with sauerkraut which was garnished with parsley and quarters of hard-boiled egg. The tableware was of silver, as were the wine goblets and the candlesticks which formed a central cluster on a large round mahogany table. A showcase filled with a collection of German porcelain stood by one wall, and against the opposite wall was a mahogany sideboard which had satinwood inlays. Its surface was covered with a collection of china cats.

I would have enjoyed the meal and surroundings more if Moira hadn't decided to fire a barrage of questions at me. Where did I live? What were my interests? Had I always wanted to be an accountant? What was my father's occupation? Had I travelled much? What were my views on organized religion?

Guessing that she might already know the answers to some of the questions I was guarded with my replies, keeping near the truth and yet not being so explicit that the situation would be revealed for the charade it was. I fervently wished I hadn't gone along with Eve's pointless deception, and very nearly blew the whole scenario when, on being quizzed as to my marital state, I confessed to being divorced.

'Oh dear,' said Moira. 'Was it a traumatic experience?'

'Fairly traumatic.'

'I assume you divorced her?'

'Yes.'

'I know it's quite unpardonable to pry, but I'm as curious as any cat. Don't answer if you don't wish to, but was it adultery on her part?'

'The grounds were unreasonable behaviour,' I replied.

Moira turned to Eve and said, 'You divorced your husband for the same reason, didn't you, Cat?'

'Did I? I'd sooner not remember things like that . . . This pork is absolutely delicious. Just the right amount of garlic.'

This praise, followed by reminiscences of memorable meals they'd shared, signalled the end of my grilling, but not before my appetite had all but been destroyed. I was beginning to dislike the scruffily dressed parody of Eve who fitted into her surroundings as naturally as a female yobbo in Buckingham Palace.

When the meal was finished Eve said, 'I've got to be up early tomorrow and don't want to be late home. Do you think we could

28

get on with the show fairly soon?' Minutes later we were back in the sitting room drinking coffee and watching the opening scenes of *Carmen*.

After the closing credits, Eve stood up. 'I don't want to break up the party, but I really must get back. I'll use your loo first, though.'

When she'd left the room Moira leaned towards me and in a confidential whisper said, 'Eve's had a tough life.'

'She has?'

'She was married to a swine of a husband. He ought to have been put down at birth. As a neighbour you wouldn't have known what went on behind closed doors. He treated her like furniture, cheap plywood furniture. He was the archetypal chauvinist pig. Things have never been easy for her. Be kind to her, Mark.'

'Be kind?'

'Don't promise what you can't deliver. That's a road she's been on too many times. I'd be very upset if Eve got hurt, and I can be quite an unpleasant customer when I'm upset.'

It sounded like a threat. 'She has nothing to fear from me,' I said stiffly.

'Good. Now then, Eve tells me you're a Mozart nut.'

We talked about the Salzburg genius until Eve returned.

Moira took us back to Aldeburgh and when she had driven away Eve and I stood on the pavement outside the café.

'It's too late to ask you in,' she said, 'but shall I see you tomorrow?'

'Probably not.'

In the half-light cast by a street lamp her face showed dismay. 'Why not?'

'What the hell have you been telling Moira about me? Treating you like furniture and all that rubbish.'

'Mark, I had to! You don't understand. I know it's despicable, mercenary, and every hard word you can name, but I badly needed that loan, and I had to say the sort of thing she wanted to hear. I didn't mean it, but needs must when the devil drives. If it's any satisfaction to you, I felt ashamed of myself and still do . . . Did she say that while I was out of the room?'

'Yes.'

29

'She can be a bitch. But I owe her so much. Don't hold it against me, please.'

She looked so earnest, so anxious, so sincere, that my resolve wavered.

'Come tomorrow,' she pleaded.

I didn't answer at once.

'Please,' she begged.

'All right. I promised to do your accounts and I will.'

She leaned forward and brushed my lips with hers.

'Thanks,' she said. 'Goodnight and sleep well.'

I didn't sleep well. Deeply troubled that Eve had the power to stir my emotions – I had felt a real anger at the lies she'd told Moira about me and a real thrill when her lips touched mine – I decided to cut my holiday short and return to London. It went against the grain to let her down but she'd have to get someone else to sort out her accounts. Having made this resolution after restless hours of inner debate I fell asleep.

When I woke the sun's rays were streaming through partly drawn curtains. It was a new day and I felt firmly in control of my emotions. I'd finish the accounting as promised, return to London, and never come back. Or, if I did, to attend the Festival, I wouldn't go anywhere near Fran's Pantry.

The café was very busy and it wasn't until evening that we had the opportunity to exchange more than two consecutive sentences. After our meal we cleared the table and I began work on the accounts. It was late when, in spite of double-checking, making allowances for variables, and taking a haphazard collection of receipts into the reckoning, I came to the conclusion that the bank statements couldn't in any way be reconciled with the café's net takings.

Eve was reading a newspaper when I asked, 'How much cash have you been withholding?'

She looked up from the paper. 'What?'

'You've been paying in only part of your takings.'

'I don't know what you're talking about.'

She only understood what she wanted to understand, heard what she wanted to hear, and did what she wanted to do. I had forgotten this trait in Eve's character.

'It's obvious to me that, unless your staff have been helping themselves liberally from the till, there's a big shortfall which is down to you.'

She folded the newspaper and put it away. 'Are you on my side or not?' she demanded.

'I'm trying to make sense of your business finances so you won't have the tax man on your back. It's obvious you must have been salting some cash away.'

'It's obvious, is it?' she retorted. 'Well, it's obvious to me you haven't changed. A petty-minded man with a petty attitude to petty cash.'

'Insults won't help, Eve.'

'So what if I've put a little aside?' she asked stridently. 'If you're any good at all at your job you should be able to write it off somehow.'

With this dismissive instruction she picked up the newspaper, unfolded it, and began reading. Her disdain, amounting almost to contempt of my professional ability and principles, made me feel like quitting but I persisted with my enquiries.

'I've already made big allowances for various expenses and there's still a huge discrepancy. How do you explain that?'

She tossed the paper away and, her lips thinning with spite, asked, 'What are you after? A slice of the cake?'

My temper began to rise but I kept my voice quiet and controlled. 'That's an insult, Eve, and you know it. Look, I've had bad experiences through other people's dishonesty. I've always had a clean sheet and intend to keep it that way.'

'Do you? How noble! Aren't you just a wee bit too perfect to live in this wicked world?'

'Do you *want* your business affairs straightened out? If not, say so, and I'll leave.'

'It's not very nice to be called a cheat.'

'I didn't call you a cheat.'

'It's what you meant.' Her voice cracked and tears came to her eyes. 'I've had it up to here,' she said. 'I've fought back from nothing. And now that I'm on my way, and putting a bit aside . . . Don't you think I work hard enough for what I've got? You've seen me working.'

'That isn't the point.'

'It's my point. Don't you think I've worked hard enough for what I've got? Do you know something, Mark? That first day when you volunteered to do the washing-up, I thought, "He's terribly lonely." I felt sorry for you. But you deserve to be lonely. That's all I can say . . . What happened in the past is past. I thought we could be good friends. And what are friends for but to help each other? I'd have helped you whatever you'd done. If you'd robbed a bank and wanted an alibi I'd have given it. But not you. You don't know what friendship is! No wonder you're lonely! I'm going upstairs. I can't bear to be in here.'

She didn't move, but I did. I stood up. 'Goodnight, Eve,' I said, and I walked out of the kitchen. She made no attempt to call me back. I let myself out of the front door and set off for the hotel. Fleetingly, and from the treacherous imagination which springs from foolish hopes, I had, ever since the divorce, wondered whether, if Eve and I met again, we could make a go of it.

It was now clear that we couldn't.

4

I slept badly, but that wasn't unusual; I was close to graduating as a fully-fledged insomniac. Next morning the sun was a giant red crab crawling over the horizon. Weather forecasts had predicted a fine day and, if correct, this extended the available options for passing the time. But what should I do? Certainly I wouldn't be going to Fran's Pantry to present myself meekly for washing-up chores and fudging Eve's accounts.

I'd thought about her during most of the night, not more in sorrow than anger, or anger than sorrow, but with a sort of sorrowful anger. However, there are no percentage gains in the three 'r's associated with regret – rue, remorse and repining. I decided to go for a long walk. I knew there was a small art gallery at the Snape Maltings and I needed a picture for a wall-space in my flat.

It wasn't easy to erase Eve from my thoughts. By taking some paths close to the river I was able to spot a variety of wildlife including birds of the duck kind such as mallard and grebe, and hosts of peewits; nevertheless, from time to time I was aware of an unfolding sense of emptiness within me. After a pub lunch I went to the Maltings and purchased a picture in oils by the artist Joan Bates in which a slate-grey sea and light brown beach dominated the scene. Sea and sky were in subdued tones of blue. In the foreground, lightly sketched, were two anglers, but they were subsidiary to the power of the beach. The beach symbolized an uncaring eternity and the anglers were merely an afterthought of creation, perishable, expendable. The beach would endure long after they had landed their last fish.

As I trudged back to Aldeburgh carrying the picture I felt I'd achieved something. I'm not sure what. Perhaps I'd managed to erect a small time and memory barrier against the previous night's storm with Eve. Back at the hotel I took a bath and dressed to go downstairs for dinner. It was as I was leaving the room that the telephone rang.

Eve's voice came down the line. 'I'm so sorry, Mark, about the argument last night. I didn't mean it.'

'You didn't . . .'

'I didn't mean it. All those dreadful things I said. I didn't mean them.'

I was aware that my heartbeat was accelerating.

'I didn't mean them, Mark.'

'So you've said.'

'We can still be friends, can't we?'

I thought carefully before replying, 'Why not?'

The timbre of her voice changed slightly. It became more confident. 'You didn't come today,' she said.

'No. I went to Snape.'

A pause. 'Did you have a nice day?'

'Fine. Very enjoyable.'

'I was wondering . . . Have you eaten yet?'

'I was just going down to the restaurant.'

'What I've got here won't compare, but if you'd like to take pot luck . . .'

It was my turn to create a pause before I said, 'I don't mind pot luck.'

I heard her chuckle. 'Great. You'll come round then?'

'Put the pot on.'

I checked my appearance in the bathroom mirror, combed my hair once more, straightened my tie, and set off for Fran's Pantry.

As I stepped through the front doorway she came forward, threw her arms round my neck, and kissed me passionately. It was a long embrace and it left me bemused and breathless.

She pulled away. 'That's enough of that. Come along in. I've defrosted a steak and kidney pie I made last month. I must have known you'd be coming. It's still one of your favourites, I hope. The gravy is laced with Worcester sauce.'

As she walked ahead of me to the kitchen she didn't know I was suppressing a longing to grab her, whirl her around, and continue the embrace. The moment passed and we entered the kitchen.

This wasn't the beginning of a relationship; it was a renewal. At the beginning of a relationship every little detail seems of interest; it is only later that the corrosive rot of ennui eats into timbers constructed from early explorations, and the stimulation of novelty becomes the boredom of routine. A renewal of the relationship heralds a period of reconstruction based on the best parts of understanding each other's ways and preferences.

The previous evening wasn't referred to. Instead she spoke of a different confrontation which had occurred early in the afternoon. A drunk had barged into the café demanding a drink. When he discovered that nothing stronger than coffee was on sale he became abusive and then over-familiar, trying to put his arm round her. She pushed him away and he almost fell over, then a young man who was seated near by grabbed the fellow and pitched him out of the café. 'The drunk kept calling me Madge. I don't look like a Madge, do I?'

'Eve suits you better.'

All our following conversation was kept well within the known limits of each other's tolerances; nothing which could become controversial was discussed, and it wasn't until after the meal that she said, 'I don't suppose you want to carry on with the accounts?'

'I will, if you want me to and you don't hide anything.'

She smiled. 'I won't. Cross my heart. But I haven't got much salted away. No Swiss bank account or jewellery in a bank's deposit box. I'm just the owner of a small café in a seaside town.'

When we had cleared the table I began concocting an account of income and expenditure which might pass muster with a not too vigilant Inspector of Taxes. She did her best to be open and honest about her financial affairs and, for my part against my professional instincts, I didn't argue about including mortgage interest due to Moira which had not been demanded or paid. It was almost midnight before I put the finishing touches to a draft statement to be submitted with the completed tax form. As I tidied away the papers Eve asked, 'How much longer are you staying here?'

'Only three more full days.'

'I've been thinking. It's absurd for you to be paying to stay at the hotel when you could have a spare room here free.'

'I couldn't stay here without giving you something.'

'You've already given me hard labour. But I don't want to force you. It's up to you. But you'd be very welcome.'

I almost said, 'I'll think about it', but then I recalled the embrace on arrival and changed this to, 'I can't check out now.'

'But you could tomorrow. And I'd really like to have you stay here.'

'You would?'

'Of course I would.'

'All right then. Tomorrow.'

'Tomorrow,' she repeated. 'I'll make up a bed for you. Come as soon as you've checked out.'

Another disturbed night's sleep followed but this time it was a pleasurable disquiet. I felt I'd found the purpose I'd been seeking and yet, if pressed to explain what exactly it was, I'd have been unable to give a reasoned answer. I knew there were still rivers of incompatability between Eve and me but with that hope which, according to Dr Johnson, triumphs over experience, I had visions of a second time around. No river is unbridgeable. I was cured of workaholism. Next time it would be better.

It was only when thoughts of Moira infiltrated my fantasies that I experienced misgivings. I didn't like Moira or the influence she exerted over Eve which, I suspected, went deeper than the hold which a lender has over a borrower. I could, if necessary, afford to pay off the monetary debt if this would mean complete freedom for Eve but first I would have to be satisfied that the freedom was total and sustainable.

Next morning I paid my hotel bill and checked out.

When I arrived with my suitcase at Fran's Pantry a young woman whom I hadn't seen before was taking orders from a family of five. She looked askance at me as I walked straight through the customers' area and into the kitchen.

Eve was talking to Mrs Andrews who was listening with her usual sour-faced discontent. Eve flashed a smile at me, finishing her instructions, and came over. Looking at the suitcase she said, 'You've done it.'

'Yes. I'm here.'

'I'll show you to your room.'

Mrs Andrews paused from cutting bread – Eve refused to provide sliced bread for her customers – and gave me a look which would have frozen all life in the tropics. I responded by baring my teeth in the imitation of a smile – or was it a snarl?

Upstairs Eve showed me into a small room sparsely furnished with single bed, ancient wardrobe with chipped veneer, and functional chest of drawers. An oval mirror hung on one wall and a framed enlargement of a photo of Joanna, aged eight riding a rocking horse, was on the opposite wall.

'I wondered where that photo had got to,' I said.

'I took it with me when I left . . . Will the room do?'

'It's fine,' I replied and dropped my suitcase.

I went to kiss her but at that moment she turned away. I don't think it was an intentional rebuff; she had simply wanted to indicate a bedside lamp. 'The bulb has blown,' she said, 'and I haven't got round to replacing it.'

It had been the same when we lived together. I had been the one who replaced broken artefacts and made good losses.

'I'll buy a fresh bulb,' I said, reverting to an earlier mode of life.

'I'd better get back,' she said. 'Mrs Andrews is in one of her moods. Do you know what she said when I told her that my friend might be staying here two or three days? She said, "Never give place to the devil. Ephesians, chapter ten." What do you make of that?'

'Unmitigated disapproval of me. Do you still need a washer-up?'

'It would help, if you could bear being in the same kitchen with her. Beryl is back. You probably saw her. But I'm still short-handed. Business has begun to boom.'

She left the room.

As I unpacked the suitcase and hung up clothes I savoured the experience of living with Eve once more. It didn't matter that the room was poorly furnished, or that the window was about four feet away from a red brick wall, or that my stay would be temporary; it was a start.

When the café closed I helped Eve to clean the floor and tables for the following day. As I wiped a table I asked if Moira knew I was staying for three nights.

Eve paused from emptying a display case of a few remaining cakes and pastries. 'No. Why?'

'There's a clause in the mortgage deed which prohibits sub-letting. I wouldn't want her to think I was a tenant.'

In saying this I was being disingenuous, but I wanted to draw out Eve on the nature of her relationship with Moira.

'You're not a tenant,' she said emphatically. 'I'm not accepting any money from you. And anyway, there's no reason why she should know you're staying here.'

'I wouldn't want to cause a rift in your friendship.'

'Why should you?' Eve put down a plate of chocolate éclairs. 'Mark, are you fishing?'

I stopped polishing an already spotless table. 'I suppose I am. But I'm puzzled. You were obviously great friends at school, and great friends now, but when we were married I don't recall her name ever being mentioned.'

Eve thought for a few moments before speaking.

'All right, I'll tell you. Do you remember being told about someone called Charles?'

I knew Eve had been engaged to a man called Charles before she met me. He had died suddenly of a heart attack while playing squash. It had been during Eve's grieving period that I'd met her at the house of a mutual friend.

'The Charles who was once your fiancé?' I asked.

'That's the one. Well, Moira hadn't liked him and she didn't want me to marry him, and when I said I was going to we had one hell of a row. She said she never wanted to see me again. We sort of made it up and then she went to Canada. I was surprised when she wrote to tell me she'd got married. She was always so anti-male. I sometimes wondered if it was' – Eve paused – 'a sort of revenge, if you can understand that. If I'd got married, so would she.'

'Odd coincidence that both Charles and Saul should die of heart attacks,' I said.

Eve nodded. 'I've sometimes thought the same.' She gave a wry laugh. 'It makes me feel literally a *femme fatale*.' And then, picking up the plate of éclairs, 'I'll put these in the fridge. They'll do for one more day.'

Moira wasn't referred to again. We had an evening meal and then went upstairs to play Scrabble, something we'd often done in the happier days of our marriage. Eve won and was so delighted that I was glad of her victory.

'I was afraid I'd never get rid of my "Q",' she said, 'and when I put down "quark" I expected you to challenge. I didn't know whether it was really a word.'

'A quark is a hypothetical elementary particle.'

'You always were the clever one,' she laughed.

On this cheerful note we put away the board and tiles. It was time for bed.

At the door of the sitting room she said, 'Goodnight. Sleep well.' She presented her cheek for a kiss.

I took my courage in my lips and kissed her on the mouth.

'Not tonight,' she whispered, 'I'm not quite clear.' In a louder voice she said, 'You use the bathroom first. I want to do one or two things downstairs.'

And so our ways parted.

She woke me in the morning with a light tug at the bedclothes.

I stirred. 'What's the time?'

'Eight.'

She put down a cup of tea.

'I'll get up and give you a hand,' I said.

She shook her head. 'I'd sooner work on my own. I know exactly what to do. Come down in about an hour and I'll give you a bite to eat.'

After I'd drunk the tea, bathed, and shaved, I went to the sitting room to write up my diary, something I'd neglected to do before retiring to bed.

In the café it was another busy day. I was deputed to look after the cash counter for some of the time so that Eve could be free for other matters including a long argument with Mrs Andrews who was in sullen mood and engaged on a go-slow in protest at an imagined affront.

The time passed quickly as it did again on the following day.

'It hasn't been much of a holiday for you,' Eve remarked at the beginning of the next day.

'I've enjoyed every minute.'

'You haven't had anything like your usual quota of walks. I insist you go out today. It's a lovely morning. I'm fully staffed. No need for you to be stuck indoors.'

I began to protest but she cut me short with, 'I insist. You love wandering along the beach. Go and find me a piece of amber.'

'You'll be lucky! With me it's not "Forever Amber", it's "Never Amber".'

'Anyway, you go. Please. Have a day off. We can spend the evening together and . . . well . . . I'm clear.'

Was this the old Eve, the one who sometimes teased and then tired? I didn't think so. It was with a light heart that I set off on a walk which was to take me almost to Sizewell and back.

A high-pressure belt reigned over East Anglia and the sky was almost cloudless. The sea, at low tide, lapped gently against a mixture of sand and shingle, and I was able to comb the margin although sometimes I zigzagged along the upper beach in a search for the elusive amber.

In the beachcombing I found a plastic ballpoint pen, an old George V sixpence, and a rusty corkscrew, as well as the usual flotsam. I picked up a number of stones but kept none. The sixpence was the only trophy I retained as I tramped back to Aldeburgh.

It was as I was in sight of the Moot Hall that my heart jumped like an electrified tuna. Amber! Or was it? Tentatively I put it in my mouth and bit on a piece the size of a small hen's egg. My teeth told me it wasn't stone. The next test was to take a Kleenex tissue from my pocket. I rubbed the piece vigorously and held it just above a fragment of tissue. Success! The tissue rose and clung to the amber.

I hurried along the beach, went inland to the High Street, and to a jeweller's shop. The jeweller examined my find carefully. 'It's amber all right,' he said, 'but I'm not buying any at the moment. I'm fully stocked.'

I didn't tell him I wouldn't have sold it for a fortune.

That evening when Eve and I sat down to supper I handed her a small gift-wrapped box.

'What's this?' she asked, her eyes lighting in anticipation.

She stripped off the paper wrapping and opened the box.

'Oh, they're lovely,' she said, picking up a pair of earrings, 'but you shouldn't.'

'It's a thank-you for having me.'

'There was no need for that.' She removed sleepers from her ears and put in the gold-drop earrings. 'How do they look?'

'Fine.'

I then produced a second box.

'Really, Mark,' she exclaimed.

'Open it.'

She lifted the little lid and peered down.

'Found today,' I said. 'It hasn't been polished but I can get that done, if you'd like. But it is genuine.'

She gave me a ravishing smile. 'Did you really find it today?'

'I did.'

'And you told me all you'd got was an old sixpence.'

She rose from the table and came across to kiss me. It was a long kiss.

When she returned to her chair she said, 'I feel like an early night tonight. How about you?'

The mundane question was accompanied with a look which pierced the limbic system of my brain like a laser strike sending heart-rate and hormones into overdrive. It was the ultimate in significant looks; the look which makes men write lyric poetry, gamble fortunes, and defy death against all odds.

But my reply to her question fell a long way short of such tributes. I could do no better than, 'Good idea. An early night.'

After the meal she said, 'We'll leave the washing-up until morning, but we'll have coffee upstairs and then I'll get ready for bed.'

I didn't ask if I could join her. After I'd got myself ready for the night I simply walked into her bedroom.

She pulled back a duvet to make space for me. It was then I noticed a thin gold chain round her neck. She was wearing a white low-cut nightdress and a small crucifix was visible dangling between her breasts. I was slightly surprised. Eve had never been religious. Perhaps she wore it all the time and I hadn't seen it before. But the necklace was only a momentary distraction; I had more urgent objectives. The first was to take her in my arms and hold her close.

There is a distinction between 'making love' and 'sex' although many people use the former term as a euphemism for the latter when referring to the most intimate of human physical contacts, and if the word 'sex' is used to describe the act it is a euphemism for 'lust'. There is a fashionable hypocrisy in descriptive usage.

I shan't attempt to define or analyse the difference between making love and sex but what we did was making love. It wasn't

41

a matter of mutual sexual release. At least, for me it wasn't. The only moment which might have caused difficulty, if I hadn't suppressed my thoughts, was when Eve moved down the bed and did something she'd never done with me before. Briefly the ghostly presence of some other lover chilled the room. But the moment passed.

It was during the aftermath as we lay contentedly in each other's arms that I enquired about the crucifix. Her body stiffened slightly.

'Does it matter?' she asked.

'I'm curious. I remember you used to be scornful of women who wore crucifixes.'

'You'll laugh at me if I tell you.'

'Of course I won't.'

She switched out the light and her voice in the darkness sounded like an insecure child when she said, 'It's stupid of me, I know, so please don't laugh. I don't know how to say this . . . It's a precaution.'

'Precaution against what?'

There was a long pause. 'Something bad,' she said. 'Not nice.'

'Evil?'

'Yes, sort of.'

'What evil?'

'Don't ask too many questions, please. It's been lovely. Don't spoil it.'

And so I didn't pursue this line of questioning. Instead, I said, 'Amber is reputed to give protection against enemies as well as bringing good luck. How would you like it if I got your piece of amber polished, set in gold, and made into a brooch?'

'I'd like it very much.'

She nestled closer.

'Tomorrow I'll take it to a jeweller,' I said, 'and see what can be done.'

She gave a drowsy murmur and moments later was asleep.

5

It was on the following day when the café was closed and my bag was packed that Eve, who was standing by the sitting-room window, asked, 'What will you do when you get back?'

'I don't know. Have a drink maybe. Open the windows.'

'And then?'

'I'll see what's left in the fridge and make a snack; see what's on the box or the radio. If there's nothing good I shall probably turn in for the night. What about you?'

She shrugged her shoulders. 'Much the same, I guess. I don't feel like calling Moira to see if she feels like meeting for a drink at the Three Tuns.'

Outside the sky was darkening and the wind was blowing off the sea. The rhythm of breaking waves was clearly audible. Normally this is a soothing sound but the steady repetitive murmur only heightened the tension growing between us.

'It's been great seeing you again,' I said.

'And to see you . . . Give me a phone call when you get in.'

'Right.'

'You've been a great help. I don't know what I'd have done . . .' Her voice trailed away.

'Let's hope the tax returns are accepted but if you have any problems . . .'

'I'll let you know . . . I'm sorry if I snapped at you once or twice. I didn't mean it.'

'It was nothing.'

'I've changed a bit, Mark. I'm more' – she searched for a word – 'responsible.

'I've changed a bit too. I hope I'm more tolerant.'

She left the window and came towards me. 'Do you really have to get back to your flat? I mean, does anything depend on it?'

I had to admit that nothing depended on my return. I said, 'I've got a ticket for a concert but I don't mind missing that. And then there's Verity, but she's got a key.'

'Who's Verity?'

'My West Indian cleaning lady.'

'Oh, yes, I remember. Then if nothing depends on it . . .'

I finished the sentence for her. 'I could stay on here for a bit.'

'I wish you would,' she said with intensity as though beseeching a favour of incredible magnitude.

'I'll stay,' I said.

She threw her arms round my neck and kissed me with a passion that sent me rocking on my heels. Her eyes, when they opened, were misty. Soon they were shining. 'I've got one bottle of champagne stashed away for a special occasion,' she said. 'We're going to celebrate.'

The following days were a second honeymoon. I helped in the café and made some useful economies, not only by negotiating with suppliers for regular bulk purchases but by reducing orders for confections for which there was little demand. I also changed the position of the cash counter so that space was made available for another table for customers.

I telephoned Verity and asked her to make a regular check that everything was in order at the flat; I told her I'd let her know when I planned to return but this wouldn't be for some time yet. Because my stay had been prolonged it was necessary to increase my limited wardrobe and I bought a whole new set of clothes. Each evening after cashing-up we would take a stroll along the front, have a drink at a hotel or pub, and perhaps have a meal out. We might play a game or two of Scrabble before going to bed. More often than not, we would fall instantly asleep. My insomnia was cured.

The only blemish in our second-time-around idyll was Moira. She would call unexpectedly, which wasn't unreasonable as Eve's backer in the enterprise, but although she had approved my work as an accountant, she was critical of almost every change I suggested for running the café. When exploring possibilities for improvements I floated the idea of installing piped classical music, Mozart or Chopin: the tentative idea was scornfully dismissed before I'd finished speaking.

44

'Why not fruit machines, too? Put in half a dozen fruit machines, and sell candy-floss and T-shirts with rude slogans! Honestly, Mark, you haven't a clue what's wanted here. Piped music! You stick to balance sheets and leave the creative side to Eve and me.'

I noticed the argument made Eve nervous and so I dropped the subject.

That night before we went to bed I said we ought to tell Moira about our true relationship, and that we had been married.

A look of horror came to Eve's face. 'Oh, I couldn't do that. Not yet, anyway. She'd never forgive me. You don't know Moira. She has a very vengeful, unforgiving streak.'

'It's a pity you weren't honest in the first place.'

She nodded. 'Yes. I regret it now. But I didn't know then that things would turn out the way they have. Please don't say anything to her.'

For three days we heard nothing from Moira but on the fourth she arrived as we were cashing-up. She gave me a curt nod before saying, 'What do you think, Cat dear, I've got a couple of tickets for a production of *Hedda Gabler* in Ipswich on Saturday night. I'd love you to come with me. What about it?'

Eve looked at me, a plea in her eyes.

'You go, if you want to,' I said. 'I shall have plenty to do.'

Moira gave a harsh laugh. 'Really! Has it come to that? Does one have to give permission to the other to have a night out?'

Eve and I were both silent.

'Will you come with me, Cat?'

'Yes.' The affirmative was almost inaudible.

'Good. Now, I've got a bit of time to spare before going to take poor Dorothy her shopping. I wonder if I could cadge a cup of tea. Not that cheap junk stuff Mark has persuaded you to buy but Earl Grey.'

She'd said she had an hour to kill but I had the impression she'd sooner have killed me. Upstairs in the sitting room she began making snide remarks about the male sex. She was trying to wind me up and for the sake of Eve, who was looking acutely apprehensive, I resisted the temptation to give better than I got. None of the slurs were obviously directed at me.

After she had left to visit her friend Dorothy, Eve said, 'I'm not going.'

'Are you sure?'

She came across the room and sat on the edge of my chair before sliding an arm round my neck. 'She's forcing me to make a choice, and this is my choice.' She lowered her head to give me a kiss.

I was touched by her loyalty but instinct told me it would be unwise to cross Moira just yet. The time to sever relations with her would be if Eve and I decided to remarry. Until then we'd play along with Moira's bitchiness.

'I'd like you to go,' I said. 'It's an outing for you and I can get on with the Puccini biography.'

Immense relief lightened her face. 'Are you sure?'

'Positive.'

She kissed me again. 'You were right when you said you'd become more tolerant. I love you, Mark. I think I always have.'

'And I love you.'

It was a moment when I should have proposed marriage, but I didn't. I held back. It was because I wanted any proposal to be at a more romantic time and place, at a candlelit champagne dinner perhaps, or at a weekend break in a five-star hotel in Paris. Instead of 'Will you marry me?', I said, 'Who is this "poor Dorothy" Moira's taking shopping to?'

'That illustrates Moira's best side. I know she can be, well, abrasive, but she can also be very understanding with some people. Dorothy is menopausal and has gone a bit funny, sort of agoraphobic. She won't go out during the day, only at night. She's become something of a recluse and Moira is the only person she'll let into her home. Moira does her shopping.'

Then Eve suggested a game of Scrabble and the moment to propose was lost.

Saturday arrived and Moira called to collect Eve. As always she was dressed in clothes that looked like the cast-offs of a garage mechanic, oil-stained and shapeless. She gave me a triumphant look as they left. She might as well have said aloud, *I've won!*

I wasn't annoyed. If Moira regarded me as a rival, someone to score off, that was her problem, not mine. I went upstairs and after writing up my diary I continued reading the biography of Puccini. When darkness fell I made some sandwiches and went on reading. I was on the last chapter, and my third whisky, when Eve arrived back from her evening at Ipswich.

I asked if I could get her a drink.

'Yes. A stiff brandy.'

She seemed pale.

'Are you all right?' I asked.

She shook her head. 'I've had one hell of a row with Moira.' She shook her head again as though it needed clearing. 'And when she dropped me off here just now she said something terrible.'

I paused from pouring brandy. 'What did she say?'

'I'll tell you in a minute. I want to sit still for a moment.'

I passed her a glass of brandy and waited until she was ready to speak.

'It started on the way home,' she said. 'We'd been talking about the play when Moira, apropos the play, said all men were fools. "Not all," I said. She didn't agree and said all men were fools where women were concerned. And then she picked on you and said that any woman who listened adoringly to your "trivial" opinions, and went to bed with you, would have you eating out of her hand.'

Eve took another sip of brandy and looked across to where I was sitting. 'I resented that,' she said, 'and I let it show. I started defending you. I said that I knew you much better than she ever would, and you weren't at all like that.'

'Thanks, but it was probably the worst thing you could have done.'

'It was. She began needling me and she's very good at that. She's an expert at finding out people's weak points and then attacking them. She used to do it at school. One girl even tried to commit suicide because of what Moira had said to her. Anyway, I got more and more on edge as she sneered at you and made sarcastic remarks. She said you probably weren't anything more than a con man and that you were conning me. I was stupid not to see you were nothing more than a freeloader. That was too much. I saw red. I said she didn't know what the hell she was talking about. I told her the truth, who you were, and that we'd been married.'

'How did she react?'

'She went very quiet.'

Eve looked at her glass which was empty. I fetched the bottle and poured another drink.

'It was awful,' she went on. 'We did the last part of the journey in a terrible atmosphere. I said mundane things about the play, the weather, anything. She didn't utter a word. When we arrived here I thanked her for taking me to the play and said next time it would be my turn to treat her.'

Eve paused and gave me a pleading look as though needing assurance that this had been the right thing to say.

'You were trying to make it up?' I asked.

'Exactly. I didn't want to quarrel. I owe her too much.'

'I understand.'

'And so I said, shall we have another outing together? Do you know what she said?'

'I can't guess.'

'She hadn't said anything for, I don't know, a quarter of an hour, and I thought she wasn't going to say anything then, but she did. She turned to me and said, "The only outing I want with you is to your funeral!" '

As she spoke Eve's hand trembled so violently that she spilt some brandy. 'Oh, damn!' she exclaimed.

'I'll get a cloth. Don't move.'

When I'd wiped up the spillage she said, 'I'm frightened, Mark.'

'Don't be. She can't harm you. Not physically. And don't let her get to you mentally.'

'I'll try not to, but do you know what I think?'

'No. What do you think?'

'You might think it sounds crazy.'

'Go on.'

She lowered her voice as though afraid of being overheard. 'I know she's got a good side. The way she helps Dorothy, for instance. But . . . I think she dabbles in witchcraft. I think she's a witch.'

I didn't laugh. I'm one with Dr Johnson when he said of the occult, 'All argument is against it but all belief is for it.' I wasn't surprised that Eve suspected Moira of possessing some sort of evil power.

I said, 'I'm not being sceptical, but have you got any evidence that she might be a witch?'

'Not really. Well, perhaps. One day, when we were children, I called at her house and she was out. Her mother told me to wait in her bedroom because she was entertaining visitors in the sitting room. I went to the bedroom and on the dressing table was a crude human figure made of plasticene with pins sticking into it.'

'Did she ever explain that?'

'Yes. She said it was her pin-cushion. I pretended to believe her although I thought it was a queer sort of pin-cushion. And I've sometimes wondered about Saul's death. He was a fit man.'

'He was overweight.' The words escaped before I could stop them.

'All right. He was overweight but otherwise very fit. He'd had a medical check only three weeks before and was, apart from the weight, rated A1 in health.' She took a swig of brandy. 'Imagine saying a thing like that to me. Do you think I'm silly to feel frightened?'

'Not silly, but she can't do anything to you physically. It's mental intimidation.'

'I wish I'd kept my mouth shut about us being married.'

'I'm not. I didn't like the idea in the first place. I'm glad it's out in the open.'

She shook her head slightly as though disagreeing but made no comment.

Although she was tired she didn't want to go to bed and we stayed up well past midnight. I tried to convince her she had nothing to fear from Moira's cruel threat. I probed for information about Moira's past because it had occurred to me, as I think it would to anyone, that she was homosexually orientated. But I couldn't believe her friendship with Eve was a lesbian one. Determined to find out what I could, I asked, 'Do you think she's a lesbian?'

'Why do you ask?'

'She seems very anti-male.'

She gave a short laugh. 'You don't have to be a lesbian to be anti-male, my dear. And I'm sure there are plenty of lesbians who are pro-male provided the male is no sexual threat. No, I wouldn't say Moira was a lesbian. Asexual perhaps.' She narrowed her eyes and gave me a piercing look. 'You're not thinking . . .'

As had frequently happened she had tuned into the direction of my thoughts. 'No, of course not.'

'I should hope not.' She gave a slight sigh. 'I suppose it must be puzzling for you. I mean, why she and I should be friends.

Well, at school I rather looked up to her. She was terrifically athletic and was school games captain before she was sixteen. I was hopeless at any sort of sport but none of the girls dared rib me for always coming in last, not if Moira was around. So there was a close bond between us at school and these things aren't easily forgotten. When she came back into my life the years melted away and it was as if we'd parted only a few weeks before.' She paused. 'I must say she seemed tougher than ever and I had moments when I felt a bit uneasy. It was about three months ago she tried to interest me in the occult, but I don't like that sort of thing, and I began to wonder about her.'

'About her being a witch?'

'Well, at least having something to do with witchcraft.'

'Apart from the pins in a plasticine figure, and the fact that Charles and Saul, both men she disliked, died suddenly of heart attacks, is there any other reason why you think she is involved in witchcraft?'

She frowned in thought. 'The first time I went to her house in Leiston I went upstairs to the loo, but I walked into the wrong room. Before I could find the light switch Moira was behind me. "Don't go in there!" she said, so loudly it made me jump. "You didn't see anything, did you?" I said, "No," but I'd glimpsed what looked like a whip hanging from a hook near the door. She explained that it was an absolute mess and she hadn't got around to tidying it up, and she'd be ashamed for anyone to see it. To be honest, I didn't really believe this but I didn't want to dwell on it. She'd been very good to me and I more or less blotted the incident from my mind.'

'Anything else?' I asked.

'No. I know it all seems a bit far-fetched. Perhaps I'm being silly and over-imaginative.'

We went to bed at two in the morning and what Eve needed was nothing more intimate than snuggling close in embracing arms. As I shifted to cushion her body my hand brushed against her necklace. I asked if, since suspecting Moira of being a witch, she'd taken to wearing a crucifix.

'Am I being silly?' she asked.

I thought she was being superstitious but I said, 'No, I don't think you're being silly.'

50

She gave a contented murmur, nestled even closer, and was soon asleep.

It must have been at least an hour before I dozed off.

The sun was clear of the horizon when I drew back the sitting room curtains. Beyond the beach the sea was sparkling like a grey-green dress covered with thousands of glittering sequins. Eve came and stood beside me and slipped her hand into mine. Neither of us mentioned the events of the previous evening.

The café was closed on Sundays so we went for a walk along the beach before I drove to Orford for lunch. After a drink at the King's Head we went across the road to Butley's Oysterage where we had oysters and crab salad, then for a stroll close to the banks of the River Ore before returning to Aldeburgh. For the first time Eve referred to the previous evening.

'I think I got Moira at a bad moment. She'll get used to the idea that we were once married. After all, it was only a little deception on my part.'

'Don't let it bother you. She'll get over it.'

It was about nine o'clock in the evening of what had been a perfect day that the phone rang. As Eve had gone out to post a letter I answered the call.

A man's voice said, 'You won't know me but I'm a friend and I'm ringing to warn you. The woman you're staying with isn't what she seems. She's a whore who's had it off with half the lads in town.'

'Who are you?' I interrupted.

'I've told you. I'm a friend. And she's not only had it off with men, she's got a friend, the Makepeace woman, a real dyke, and the two of them have been seen—'

I hung up the phone.

When Eve returned she looked so bright, fresh and happy, I couldn't immediately tell her of the call; but later in the evening I mentioned it in an off-hand, dismissive way. I didn't want her to think I gave any credit to the slanders.

She listened, aghast.

'I hope you don't believe it!' she exclaimed.

'Of course I don't. But who could it be? He had a local accent and sounded quite young.'

51

Still looking shocked she replied, 'I can't think.'

'Could Moira be behind it? Could she have got someone to ring?'

'I can't believe she'd stoop so low,' Eve said firmly. 'No. It must be a nut-case. What a pity I'd just gone out. I wonder what he'd have said if I'd answered the phone.'

Three nights later we discovered what he would have said. It was at about the same time, nine o'clock, and Eve left the table where we were playing Scrabble to take the call.

I saw her jaw fall open, not to speak, but in shock, and then she slammed down the phone. Her face was pale.

'Who was it?' I asked.

'I don't know. He talked fast . . . I must sit down.'

'Was it an obscene call?'

'Yes.'

'What did he say?'

'I don't remember. It was a stream of filth.'

'We must report it to the police.'

'No! It won't do any good. Moira had the same problem when she first came to Leiston and tried the police and British Telecom but didn't get anywhere so she got a police whistle and, when the fellow started his rubbish, she blew it close to the mouthpiece. He tried once more and she gave him the same treatment. He never called again. Needless to say, it didn't improve her opinion of men.'

'Perhaps it's the same guy, a pathetic pervert.'

'Maybe.' She gave a weak smile. 'If it happens again I'll buy myself a whistle. Come on, let's get on with the game. Have you put down my score?'

She was in the bathroom getting ready for bed when the phone rang once more. Whoever was calling put down the handset when I answered and the line went dead.

When Eve came out of the bathroom she asked, 'Who was it?'

'The same guy, I guess. He hung up without speaking.'

'Let's leave the phone off the hook tonight,' she said. 'We want a good night's sleep.' And then, coming closer and looking up seductively, she added, 'Besides, we don't want any interruptions before we go to sleep, do we?'

Such was her power to arouse that this hint of pleasure in store was enough to create a quickening tumescence in what had been an inert appendage.

'No telephonus interruptus, you mean?' I said.

She laughed. 'You've got it in one.'

After a love-making which was even more erotic than usual due to a variation she initiated she fell asleep in my arms.

As was customary on working days Eve was the first to rise in the morning. She had a range of jobs she liked to do before Beryl or Sandra arrived.

When I joined her in the kitchen for a light breakfast she handed me a letter. 'This came in the post this morning,' she said. 'Read it.'

6

The letter was from a prestigious firm of London solicitors; not the solicitors who held the mortgage deeds. I read it carefully.

Dear Madam,

We have been consulted by our client, Mrs Moira Makepeace, with regard to the regular monthly payment of £366 due to her under the terms of a legal charge on property known as Fran's Pantry.

We understand that to date you have made no payments of interest and accordingly we have to inform you that if payment of all arrears up to and including the first May is not forthcoming within the next fourteen days we shall reluctantly be compelled to institute proceedings against you for possession of the property. We compute the sum in question to be £6,954.

We further understand that our client made an unsecured loan to you in the sum of £10,000 for the purpose of making improvements to the aforementioned property. Although this loan was made on a somewhat informal basis we have no doubt that its repayment could be secured through an Order by the Court. However, our client does not wish to be unreasonable, or put you to the expense of a Court action, and is prepared to allow six months' grace for the repayment of the unsecured loan.

We shall be glad to hear from you as soon as possible with a draft in the first instance of £6,954. Of course if you wish to clear your total indebtedness to our client we should be pleased to receive a draft in the sum of £16,954.

Yours faithfully,
(Signature indecipherable)

Eve looked at me with eyes wide with dismay. 'What shall I do?' she asked. 'I can't possibly pay what she wants.'

'What a cow!'

'When she gets her knife into someone it goes for the vital organs.' She swung round and dashed to the cooker. 'I forgot your egg. It'll be hard-boiled!'

'Don't worry about that, and don't worry about the letter. I'm sure they'll be prepared to negotiate.'

'Negotiate?'

'Foreclosure isn't quite the straightforward business some people think. If you offer to pay off the debts by reasonably substantial instalments they'll probably recommend Moira to accept.'

'Negotiate,' said Eve once more as though the word was from a foreign language she didn't understand.

'Offer to pay off at the rate of, say, five hundred and fifty a month. On your takings and projected increases during the summer you could afford that.'

'You mean – give in?'

'For self-preservation it's sometimes necessary to be flexible.'

'Flexible.'

Her clipped replies to everything I said made it seem she was as much out of her depth as a baby tossed into a whirl-pool.

'They would want more than five hundred and fifty, but that's when the hard negotiating would start.'

'I can't think how Moira could do this to me,' she said.

'She's jealous of you and me. That's what it's about.'

Eve frowned thoughtfully as she considered this piece of ama-teur psychoanalysis. My thoughts were on a different track. Should I offer to pay off her debts? If possible I wanted to avoid raising £16,000 from my resources as this would mean selling shares during a depressed bear market.

'I suppose you're right,' said Eve at length. 'She's jealous. It was like that at school. She didn't like it if I got too friendly with anyone else. Half a dozen of us had a secret society; we were all "Cats". At our little meetings I always had to sit next to her. I was designated Cat Vice-Chair. But I can't give in and "negotiate" as you call it. I know her. She wouldn't negotiate, she'd just turn

55

the screws tighter . . . Oh, Mark, my love! What can I do?'

I had already told her what she should do. Negotiate. Almost every problem or difference between two people can be overcome by negotiation, given sanity and goodwill on both sides.

'Do you want to sit tight, then?' I asked. 'Do nothing? See if it's a bluff?'

'It won't be a bluff.'

I cracked the shell of a hard-boiled egg with a spoon and could happily have cracked Moira's head instead.

Eve started cutting a loaf of bread, which had recently become one of my jobs. Perhaps she was wishing it was Moira's throat. 'I'm not giving in,' she said. 'Let her do her worst.'

'That's the stuff.' As I spoke I knew that if the worst came I'd find the money. In the mean while we'd do nothing. Masterly inactivity would be our strategy.

A few days after receiving the letter from Moira's solicitors we were faced by a problem from a different quarter. I don't know what it is about me, perhaps I lack that elusive magic called charm, but I have never beguiled women by looks or chat and certainly I didn't appeal to Mrs Andrews. I tried to be friendly but might as well have tried to befriend a stick-insect. She would have nothing of my sociable commonplaces and attempted pleasantries. It was clear she disliked my presence in the kitchen. She gave in her notice. She said she'd stay one more week and then go. She thought I was spying on her.

Eve told me all this while we were going for our usual stroll along the Crag Path after the café had closed. I felt her take my arm and hold it tightly.

'At least I've still got you,' she said.

'I'll have to go back to town sometime.'

'Oh.' Her grip slackened.

'I've got to check that all's well, but I'll be back. Now that I've found you I'm not going to lose you again.'

Her grip tightened once more and she gave my cheek a quick kiss.

'I was a fool,' she said. 'I wasn't really in love with Saul. I liked him a lot, but it wasn't really love. It was just that I was—'

She broke off and I supplied the missing words. 'Bored to death.'

56

'We agreed not to go back,' she said. 'Sorry I started it. From now on, no explanations, justifications or recriminations.'

During the following week I found it difficult being in the kitchen with Mrs Andrews. How does one demonstrate that one isn't spying? I took pains not to say anything more than was necessary although Eve, for reasons of her own, played the game we had played when first married of jokingly insulting each other. Maybe she thought it would annoy Mrs Andrews.

It was two evenings before her notice was due to expire that we had another obscene call. Eve, who hadn't bought a police whistle, slammed down the phone.

'Was it him again?' I asked.

'Yes, but he didn't get beyond calling me a whore.'

It suddenly occurred to me that Mrs Andrews might be behind the calls. 'Hasn't Mrs Andrews got a son?' I asked. 'I know she's a widow.'

'Yes. He works for Eastern Electricity and drives to Ipswich each day.'

'Could she have got him to make the calls?'

Eve pursed her lips. 'I doubt it. No. It's some nut-case who's got my number.'

The calls had all been made at or around nine o'clock in the evening. I suggested that while I was staying with her I should take all evening calls. She agreed.

Mrs Andrews walked out at the end of her period of notice without troubling to say goodbye to me. The only trouble she took was to count out her final wage packet before marching out of the café like an outraged stork.

Eve hadn't found a replacement and during the following week we both worked flat out to keep the café going and the customers satisfied. Eve took over Mrs Andrews's duties and I trebled up as waiter, dish-washer and cashier. We rose early every morning and got to bed late at night. Neither of us mentioned the threat issued by Moira's solicitors but I knew Eve was worried. Each day when the mail arrived Eve would rush to the door to see what the postman had delivered, and there would be relief on her face when she discovered there was no solicitors' letter.

It was about nine on a Saturday evening when the phone rang. We were upstairs having just returned from having dined out at a hotel near the Moot Hall. Eve was wearing a pretty dress with

57

low neckline and I knew from her manner that tonight we would be making love. Annoyed by the ringing telephone I picked up the handset and in a brusque no-nonsense voice said, 'Who's that?'

The caller said, 'Oh, hello, Mr Markby, this is Verity. I'm sorry but I've got bad news.'

Either there was interference on the line or she was speaking from a place exposed to noise. I had to ask her to repeat her last words.

'I'm sorry but I've got bad news. It's your flat.'

'What about it?'

'It's been vandalized. The place is in a terrible state.'

Although background noise interfered with what she was saying, something in her voice didn't sound quite right. It seemed curiously inexpressive whereas normally it rose and fell in musical cadences.

'Have you reported this to the police?'

'Yes, I've reported it.'

Before I could ask any more questions the line went dead.

'Who was that?' Eve asked.

'Verity. She says my flat's been vandalized. I'd better go and see what it's all about.'

'Vandalized? Who?'

'I don't know. We got cut off. I don't think she was calling from the flat but I'll ring back.'

I keyed my own number. It rang and rang. There was no reply.

'I'll have to go back and see what the damage is,' I said to Eve.

'It's late.'

'I know, but I must go.'

'Can't it wait until tomorrow? I'd been hoping . . .'

'So had I, but I must see what the damage is. I wouldn't sleep or be a good lover if I waited until tomorrow.'

She sighed. 'Oh, all right, if you must, you must.'

'It's Sunday tomorrow so you won't need my help and I'll be back before you open up on Monday. But I want to assess the damage and see if the police have any clues. You'll be OK. It's only one night.'

She gave a weak smile. 'I'm being selfish. Yes, you go.'

I gave her a quick kiss and hurried from the room before she changed her mind and begged me to stay.

She came out to the car park with me and when I wound down the window ready to wave goodbye she poked her head through the open space and gave a final kiss. 'Drive carefully,' she said.

'I will.'

'Let me know you've arrived safely.'

'I will.'

'See you sometime tomorrow then.'

'Without any doubt.'

'I love you, Mark. I really do.'

'I love you too.'

On that sweet note I engaged gears and backed out of the car park.

The last glimpse I had of Eve was of a forlorn figure standing under the pale light of a street lamp, waving an arm.

Apart from a very minor collision with another car at the A12 junction in which there was no damage to either vehicle the journey was uneventful.

Normally I make a note of journey departure and arrival times but on this occasion I was so preoccupied with wondering what damage I should find that I didn't note the time I drove into the underground car-park beneath my flat. I think it was around midnight.

I ran up three flights of stairs and unlocked the front door. Having half expected the lock to be broken I was glad the key worked perfectly. How had the vandals entered, I wondered as I switched on the light.

The small hall was undisturbed. The vandals hadn't bothered to desecrate this part of the flat. And then I entered the sitting room. To my amazement everything was as I'd left it. I went round the flat room by room. Nothing had been touched. I was both immensely relieved and mystified. Why had Verity made the call? She didn't seem the type to play practical jokes; she was quiet and unassuming, even timid, and I had the impression that she'd been bullied into earning money by her unemployed husband.

I telephoned the place in Balham where they and their children lived. It was a Victorian villa which had been converted into six flats and there was a communal phone in the downstairs hall. After about a minute a man's voice came on the line and I asked if I could speak to Verity da Costa who occupied Flat Four.

'No, you bloody well can't. What do you think I am? A bloody messenger boy?'

The line went dead.

I waited a moment or two and then keyed Eve's number. It was engaged. A few minutes later I tried again but the line was still engaged. Who would she be calling, or calling her, at this late hour? I tried once more, a quarter of an hour later, but with no better result. Either there was some technical malfunction or she'd left the phone off the hook.

I decided to spend the night at the flat. In the morning I'd try to contact Verity, who had a lot to explain. And I'd try again to get in touch with Eve to inform her of the situation and say I'd return to Aldeburgh as soon as possible.

My sleep was deep and I didn't wake until eight thirty.

It was as I was about to phone Eve that the doorbell rang. Wondering whether the caller was Verity who had come to apologize for a rotten joke, I opened the door. Two casually dressed men stood outside, their faces as about expressive as a couple of chunks of granite. One of the callers, a man with close-set grey eyes and mouth downturned at the corners, said, 'Are you Mr Mark Markby, sir?'

'I am.'

He thrust a card at me. 'Detective Inspector Clench,' he said. 'May I have a word with you? This is my colleague, Detective Constable Baker.'

Verity had said she'd reported vandalism of my flat to the police. But there had been no vandalism. Were the two callers true policemen or were they participants in an elaborate and bafflingly inexplicable hoax. The identity card looked genuine.

Clench's voice became harder. 'I said, may we have a word, sir?'

'I wasn't expecting you to call on me.'

'You weren't expecting us to call on you yet, you mean.'

'No, I wasn't expecting you at all.'

'Really? I'd be glad to know why you weren't expecting us sooner or later.'

His incomprehension irritated me but it seemed sensible to comply with his request to "have a word". I would then get to the bottom of Verity's vandalism story.

'You'd better come in,' I said.

7

I took them to the sitting room. 'As you can see,' I said, 'there hasn't been any vandalism. I don't know what Mrs da Costa's game is, but I've been brought back here on a wild-goose chase.'

While I was speaking I noticed Baker wandering around the room, peering here and there, as though looking for something. It passed through my mind that the two men were professional thieves using stolen or faked identity cards. But Clench looked and sounded exactly like the stereotype of a plain-clothes detective as seen on television when he said, 'I'd like you to explain that remark, sir. What's this about vandalism, and who is Mrs da Costa?'

'I've assumed you are here,' I said slowly, 'to check out a report made by a Mrs da Costa, who does domestic work for me, that my flat had been vandalized.'

Clench turned to his colleague who was impudently toying with an ivory paper-knife which had been lying on the top of a cabinet. 'Have we had such a report, John?' he asked.

'Not to my knowledge,' the other replied. 'I've not heard anything about reported vandalism, sir.'

'Nor have I. No, Mr Markby, we're here on a more serious matter. Might I ask where you were last night?'

'Why do you want to know?' Although the question was addressed to Clench I kept my eyes on Baker who was still fiddling about with the paper-knife. I wanted to make sure he didn't pocket it.

'I'm pursuing an enquiry,' said Clench, 'and for the purposes of elimination it would be helpful to know where you were last night.'

I disliked his air of studious politeness and the way Baker, having put the paper-knife on a coffee table where it didn't belong, was now examining a small bronze bust of Mozart. I wanted these intruders out of my flat without delay and so I said, 'If it's of any real concern to you I was at Aldeburgh in Suffolk during the first part of the evening. I had a call from Mrs da Costa to say, quite wrongly, that this place had been vandalized. I came back to London to find everything in order. I don't know why she did it but I intend to find out.'

'Could you say what time you left Aldeburgh?'

'What is all this about?'

'The time, sir.'

'I think it was about ten. So what?'

Baker had stopped prowling around and was watching me intently. He and Clench exchanged glances and Clench said, 'I must ask you to accompany us to the police station.'

'Why?'

'To make a statement about your movements last night, sir.'

This was very annoying, but I guessed that if I prevaricated my departure would be further delayed.

'I'll come with you,' I said, 'if you'll tell me what this enquiry is about, but first I want to telephone my friend.'

'Which friend is that, sir?'

'I don't see that it's any of your business but it's a lady who lives at Aldeburgh and who will be expecting me. I was just about to make a call to her when you turned up.'

Baker moved in closer, still staring fixedly at me, as Clench asked, 'Can I enquire, who is this lady?'

'You can, although I don't see that it's any concern of yours. It's a Mrs Harris.'

'A Mrs Eve Elaine Harris?'

I was surprised. How did he know Eve's forenames?

'Yes.'

'Then I have to tell you that such a call would be a waste of money, an unnecessary addition to your telephone account.'

Clench gave a smile as bleak as the beach in winter and Baker smirked at what seemed to be an attempt at sardonic humour by his superior officer. But I was gripped by a terrible fear.

'What do you mean?'

'I think you know what I mean but I'll spell it out. Mrs Harris is dead, almost certainly murdered. She was your ex-wife, or so I have been informed. Is that correct?'

I nodded my head, unable to speak.

'And that is why I want you to come with us to make a statement.'

'How did it happen?' I managed to say.

Clench didn't reply.

'I need to know!' I shouted. 'What happened to Eve?'

'It's my duty to find out what I can about the deceased and it would assist me if you would accompany us to the station to make a statement.'

I realized that Clench regarded me as a suspect and this awareness somehow temporarily numbed feelings of loss.

'Give me a moment to close and lock the windows,' I said, 'and I'll be with you.'

Clench made an impatient gesture. 'Do whatever you want to your windows, but let's not waste any more time.'

Like a dog keeping close to its handler Baker followed on my heels as I went round the flat fastening all windows; maybe he thought I might try to abseil to freedom.

Throughout a very long drive to a police station Clench sat tight-lipped and refused to answer my questions. It was only when we were closeted in a very clean but functional interview room which smelled faintly of emulsion paint that he became more forthcoming.

'Mrs Harris's body was found in her kitchen,' he said. 'We shall be taking a number of statements, not only from persons who worked in the café and had access to the kitchen, but also from any regular customers, or others, who may be able to assist us in our enquiries. I now propose to interview you and I presume you will have no objection to a tape-recording being made of the interview.'

'None at all,' I said. 'I want to get this over and go back to Aldeburgh.'

Baker ripped cellophane wrapping from unused tapes and loaded a double-deck recorder and then Clench went through the prescribed code of practice relating to police interviews by stating the names of those present, the time, date, and place, before concluding, 'You do not have to say anything unless you wish to do so, but what you say may be given in evidence.'

'I understand.'

We were seated at a table opposite each other. It had occurred to me to ask for my solicitor to be present but I didn't want to interrupt his Sunday leisure-time. Moreover, I felt sure I could cope unaided with the situation.

Clench fired his first question. 'What exactly were you doing in Aldeburgh, Mr Markby?'

'I went there initially for a holiday, for a break.'

'A break from what?'

'A break from a rather humdrum life in town. I wanted a change of scene and to consider my future. I felt a break would enable me to review my life which didn't seem to have a great deal of purpose.'

'And did you find a purpose?'

'In an unexpected way, yes. By chance I met my former wife and—'

'By chance,' he interrupted. 'Tell me about this chance.'

I explained.

'Some people would think that an extraordinary coincidence.'

'They might, but life is full of coincidences. Koestler wrote a book about it.' With a touch of sarcasm I added, 'I expect you've read it, Inspector.'

His thin lips became invisible. 'As it happens, Mr Markby, I have. I'm not an ignoramus. I've read a number of the late Arthur Koestler's books. I admire his intellect but wasn't convinced by his theory on coincidences. But we mustn't digress. You met your ex-wife by coincidence and then what?'

'She was plainly short-staffed and I offered to help out.'

'And how did you think you could help out? By becoming a waiter?'

'I offered to do the washing-up.'

'You offered to do the washing-up.' As he repeated the words the extremities of Clench's lips twitched slightly as though he was suppressing amusement. 'Was that the purpose you were seeking?' he went on. 'Washing dishes at a little café?'

'She was in a fix. I was helping out.'

'Very commendable, I'm sure. And then what?'

'What do you mean – then what?'

'Did she pay you, thank you for your help, and say goodbye?'

'No. It wasn't like that.'

65

'Then tell me what it was like,' he said, and he spoke in a curiously flat voice as though the words had been used so often they'd ceased to have much meaning.

I realized there would be no escape from his probing questions. Co-operation, not evasion, would be in my best interests. Beginning with, 'We had a lot of news to catch up on,' I gave a summary of events from the time I had arrived at Fran's Pantry. Every so often I was interrupted so that a point could be cleared up. One interruption came when I mentioned seeing the video of *Carmen* at Moira's house.

'Mrs Makepeace was a close friend of your ex-wife?'

'Yes.'

'I gather they were *very* close friends. Would you agree?'

What was he getting at, I wondered. 'I can't comment on the degree of closeness. You'd have to ask Moira Makepeace about that.'

'For your information Mrs Makepeace has already been interviewed. It was she who found the body of your ex-wife.'

'Found her in the kitchen? How did it happen? How did Eve die?'

A phantom smile hovered over Clench's mouth and vanished.

'I wondered when you were going to ask that.'

'I have already asked,' I said indignantly. 'I asked in the flat! So don't imply that I haven't been concerned about the manner of her death.'

Clench's eyes didn't waver from mine. 'I don't recollect you asking anything about the manner of Mrs Harris's death.'

With this lie Clench made it clear he was no longer a police detective impartially attempting to discover who had murdered Eve, he was an adversary bent on putting me in the frame as her killer. Co-operation was out. I would have to monitor carefully every word I spoke before it was uttered. Self-interest and survival were paramount.

'I did ask you,' I said, 'and I don't want it erased from the tape that I did. And if I'm to sign anything I want a reference included that I asked.'

'Very well,' he said.

'So now, at last, you'll tell me how she met her death.'

Clench didn't reply immediately. It was as though he was weigh-

66

ing up how much longer he could cat-and-mouse over the issue. When he spoke he said, 'On the assumption that you have no idea how Mrs Harris died—'

'It's not an assumption,' I interrupted angrily, 'it's a fact that I don't know how she died.'

'Very well. The woman who you met purely by chance and was your ex-wife was found on the floor of her kitchen with a bread-knife half-buried in her abdomen. It had pierced her heart.'

I had a vision of my lovely Eve lying on the cold tiles of the kitchen floor, blood congealing from a lethal wound, and suddenly felt very strange. The walls of the interview room seemed to contract to box me in and I felt slightly dizzy. 'I'd like a drink of water,' I said.

Clench turned to Baker. 'Stop the tape, John, and fetch some water, will you?'

When Baker had left the room Clench said, 'You're off the record and there are no witnesses. Is there anything you'd like to say? Anything you'd like to get off your chest?'

'There's nothing to say I wouldn't want on record.'

'Suit yourself,' said Clench in an offhand manner. 'It's no skin off my nose if you want to play it the hard way. I've got all day.'

'How long is this interview likely to last?'

He gave a shrug of indifference. 'Can't say.'

An uneasy silence fell between us. It was broken by Clench yawning audibly. He rubbed his eyes. 'I'll be as glad as you to get this over with,' he remarked. 'I've been up all night.'

When Baker had returned with a glass of water and after I'd drunk from it, the tape-recorder was restarted with the words, 'The interview recommenced at eleven-thirteen hours.'

Clench said, 'Mrs Harris was killed with a bread-knife. Have you had occasion to use such a knife?'

I had anticipated that Clench would ask this question and, apart from an ingrained aversion to telling lies, I guessed that he would know that one of my chores was to cut bread.

'Eve didn't use sliced bread,' I said. 'It always had to be loaves fresh from the bakery. It was one of my jobs to cut the loaves for sandwiches.'

'Most helpful of you,' said Clench. 'Washing up dishes and cutting bread. What were you paid for your valuable services?'

'I wasn't paid.'

'You did it for free?'

'Yes.'

'Mrs Makepeace has told us you prepared accounts for Mrs Harris. Did you charge for that work?'

'No.'

'You did all this for love?'

'If you like, yes.'

'You loved her?'

'Yes.'

'And did she love you?'

'I think so.'

'Love is a strange thing,' Clench mused. 'When a lover is repulsed violent words and, sometimes, violent actions can follow.'

I said nothing.

'That's what happened last night, isn't it?' Clench asked.

'No, and I've had enough of this. I'm going.'

I stood up.

'I wouldn't be so hasty if I were you,' said Clench.

'You haven't any power to stop me.'

'Oh, yes I do. If I arrest and charge you I have the power.'

'If you arrest me and hold me here I shall sue for false imprisonment.'

Clench gave a weary smile. 'I've heard that one before a few times. You'd make it a lot easier for yourself if you tell me what happened before you left Mrs Harris to drive back to town.'

'I've already told you.'

'Tell me again.'

Clench listened intently for any discrepancy as I went through my account once more. But there was none. Why should there be? I was telling the truth.

He tried a different tack. 'Did you know that before you came on the scene Mrs Harris was friendly with one of the local lads, a boy of nineteen?'

This shook me but I tried not to show it.

'I didn't know,' I said, 'but I don't understand what that has to do with anything.'

Clench raised his eyebrows. 'No?'

'No.'

'Jealousy is a dreadful thing,' remarked Clench in a ruminative voice. 'You're telling me you weren't jealous of this lad?'

'I don't know anything about a lad. I thought I'd made that clear.'

'Even though he came to the café two or three times while you were there?'

I tried to recollect a young man who had come into the café two or three times on his own.

'Take your time,' said Clench. 'Think about it.'

It was then I remembered a lean, pallid fellow who looked as though he needed a good meal and I recalled that Eve had spent some time talking to him and that he'd left in a hurry without paying. I had been keen to pursue him but she had said, 'It's not worth it. Forget it.' At the time I'd thought this dismissive attitude uncharacteristic of her but soon forgot about the incident. But now that I'd recalled it I realized he had looked like the young man who had come in from the rain with his hair hanging in rat's tails.

'Have I jogged your memory?' Clench asked.

'There was a young man . . .'

'I thought so. But you didn't know about him. That is, not until now. You didn't know about him until the fateful evening.'

'This is ridiculous,' I said, 'are you trying to suggest I killed my ex-wife in a fit of jealousy?'

'It's a workable hypothesis.'

'It's a hypothesis, and it's wrong.'

'But it's not wrong that Mrs Harris, when she was your wife, left you for another man and you divorced her?'

I couldn't deny it.

'And when you discovered there was another man in the offing, a much younger man, you saw red. You didn't want the same thing to happen again.'

'That's absolute rubbish.'

'Is it? I think robbery can be ruled out as a motive. So far as we can tell, nothing was taken. There was money lying around. It wasn't taken. Like your mythical vandalism, there was no evidence of anything out of place or that she'd disturbed an intruder. No sign of a struggle. Her assailant was obviously known to her.

Years of experience, and a nose for such things, tell me that the motive for Mrs Harris's death wasn't connected with theft by a stranger but resulted from jealousy.'

'I've had enough of this,' I said. 'I'm going.'

Clench jumped to his feet. 'You're not going anywhere. I'm detaining you.'

'I haven't been charged with anything.'

'I have power with regard to serious arrestable offences to detain you for twenty-four hours and this can be extended under certain circumstances.'

'In that case,' I said, 'I want my solicitor present. I refuse to answer any more questions until he is here.'

8

The tape was switched off while I made a call to my solicitor, Mr Frobisher. Although an agnostic I prayed to some unknown god that Mr Frobisher would be at home and that, in spite of it being Sunday and he would need to travel some forty miles, he'd be willing to stand by me. It was with a sense of immense gratitude I heard his reedy voice say, 'Yes, of course.'

When the call was finished Clench said, 'We shall require your fingerprints and we might as well do that little job while we wait for your brief. This is normal procedure in such cases. We shall do the same for everyone on Mrs Harris's staff.'

As soon as I'd been told the murder weapon was a bread-knife I realized my prints would almost certainly be on its handle. I could only hope the killer had left his, or hers.

'What if I refuse to let you take them?' I asked.

Clench turned to Baker. 'You answer that one, John. Tell Mr Markby about section 61 of the Act.' He was clearly testing his junior colleague and giving him a chance to shine.

Baker braced his shoulders, looked blankly ahead, and intoned, 'Section 61, sir, states the circumstances when a person's fingerprints may be taken without the consent of that person. First, if a superintendent authorizes such a course on reasonable grounds for suspecting the involvement in a criminal offence of the person whose fingerprints are to be taken. Secondly, if—'

'No need to go through the subsections, John. Can the super give his authorization orally, or must it be in writing?'

'Orally, sir, but it must be confirmed in writing.'

'And do you know if the super is available today?'

'I know for a fact he is, sir. Shall I get him on the blower for you?'

Clench turned to me and said, 'Do we do it the hard way or do you voluntarily consent?'

I had listened to the exchange of professional know-how with dismay and knew it could only go against me, and probably be construed as implying guilt, if I tried to delay the inevitable.

'All right. I consent.'

After staining, my thumbs and fingers were pressed down on the record card by a police officer. I then signed the card and, when I'd washed my hands, I was taken back to the interview room.

'Painless, wasn't it?' said Clench. 'The kids love it when we have a school visit. Can't wait to have dabs taken. The cards make nice souvenirs.'

I wasn't in the mood for discussing police public relations exercises and made no comment. After a while Clench said, 'We're off the record now, do you know the Aldeburgh area well?'

'You can ask me that,' I replied, 'when my lawyer arrives.'

Clench gave a prodigious yawn. 'I hope he won't be too bloody long,' he said.

It was both to his and my relief when Mr Frobisher was shown into the room. He was a small man, in his fifties, and bald except for two wings of dark hair above his ears. Thick-lensed spectacles perched on a button of a nose which looked as though it was in danger of being overrun by a luxuriant black moustache. He invariably wore a white shirt and black tie and his suits were dark grey. We had become friends during the fraud trial when he had briefed counsel on my behalf and I had great respect for his ability although in appearance he looked as though he would be more at home as an actor in a Victorian melodrama than in a courtroom.

'Well now then, what's all this about?' was his opening remark.

When he was satisfied that he understood the position he asked the policeman standing at the door to send in the officer in charge of the case. When Clench arrived Mr Frobisher said, 'Have you any objection to granting bail to my client?'

'I have.'

'On what grounds?'

'The gravity of the offence and the fact that although your client has a fixed address he's only been there a relatively short while and has been living away as a casual worker.'

'That's not good enough,' Mr Frobisher protested. 'My client is a chartered accountant, a man of integrity and high repute. He is emphatically *not* a casual worker. Do you have a warrant for his arrest?'

Clench gave his thin smile. 'I don't need one. An arrestable offence has been committed. And as for bail, you can put your case to the magistrates tomorrow. In the mean while I'm applying for a warrant to search your client's so-called fixed address.'

'I will stand bail on behalf of my client and undertake that he will attend court tomorrow. It would be more than my professional life is worth to allow Mr Markby to abscond.'

I could see Clench was enjoying the situation. He was relishing a sense of power. My heart sank.

'Sorry,' said Clench, 'but my decision stands. I'm detaining your client and let me remind you that I am entitled, by rank as an inspector, to make the final decision.'

'There has been no charge.'

'True. But I'm convinced I have the right to hold your client. If you want to ferret through the relevant rules, regulations and procedures and find you don't agree, take the matter up with the appropriate authority. I don't mind getting my wrist slapped if I'm proved to have been in the wrong. In short, your man stays here, in the nick, until the sitting of the magistrates' court.'

'This is outrageous,' said Mr Frobisher vehemently. 'I shall certainly ferret, as you most graphically describe a search for accuracy and truth.' Turning to me he said, 'It'll only be for one night. I'm sure of that. You'll get bail and I shall make a point in court of your integrity in the fraud case and I think there might be a red face or two in this police station.'

Clench, sensing trouble, said, 'What case was that?'

Briefly Mr Frobisher outlined my part in the fraud case. He said: 'How can you think that a man of this calibre would now jump bail?'

Clench's eyes assumed a sightless look as though he was retreating into himself and for a few seconds I thought Mr Frobisher had won the day. But stubbornness linked to a craving for power was the decisive factor.

'He stays here,' said Clench. 'Make whatever points you like in court.'

'Very well.' Mr Frobisher patted my arm. 'Try not to worry. I'm sure you have an excellent case. And remember, chin up.' He turned to Clench. 'You are making a very grave mistake. I shall be taking the matter to the Police Complaints Authority. My client hasn't been charged with any offence.'

An argument followed between the two men on technicalities I didn't altogether follow but obviously related to the difference between detention without charge and custody after being charged. The dispute ended with Mr Frobisher storming out of the interview room.

As the door closed on him Clench said, 'Take Mr Markby to the cells.'

Shortly before I was due to be taken to court Clench, now looking haggard with fatigue, said, 'I've been making further enquiries which confirm my suspicions. Moreover, a spot-check on your prints indicates yours are the only ones. A detailed analysis and confirmation won't be available for another couple of days but I think I've got enough to bring you to court as an accused.'

He then formally charged me with the murder of Eve Elaine Harris and gave the necessary caution. In reply I said, 'I am completely innocent,' and nothing else.

It was evident from snatches of conversation I overheard that action on the case had been exceptionally swift and there was concern that the prosecution lawyer would be adequately prepared.

Mr Frobisher was already at the court. 'They've pulled a fast one,' he said, 'but never mind. It's bail we want while both sides look at the evidence and prepare their cases.'

Eventually I was summoned and taken to a courtroom where three magistrates were sitting. The prosecution lawyer opened by requesting an adjournment of committal proceedings. Mr Frobisher stood up and said he had no objection to an adjournment but he did respectfully request that I be released on bail until such proceedings took place. He painted a glowing picture of my integrity and concluded by stating that he would act as surety and would personally guarantee my appearance at court whenever required.

'Have the police any objection to bail being granted?' the chairman of magistrates asked.

Clench entered the witness box and from that moment my chances of freedom began to drain away like the waters of a spent wave on a pebble beach. He said that this was a case of cold-blooded murder, not manslaughter by accident such as could occur when the accused had been drink-driving. The murder had been committed with a bread-knife and the accused had admitted in a taped interview after being properly cautioned that the knife was what he used when working in the premises where the murder occurred. Fingerprint tests on the knife had yet to be completed but these should be ready within two or three days. Clench went on to say that it appeared that the accused had effectively abandoned his London home to live with the deceased and yet had been found, the morning after the murder, at his London address. Clench said he feared that if bail was granted the accused might attempt to leave the country. Accordingly he respectfully requested that bail be refused.

Mr Frobisher rose to his feet, adjusted his spectacles, and launched into a eulogy lavishly praising my trustworthiness, integrity, honesty, rectitude, etc., etc., and expressing his complete confidence in my innocence, and imploring the magistrates to grant bail. His speech lasted about ten minutes and when he sat down he took off his spectacles and wiped them with a demisting lens cloth, such had been the heat and passion of his appeal.

'I can't do more than that,' he murmured.

'Thank you very much.'

'I doubt if it will be enough.'

It wasn't. After a brief muttered conference between the magistrates the chairman said, 'Bail is refused. The accused is remanded in custody. The case is adjourned for a week.'

I was taken to a cell beneath the courtroom. A huge weight of despair descended on me. All my life I'd tried to do the right thing. I'd done the right thing at school by owning up to a minor misdemeanour when I could have evaded punishment. As it was, I was caned for my honesty. I had done the right thing by trying to make a citizen's arrest on a man I saw pilfering goods from a department store only to be rewarded by a hard punch on the nose from the thief (who escaped) and to be reproved by the store manager for "causing a scene". I'd done the right thing by taking up a career in accountancy to please my parents although I'd sooner have become a journalist, but my father had quoted Coleridge – I think it was Coleridge – who had once said that writing made a good stick but a poor crutch. I had done the right thing by proposing marriage to Eve after sleeping with her for one night. I had done the right thing by ensuring that Joanna had the best of everything, including education, at whatever cost. I'd always done the right thing by my clients and done the right thing in giving evidence against my partners when I'd discovered their malpractices. And what was the reward for doing the right thing and a life of honesty? It was to find myself incarcerated in a cell suspected of a murder for which I was guiltless in thought and deed.

Mr Frobisher was shown into the cell. He sat down, unzipped a brief-case and took out a writing pad.

'Now then,' he said, 'let's get down to brass tacks. The first priority is to obtain a statement from your cleaner, Mrs da Costa.'

I told him everything I knew about her, which wasn't very much. I had obtained her services through an employment agency but she had never been communicative and I had never asked personal questions. Mr Frobisher said he'd send a private enquiry agent to her address to ask some questions.

'Now,' he went on, 'I'd like to know if you have any views on who could have committed that dreadful act.'

'I've wondered about her close friend, Moira Makepeace, who seemed jealous of my relationship with Eve. We only have her word for it that she found Eve's body. She could have killed Eve and then phoned the police and pretended she'd found her dead.'

'The fingerprint evidence may throw light on that. Now tell me what you know of Mrs Makepeace.'

For the next few minutes I told him everything I knew about Moira including the demand for repayment of loans to Eve and the threatening remark about Eve's funeral.

Mr Frobisher hesitated before asking, 'Was there any sort of Sapphic relationship between the two women?'

'Not that I know of, but Eve did seem, in a strange sort of way, more under an obligation to her than I'd have thought necessary. And there were the obscene phone calls.'

Mr Frobisher perked up. 'Obscene calls? Tell me about them.'

I outlined the substance of the calls and mentioned that I had speculated that a youth who had come two or three times to

Fran's Pantry had got a crush on Eve. It had occurred to me that he might have been responsible.

Eventually, after asking a few more questions about my relationship with Eve and who I thought might dislike this relationship enough to commit a murder, to which I was guardedly honest about the former – an honourable man doesn't boast or expound on his sexual life – and unable to simplify what I'd already said on the latter, Mr Frobisher put away his pen.

'Don't give up hope,' he said. 'I shall pursue enquiries relentlessly. I shall make it my business to see that you are not committed to trial for murder and, if you are, to see that you are acquitted.' He stood up and extended a hand. 'Good luck, and keep your chin up.'

We shook hands. 'I'm relying on you,' I said.

'And so you should. What is a lawyer for but to look after the best interests of his client? I'll do everything humanly possible.'

With that, he left the cell.

9

The week on remand was spent in a police station cell as it was difficult to find a place elsewhere. I was provided with regular meals from the canteen, newspapers, radio and plenty of writing materials. Mr Frobisher had arranged for mail to be collected from both my London and Aldeburgh addresses. Among the letters was a note from a jeweller stating that my piece of amber had been set to make a brooch and was ready for collection. I had forgotten about the amber and his note brought back a flood of memories and almost a flood of tears.

I wondered and worried endlessly about who could have committed the murder. It was in the middle of the night that I remembered how, the first time I met Moira, she had walked into the kitchen and said, 'You're hopeless, Cat. Front door unlocked again.'

Had Eve, after she'd waved me goodbye, gone indoors and, preoccupied by thoughts of our parting, forgotten to lock up? And had our parting been watched by a man on the Crag Path? He might have followed Eve and, intent on theft or rape, have cornered her in the kitchen. When she refused to give in to his demands there might have been a struggle during which he seized the bread-knife and stabbed her fatally. If he had been wearing gloves at the time of the attack there would be no fingerprints.

As soon as Mr Frobisher arrived on his next visit, and while he was taking off his raincoat, I put forward my theory. 'What do you think?' I asked. 'It's a possibility, isn't it?'

He slung the raincoat over the back of a chair, sat down, and unzipped his brief-case. 'Well now,' he said, 'how are you keeping? In good heart, I hope.'

'I'm all right, but what do you think of my theory?'

'Were you aware that someone was watching you and Eve?'

'No.'

'So it is pure conjecture on your part, nothing more?'

'Yes.'

His eyes, like small aquatic mammals sheltering under goldfish-bowl lenses, regarded me compassionately.

'Theories about who may have murdered Eve are of little practical use unless they can be substantiated by proof so overwhelming that the prosecution would be forced to drop its case against you.'

'I want to find out who murdered Eve.'

'And so do I. But who murdered her is secondary to your acquittal. That's what we must concentrate on. If we don't, and divert our energies to finding the murderer, we shall be in danger of falling between two stools.'

'I don't give a damn about myself!' I shouted. 'I want to get whoever murdered Eve!'

'I *do* give a damn about you and so let's get on with the facts of the case. Let's consider your defence. So far, I'm afraid, I haven't made much progress.'

'What about Mrs da Costa? Have you found out why she made that call?'

'Ah, that is a disappointment. I have the report of our enquiry agent,' he said. 'He states he called at the address you gave for the da Costa family and found they had left. Our man checked on flights from Heathrow on Saturday night and, sure enough, the da Costas left for the West Indies.'

'She must have called me from the airport concourse,' I said. 'That would account for the background noises I heard.'

'You had no idea she planned to return to her homeland?'

'None at all.'

'I assume they weren't a well-off family.'

'They were on Income Support. I've no idea how they got enough money for the fares.'

'It passes my mind,' said Mr Frobisher thoughtfully, 'that someone may have paid them a considerable sum for some sort of service. It wouldn't be easy to find them in the West Indies, and it would be an expensive process. Further, I'm not sure what benefits there would be. Mrs da Costa might deny making the call.' He paused. 'I can't help wondering why she should have made the call at all. Why not just leave the country?'

Before I could answer he went on, 'It may have been made to

get you away from Fran's Pantry. On the other hand she might have thought you should know that your flat would be unattended. Was she a conscientious sort?'

'Very. She took pride in her work. Never skimped.'

'You are sure it was her and not someone impersonating her?'

I said that the voice had been somehow different, flatter, not so musical.

'She might have been reading out a message written for her to speak,' said Mr Frobisher. 'We shall probably never know. But you must stick to your account of what happened. That can't be disproved.'

'But not proved either,' I said.

'True. That's the difficulty.' He shook his head. 'But how could they pay for a flight for two adults and three children? If we knew that we might be getting somewhere.'

My thoughts, as they had often, turned to Moira. She was affluent and she disliked me, but I couldn't fathom what motive she would have for arranging for Eve to be killed and myself framed for murder. Because Mr Frobisher had made a strong point that theories weren't of much help I said somewhat tentatively, 'There's Mrs Makepeace.'

'Yes, you've told me about her. She was the one who found Eve. I understand she has made a full statement and will no doubt be called as a witness.' He sighed. ' "Dangerous woman" is a cliché but it seems to fit her. I shall obtain a copy of her statement. We must be fully prepared.' He scrutinized the paper he held. 'Now then, our agent would like to know how many people have keys to Fran's Pantry. Can you help on that?'

'I've got one, a Yale, but there's also a dead lock on the front door and I haven't the key for that. Unfortunately Eve was in the habit when she went out for a short while of slipping up the latch to hold the mechanism back.'

'She might well have fastened the holding latch before bidding you farewell.'

'She might.'

'Apart from you, who else holds a key?'

'I don't know but it wouldn't surprise me if Moira Makepeace had one.'

'What about staff?'

'I wouldn't think so.'

Mr Frobisher's next set of questions concerned Saul Harris and his son. I couldn't see the purpose of this line of enquiry. Saul was dead and his son, so far as I knew, was still living in France. Maybe Mr Frobisher was trying to learn as much as he could about Eve's life. Certainly the next batch of questions were directed to this end. After shuffling his papers around like someone preparing a card trick but not sure which card should be at the top of the pack, he looked up at me and said, 'This is a delicate matter but it could have relevance. I have to ask, what were the sexual relations between you and Eve like? By that I mean, were they good? Bad? Indifferent? I have to advise you that if you are committed to trial the subject of sex is almost certain to be raised. Sexual frustration is often at the root of domestic murders.'

I laughed. It must have been the first laugh I'd had since my arrest.

'Frustrated? I wasn't at all frustrated. Usually we'd been too busy during the day to want anything but sleep when we went to bed. But when we weren't too tired, it was very good indeed.'

'I'm glad,' he said. 'No hang-ups on either side, then?'

'None at all.'

'Everything straightforward? No, er, unusual practices? The reason I ask is that there are no holds barred in cross-examination. The most embarrassing questions might be asked if counsel can cunningly lead a witness in that direction.'

'No unusual practices,' I said firmly, although the memory of one of Eve's naughty variations flashed in and out of my mind.

'Good. Good. Now then, as to the obscene calls. It didn't disturb you that the unknown caller referred to Eve as a whore? You didn't quarrel about this?'

'Of course I didn't. It was a lot of nonsense. You must be aware that sexually inadequate males get a kick from dirty talk on the telephone.'

'Yes, quite.'

He took off his spectacles and polished them vigorously. It was a protracted operation which served as a pretext for avoiding eye contact with me when he said, 'I'm afraid I must tell you something you won't wish to hear, but if you are committed for trial the matter may be raised by the other side. Our agent has spent a day making enquiries – discreet enquiries – in Aldeburgh. He gathered that, before your visit, Eve was in the habit of going to a pub on some Saturday or Sunday nights and, although arriving alone she left, at least on one occasion, possibly more, with a young man, a man much younger than she.' He replaced the spectacles on his button nose. 'Did you know about this, Mark?'

The information shook me. 'I knew she'd sometimes gone on her own to a pub,' I said. 'I thought she met Mrs Makepeace there. I don't know anything about a young man.'

'So there were no arguments or resentments about this?'

'None.'

'Good. Enough of all that. Let's change the subject. Although I haven't yet seen a copy of Mrs Makepeace's statement I've managed informally to acquire some details. I gather she arrived at Fran's Pantry at approximately ten thirty. She immediately called the police who came within a few minutes. They, in turn, called the police surgeon and a Home Office pathologist. All the forensic evidence, so far as I can ascertain, points to Eve being murdered at some time between eight thirty and a time shortly before Mrs Makepeace arrived. The actual time of death cannot be precisely—'

'Hold on,' I interrupted. 'I know I'm the one who's accused of murder, but Moira could have done it. Can she prove she didn't?'

Mr Frobisher shook his head. 'I understand what you're saying but there isn't a scintilla of evidence, circumstantial or otherwise, that she did, nor did she have any motive that is apparent. Moreover, it is your fingerprints, not hers, on the bread-knife. Finally, although there are one or two rare exceptions, women do not usually commit murders with knives. Poisons, I believe, are the most popular method.'

'She was conveniently on the scene.'

He gave me a somewhat baleful look. 'I was coming to that before you interrupted me. I understand that in the comprehensive statement made to the police she referred to the demand for repayment of loans made by her. She alleged that this was nothing more than a ploy to upset Eve on account of a tiff they'd had. Mrs Makepeace stated that she hadn't the slightest intention of going through with the threats. She stated that on sober reflection she decided she was being petty. She used that word. Petty. On

Saturday night she telephoned Eve to tell her not to worry. She remembers the time she made the call. It was five minutes past ten. There was no reply. She assumed that you and Eve were out somewhere as it was Saturday night. So she scribbled a note in which she said she had no intention of calling in the loans and was sorry about the tiff they'd had. She drove to Aldeburgh from Leiston to put the note through the letter-box. But when she got to Fran's Pantry she found the front door was unlocked. She went inside intending to write a postscript to the effect that Eve must be more careful about locking up. This wasn't the first time it had happened. She intended leaving her note on the kitchen table to show that anyone could have walked in. It was then she saw Eve's body on the floor by the refrigerator.'

I said nothing.

'You must admit it's a plausible explanation of her presence,' said Mr Frobisher. 'She seems a sensible and competent woman.'

'She's a bitch. Why did she put the police on to me? Why couldn't she have left me to return to Aldeburgh of my own free will? How did she find my address? Snooping? I wouldn't put anything past Moira.'

'I think you're over-reacting,' said Mr Frobisher gently. 'She obviously knew a lot about Eve's affairs. She was the one who told them how to contact a cousin of Eve's for the purpose of identifying the body. Whatever you may think, she seems to have given the police every co-operation.'

'That doesn't alter the fact that she'd said she wanted Eve's funeral.'

'I'm afraid we only have your word for that,' said Mr Frobisher, and he sounded weary. 'As evidence it would be regarded as mere hearsay. And anyway, it could be something said in the heat of the moment and later regretted.'

'Moira meant what she said.'

Mr Frobisher sounded even more weary when he continued, 'Your personal animosity to Mrs Makepeace, and your belief that she may have committed the murder, won't hold water in a court of law unless you can back allegations with proof. And that you can't do. Put your prejudices against Mrs Makepeace to one side. What I want to know is whether anyone, any passer-by, someone out for a late-night stroll, saw you leave Fran's Pantry and that

Eve was alive and waving you goodbye. I know you've been asked this before, but rack your memory. Wasn't anyone else around?'

In the private cinema of the inner mind which is known as memory I could clearly see Eve standing under the pale light of a street lamp.

'I didn't notice anyone,' I said. 'I had eyes only for Eve.'

'Of course, but this is so important that I propose advertising through the press for anyone to come forward who was walking along King Street or the Crag Path at approximately ten o'clock on the Saturday evening. Now then, Mrs Makepeace says she phoned at five minutes past ten. Did you hear that call?'

'No.'

'It could have been made at just the time you and Eve were outside the house.'

'It could. And all these calls which were being made by the police, and possibly others, presumably on Eve's telephone, must have been the reason why I got an engaged signal when I tried to call Eve to say I'd arrived in London.'

Mr Frobisher nodded in agreement and began gathering up his papers.

'I'll leave now but I shan't rest on this case.' His eyes seemed to swim towards me. 'Don't worry if I ask for another adjournment. Our defence is far from complete. But we'll win. I'm sure we'll win and you'll be a free man again.' He put the papers in his brief-case. 'Goodbye for now, Mark, and remember that Giant Despair was regarded by Bunyan, who knew a thing or two about imprisonment, as the great enemy. Never give in to despair. Keep your chin up.'

With this encouragement, he left.

10

After Mr Frobisher's departure I made notes of our conversation including my foolish outburst about not giving a damn about myself but wanting to get whoever murdered Eve. And yet, was it so foolish? In anger I had spoken the truth and in articulating my pain at Eve's death and a desire for vengeance I had exposed the nerve-ends of my psyche.

I had gone to Aldeburgh in a low state of mind, hoping somehow to find a purpose in life other than going to innumerable concerts and preparing accounts for a few old faithfuls. I had found a purpose – helping Eve. At the back of my mind, almost from the beginning of the renewed relationship, was the idea that we might make a fresh start together. In bed we had warily skirted around this subject and had agreed that if there was to be a second time it must be when both felt ready and not the result of a misguided sentimental impulse.

The outburst had been ill-timed but it had illuminated something fundamental. Eve had given me a sense of purpose. That sense had been snatched away. But now I had a new purpose – to find and punish whoever was responsible for her death. Even if I was convicted, that purpose would sustain me. One day I would be free and then I would hunt down and destroy the killer.

That night I slept well. It wouldn't be an exaggeration to say that from this time the purpose became an obsession. Incredible as it may seem, any court trial was nothing more than a nuisance. All that mattered was to find and punish Eve's killer even if I bankrupted myself in the process.

Moira Makepeace was my principal suspect although I couldn't figure out how she had been able to use the bread-knife keeping my prints on it, unless she had worn gloves. But why should she be wearing gloves unless murder was in her heart when she came to Aldeburgh? Clench had told me that tests had shown my prints to be the only ones on the knife but this wasn't surprising as, before using it, I'd noticed a smear of jam on the handle and had washed the knife before use. I would mention this detail to Mr Frobisher the next time he visited me.

Mr Frobisher requested a further adjournment of the committal trial and each time he came to see me I detected a lessening of confidence that there would be no case to answer. I would probably have to go through the ordeal of a full trial before a High Court judge.

'You have no alibi,' he complained. 'If only someone would come forward to testify that they'd seen you leaving Eve and then noticed somebody follow her into the café then you'd be in the clear. But in spite of all our efforts nobody has come forward. One would have thought that at ten o'clock on a Saturday night somebody would be around.'

'You don't know Aldeburgh,' I said wryly. 'The night-time peace and quiet is part of its charm.'

'Myself,' said Mr Frobisher, his eyes glinting roguishly, 'I prefer a bit of life when I'm on holiday. Italy or the south of France suit me. The people there really know how to enjoy the night. But each to his own diversions.' And then, extinguishing all thoughts of pleasure, he continued, 'I can't protract a hearing indefinitely. But we won't wallow in the Slough of Despond if you're committed for trial.'

'I want this business over and done with. The sooner the better.'

And so it was on the following Tuesday that I was taken to court in a Black Maria and a coat thrown over my head before I was hustled from the van to a back entrance of the courtroom. I was taken to a cell and moments later a young man carrying a black attaché case walked in. He extended a hand. 'My name is Smithers,' he said. 'Unfortunately Mr Frobisher became ill at a function last night and was taken by ambulance to hospital. Cystoscopy has revealed a kidney stone. They hope to operate today.' He opened the attaché case. 'I've been reading up the papers on my way here. We've taken the opinion of Gregg QC who, as you may know, is a top counsel in criminal law. He considers the Crown has an irrefutable prima-facie case and accordingly we should acknowledge this and agree that you should stand trial. I trust that's OK by you.'

I don't normally make snap judgements but Smithers struck me as brash, self-opinionated, and totally indifferent to my fate.

'Just a minute,' I said, 'aren't the magistrates going to be told my side of the story?'

'No way,' he replied with a half-laugh as though I was a simpleton for asking. 'We keep any defence evidence we can string together for the main trial. That's when Gregg will do his stuff, and he's got a well-deserved reputation for ruthless cross-examination. The magistrates will merely formally commit you for trial at the appropriate Crown Court.'

'What about bail?'

Again he gave an irritating half-laugh. 'Not a chance. When did you last hear of bail being granted to someone with a prima-facie case of murder against him?'

I didn't reply.

'Never is the answer to that one,' he said. 'Of course I'll make an eloquent appeal but it'll be a no-hoper. I think I can do that quite as well as old Frob would have done.'

I felt like kicking the insufferable Smithers but prudence prevailed. 'Shall I see this eminent Queen's Counsel before the trial?' I asked.

He looked doubtful. 'I can't really say. He may spare you a few minutes before we go into court. Time is money for men of his calibre.'

'It would be most kind of him to deign to see the client who will pay his fees,' I said, and I don't think Smithers appreciated the biting sarcasm.

'We'll just do a quick run-through of your evidence,' he said. 'Beginning at the beginning, why did you go to Aldeburgh in the first place?'

Because he was my representative, however unsympathetic, I went through my story for the umpteenth time. But he seemed less interested in my movements than in probing Eve's private life. He seemed to gain vicarious pleasure from the allegations that she'd habitually frequented a pub at the back of town and had been seen leaving with a youth. When I said I didn't understand what relevance this had to the case against me he had the nerve to say, 'Sexual jealousy is a common motive in murder cases.'

I was glad to see the back of him and just before he left I asked him to convey wishes for a swift and full recovery to Mr Frobisher. My message was heartfelt.

'I'm not deserting you,' he said. 'you'll see me again in court.'

I did; nearly two hours later. To his credit he spoke eloquently of my trustworthiness, but it was of no avail. Bail was not granted. I was remanded in custody for the Crown Court trial.

The period on remand was grim but not too long. I had plenty of writing paper and was able to listen to classical music on Radio Three. My determination to discover who had murdered Eve never wavered. Just as some find solace in religion, I found comfort in dedication to a supreme purpose. No knight questing for the Holy Grail, no Orpheus seeking the return of his Eurydice, no Flying Dutchman in search of a haven, could have pursued his purpose with greater commitment.

As the time for the trial drew closer I experienced misgivings about its results. Mr Frobisher, who had recovered from his operation, came to visit me and although he tried to be cheerful I sensed that heavy doubts lurked behind a façade of good humour. I was also visited by an elderly colonel for whom I regularly prepared accounts. He never stayed long but in his blimpish manner he tried to be encouraging. 'Don't let the troops see you're nervous,' he advised. 'Show you've got mettle. You're a fine fellow. You'll get off.' He pronounced 'off' as 'orf' and would beam at me. I was grateful to him for his loyalty.

The big day arrived and I was ferried to a town many miles away. I glimpsed the courthouse, a modern red-brick building, before, head covered, I was hurried inside. Clear of newshounds and morbidly curious onlookers I was conducted to a cell which, although it had the usual minimum of furniture, was clean and well lighted.

Within a few minutes the cell door opened and Mr Frobisher entered followed by a portly man in wig and gown. His face had the flushed and fleshy look of someone accustomed to gratifying sensual appetites and his bulk almost obscured a third person, a young woman whose wig was precariously perched on a mass of auburn hair. She too wore a gown.

Mr Frobisher made the introductions. 'This is Mr Gregg. Miss James is his junior on this case.'

After a curt nod Gregg sat down on the only available chair and placed a sheaf of papers tied with pink ribbon on a bedside table-cum-locker. His first question startled me. 'How are your legs?', he asked.

'My legs?'

'Your legs. The two lower limbs you use when you wish to stand, walk, or run.'

'My legs are fine. Why?'

He tapped the papers with a plump forefinger. 'Because on the reading of this brief you haven't a leg to stand on.'

Could this be the top counsel in criminal law Smithers had promised me, I wondered.

'Anyone reading this,' Gregg went on, 'with its extraordinary tale of being summoned to your London flat by someone who has vanished, and with your fingerprints clearly defined on the lethal weapon, to say nothing of the motive being attributable to sexual jealousy, could be forgiven for thinking you guilty. What do you say to that?'

He looked unblinkingly into my eyes.

'I most certainly am not guilty,' I said indignantly. 'I loved Eve.'

'Quite so. All the more reason to kill her. You wouldn't bother to attack a woman to whom you were emotionally indifferent.'

Controlling my anger with an effort I said, 'Mr Gregg, I am not a jealous man by nature. Furthermore, Eve didn't give me the slightest cause to be jealous. The opposite.'

'What about the obscene calls? Didn't those stir doubts about her?'

'Not in the least.'

'You had intimate relations with her, did you not?'

'Yes.'

'Then I find it hard to believe that the calls didn't excite suspicion, even a twinge of jealousy, on your part.' Gregg shook his head and a flutter ran through his flabby jowls. 'It's a pity you ever mentioned the calls when you made a ridiculously informative statement to the police. If the matter is raised by the prosecution why don't you say you were grossly exaggerating? Say that you and Mrs Harris, far from being offended, had a good laugh.'

I was aghast at his suggestion. 'I couldn't say that!'

'Why not?'

'It wouldn't be true.'

'It could help your case.'

'But not my self-respect,' I replied hotly.

Gregg rose to his feet and picked up the beribboned sheaf of papers. 'I'll do my best for you,' he said, 'even though you only have a far-fetched story for your defence.' He glanced towards his junior, who had not taken her eyes off me. 'Come, Fiona,' he said imperiously.

He had almost reached the door when he turned and gave me a look as though I was a zoo animal he'd never seen before, a rare specimen of an endangered species. 'What I can't make out,' he said, 'is whether you are a truly honourable man or simply an honest fool.'

His gown swished as he breezed from the cell followed by his young acolyte who paused fractionally to give me a nod and a smile.

When the door had closed I gave vent to my feelings. 'I didn't like that one little bit.'

'Don't take any notice,' said Mr Frobisher. 'He's noted on the circuit for his rudeness. In time that'll make him an excellent judge. Meantime, he's one of the best advocates around.'

'He as good as accused me of murdering Eve.'

'It's his method. He likes to test the people he's defending, and he's clever at it. If you'd agreed to water down the nature of the obscene calls and pretended that you'd had a good laugh about them then he'd have been at your throat. He'd have said that if you were willing to lie about that, you would be capable of lying about your innocence.'

'He didn't ask one question about Mrs Makepeace. I think she's the one behind all this.'

Mr Frobisher stiffened slightly. 'Look, Mark, you're the one on trial, not her. When the time comes Mr Gregg will do his best to discredit her as a witness. More than that, you can't expect. But I guarantee that by the time the jury retire to consider their verdict Gregg will have earned your admiration and respect.'

'I hope so. Anyway, thanks for all you've done on my behalf.'

He gave a little smile. 'Good. Good. Now I must go. Good luck.'

A flight of stairs led directly from the cell to the courtroom. I was escorted up the stairs by two officers one of whom always seemed to be on duty. I never knew his official title but his surname was Fluck and I always thought of him as 'Warder Fluck'. He had a saturnine face and radiated gloom.

We entered the courtroom and I stepped straight into the dock. It was at one end of the room and directly opposite the witness-box. The judge's bench which was on a raised level and surmounted by the royal coat of arms was sited equidistant between dock and witness-box. I could see my legal team among two rows of lawyers and clerks; they would all be facing the judge when he appeared. The jury were already seated close to the witness-box. Opposite them, the press bench was crowded with journalists and reporters. The public gallery occupied the width of the far end of the courtroom; it was packed with people who had come to enjoy free entertainment offered by the theatre of a criminal trial.

I was the focus of all eyes for the minute or so before a tipstaff bellowed, 'Everybody stand!'

Warder Fluck muttered, 'And you stand to attention, Charlie.'

As the bewigged and red-robed judge entered the courtroom a silence fell which was as acute as the ghostly hush which descends on the Cenotaph at eleven o'clock on Remembrance Sunday.

The judge sat down. Everybody breathed again. The clerk of the court remained standing while those who were to be the audience, and the handful who had parts to play, settled down.

The show was about to begin.

My trial had started.

PART II

1

The clerk of the court concluded reading the indictment by asking whether I pleaded guilty or not guilty.

'Not guilty,' I said in a firm voice. I know it was a firm voice because every newspaper report I read the following day referred to it as such. What wasn't recorded in print was Mr Frobisher's slight nod of approval and Miss James's encouraging smile. Gregg looked as though he'd breakfasted on a surfeit of food and wine and was about to fall asleep.

Prosecuting counsel, Spendlove QC, in contrast to Gregg, had the thin and drained appearance of a man who practised the ascetic virtues of austerity and abstinence. Occasionally peering at the jury over half-moon spectacles he outlined the case against me, emphasizing that facts were a matter for the jury while questions of law were for the judge.

I looked at the jury. Five women and six men were white; one man was black. Would there be prejudice on his part, I wondered, if Gregg tried to denigrate Verity.

The case against me, cogently presented by Spendlove in a restrained and yet compelling manner, sounded formidable. There was no dispute, he said, that Mrs Harris had been killed by a bread-knife bearing the accused's fingerprints. As for motive, this would become overwhelmingly apparent during the course of the trial. It was a motive endemic to human nature, a motive which must have been present when hominids first prowled the earth, a motive rooted in the desire of a man to possess, against all comers, the woman of his choice. He paused at this juncture and then, after surveying the jury over the rims of his spectacles, he added, 'to possess against all comers, and at all costs, even the cost of the beloved's life'.

After pausing to allow his sickly description of jealousy to be digested, he craftily tried to appear even-handed by stating that hearsay and gossip could not be regarded as fact, nor, indeed, were admissible as evidence. Accordingly, the prosecution would not be calling a number of witnesses which otherwise they might have wished to subpoena. The jury must rely on established facts and not be diverted by suspicions as to Mrs Harris's over-friendly attitude to the opposite sex.

Having implied that Eve was promiscuous and I was a jealous suitor there should have been no need to say more. But, in between pauses while he studied his brief, Spendlove continued on the repetitive theme of bread-knife and jealousy, and it dawned on me that his method was to hammer home the prosecution case until its nails sealed the coffin of my future. He could have summarized the salient points in a few minutes; instead he laboured for at least an hour.

His first witness was Clench who was asked what he had found on arrival at Fran's Pantry, whether he had checked for signs of robbery, and what immediate action he had taken.

On these matters Clench's evidence was unremarkable and uncontestable. In giving his replies he looked easy and unflurried, the perfect example of an experienced police officer as capable of dealing with the armoury of a barrister's vocabulary as with a robber's sawn-off shot-gun.

It was when Spendlove asked him how I'd reacted when he appeared on my doorstep that Clench, for the first time, looked across the well of the court at me and seemed to hesitate before replying, 'He seemed completely taken aback, sir.'

This wasn't true. I hadn't been *completely* taken aback. I had assumed his visit was a police response to Verity reporting vandalism.

Clench continued to stare fixedly at me as though defying me ever to deny his slanted opinion as Spendlove asked, 'Did the accused say anything?'

'Oh, yes, sir.' Clench looked away from me. 'He said he hadn't been expecting us and then, after we had been invited inside, he tried to explain why he had returned precipitously from Aldeburgh to his home address in the middle of the night.'

When asked about my explanation Clench, without being inaccurate on detail, made my reason for going to London seem a preposterous alibi. He implied I'd made the first excuse that came into my head. There was no evidence of any vandalism at my flat; no evidence of reported vandalism; and he had felt it his duty to take me in for further questioning. Procedures had been scrupulously followed. I had been cautioned and the interview recorded on tape. After salient points from the interview had been extracted by Spendlove Clench's evidence concluded with my arrest.

Gregg aroused himself from half-slumber, stood up, hitched his gown on his shoulders and said, 'Detective Inspector, am I correct in thinking that as a conscientious police officer you keep your fingers on the pulse of local affairs so far as you are able?'

'So far as I am able, yes. I have a fairly large manor.'

'In doing so you must sometimes frequent places used by the general public – pubs, cafés, and so on?'

'Yes.'

'Have you ever been a customer at Fran's Pantry?'

Clench appeared to search his memory before replying, 'I believe I went once, sir.'

'Why?'

Clench had been standing in a relaxed posture, arms hanging loosely, but at Gregg's question he tensed slightly and clasped his hands in front of his pelvis.

'I happened to be in the neighbourhood and wanted a little light refreshment.'

'Also you wished to see what the new proprietor was like, didn't you?'

'Perhaps. I don't recall.'

'Then let me try to jog your memory. You had heard, had you not, that Fran's Pantry had a new proprietor?'

'Maybe.'

The judge intervened. 'Mr Gregg, I can't see where this line of questioning is leading.'

'I am endeavouring to ascertain the reliability of the witness's memory, my lord. It is germane to the principal issue.'

The judge, whose face was like a hard-boiled egg on which a child had drawn two black eyebrows and a pencil-line downturned mouth, said, 'Very well,' in a bored voice.

Gregg bowed his head and resumed questioning.

'You say you believe you went once to Fran's Pantry, Detective Inspector. Would it surprise you to know that I could call a witness who will swear on oath that you were seen in the café on at least two occasions?'

Tiny flush spots appeared on Clench's pallid cheeks, and I wondered how Mr Frobisher had unearthed a witness to Clench's patronage. He must have interviewed Beryl.

'I may have been there a couple of times,' said Clench.

'Your duties embrace, in your own words, a fairly large manor. And yet you visited this fairly insignificant café at least twice. Was this simply for a little light refreshment, or were there other reasons?'

Spendlove looked as though he was about to make a protest but before he could speak the judge said, 'Mr Gregg, whether the witness went to the café for refreshment, or to get out of the rain, or to have somewhere to sit while writing up notes, is neither here nor there. I'd be obliged if you'd address yourself to matters at issue.'

'As your lordship pleases,' replied Gregg. 'Detective Inspector, you've stated that you looked around for any evidence of robbery and found none. I believe there was even a sum of cash on the kitchen table.'

'That's right, sir.'

'And presumably you went right through the house to see if anything was amiss?'

'Yes.'

'Then you must have noticed a blue cheque book lying on the dressing table in the bedroom.'

I now understood why Mr Frobisher had persisted in scratching around for the slightest detail which could be of use. I had told him that in my hurry I'd forgotten to take my cheque book and credit cards.

Clench shifted uncomfortably in the witness-box.

'I can't say I noticed a cheque book.'

'You must have noticed it. It was plain for anyone to see. The deceased's cousin found it lying there. On top of the dressing table in the main bedroom. The room in which, so I understand, the accused and Mrs Harris slept.'

'I was making a quick search to see if anything was obviously disturbed. I also considered the possibility that the assailant might have been hiding upstairs. I don't specifically recall seeing a cheque book but, if there was one on the dressing table, I would have assumed it belonged to Mrs Harris.'

This last sentence was spoken by Clench as though it was the final word on the irrelevant subject of cheque books.

Gregg had other ideas. 'Your assumption would have been wrong, Mr Clench. If you'd bothered to examine the cheque book you would have seen at once that it belonged to the accused. Now, drawing on your extensive experience in criminal investigation, would it not be true to say that people who intend to abscond, or disappear, wouldn't be likely to leave behind not only a cheque book but no fewer than five credit cards?'

Clench fidgeted. 'No, sir. Not likely.'

'It would be perfectly reasonable in the circumstances for the accused's insistence, during your questioning, that he intended to return to Aldeburgh to be a true statement of his intention. Is that not perfectly reasonable?'

'I suppose so.'

'I suppose so too. On that we are in agreement. A man who has committed a hideous crime and plans to disappear or flee the country isn't likely to leave behind his cheque book and credit cards. On the other hand, a man who has committed no crime at all and intends to return to the house from whence he came is very likely to leave all sorts of valuables behind. That is a reasonable view, is it not?'

Clench's jaw had tightened during this exposition. He unclamped it to ask the judge, 'Do I have to speculate on this, my lord?'

He didn't receive a direct answer to his question. Instead, turning to Gregg the judge said, 'I think we are all abundantly clear on the point you are making, Mr Gregg. Must it be pursued any further?'

'No, your lordship, I would not wish to weary the court by positing any further that a guilty man is most unlikely to leave a cheque book and credit cards at the scene of the crime. But if your lordship will bear with me I have one or two more questions to ask.'

'Oh, very well. Go ahead.'

Gregg's head moved fractionally in what was more a nod of acknowledgement than a respectful bow and he muttered, 'I'm much obliged,' before facing Clench once more.

'I believe that almost your entire police career has been spent in criminal investigation and you have risen from humble police constable to the rank of detective inspector. Is that correct?'

'It is, sir.'

'And during all these years of service have you ever had cause to investigate a case more or less on all fours with this one?'

'No, sir.'

'And so you must have found yourself wandering into uncharted territory?'

'I was not wandering!'

Like a predator which had been stalking its victim, Gregg pounced. 'Exactly,' he exclaimed. 'Far from wandering you went bald-headed for the first person you thought could be suspected without first considering others who might be responsible.'

Spendlove jumped to his feet but didn't have to speak. The judge spoke for him.

'Mr Gregg, if you are implying that the detective inspector was, regardless of considerations of guilt or innocence, bent on securing a conviction on someone, anyone, you are treading very dangerous ground indeed. I won't have my court used for unsustainable imputations of bad faith.'

'As you wish, my lord. I was merely commenting on what appears to be a remarkably precipitate arrest and charge of a man who, I most sincerely believe, is entirely innocent. I was not imputing bad faith to the inspector but simply a reckless disregard of other possibilities. Bad faith is one thing; reckless disregard, quite another.'

The judge's eyebrows seemed to perform a mating dance before they locked together in the most ferocious of frowns.

'Are you bandying words with me, Mr Gregg?'

'Certainly not, your lordship,' Gregg replied unctuously.

'I should hope not. Have you any more questions?'

'Counsel like dogs, my lord, cannot bark when they are muzzled.'

'I am not muzzling you, Mr Gregg! But I am tempted to report your conduct.'

'I have no further questions, my lord.'

Gregg sat down and the public gallery which had been silent buzzed with chatter.

The clerk of the court motioned to an usher who bellowed, 'Silence!'

The hum quietened as Spendlove rose to his feet. 'Mr Clench,' he said quietly, 'have you always discharged your duties to the best of your ability and without fear or favour?'

'I have, sir.'

'Have you ever been on a disciplinary charge?'

'No, sir.'

'In fact, I believe you have received a number of commendations.'

'That's true, sir.'

'Thank you. That is all. You may stand down.'

With evident relief Clench left the witness-box.

The next witness was a big, bearded, middle-aged man called Kimble. Spendlove's opening questions established him as a fingerprint expert. He exuded the sort of confidence which comes from being a specialist among laymen. The lethal bread-knife, designated 'Exhibit A', was produced for his inspection and identification. In reply to Spendlove's questions he stated that the prints on the knife's handle corresponded exactly with my fingerprints and that there were no other prints. His evidence was exact and concise.

While listening to the testimony the judge prodded and poked at his wig with the blunt end of a ballpoint pen as though trying to satisfy an itch on the scalp underneath. When he'd finished this operation the wig was slightly askew and looked like a slipped egg-cosy.

When Spendlove sat down the judge stopped scratching.

'Do you have any questions, Mr Gregg?' he enquired.

Gregg stood up. 'One or two, my lord.' Turning to Kimble he asked, 'Am I right in thinking that the fingerprints were nearer the bottom of the knife-handle than to its centre?'

'That is correct.'

'Consistent with the way a person would normally hold a knife when cutting bread?'

'Yes.'

'When one is cutting bread into slices the grip would be different from that used for an upward stabbing motion?'

The silence in the courtroom was so acute that when a woman juror tried to muffle a sneeze it sounded as though a small bomb had been detonated.

After a pause which seemed endless but couldn't have lasted

101

more than six or seven seconds Kimble said, 'I imagine the prints would be in a slightly higher position, but I can't be sure.'

Addressing the judge, Gregg said, 'With your lordship's permission I should like to conduct a small experiment. I should like the witness to hold the knife and cut an imaginary loaf of bread, put the knife down, and then seize it and make an upward stabbing thrust.'

'What do you say to that, Mr Spendlove?' the judge asked.

'I think we should ascertain that the witness and the accused both naturally use the same hand, be it right or left. If one is right-handed and the other is left-handed I see no value in the experiment which in any event is bound to be inconclusive since there is no rule of absolute consistency in the manner human beings hold things. We are not robots.'

'I agree,' said the judge, 'but as we are so frequently being told, justice must be seen to be done.' He turned to Kimble. 'Are you right-handed?'

'I am, your lordship, and the knife was held by someone in the right hand.'

The judge hoisted his beetle-black eyebrows. 'Mr Spendlove?'

'No objection, your lordship, although I may exercise my right to ask further questions of the witness.'

'Of course, of course.' The judge beckoned to an usher. 'Here, take this book to the witness.' He handed over a thick tome which had been lying close to his elbow. Moments later when the book was in place on the ledge of the witness-box he said, 'Imagine you have a loaf of bread in front of you and pretend to cut it.' For the first time his lips twitched in the ghost of a smile. 'And be careful about it. If you cut yourself, that's your fault, but I don't want my book damaged, not with the cost of law books these days.'

This trite attempt at humour was greeted by laughter from the public gallery. Even Warder Fluck gave a slight guffaw. The judge looked all around like some entertainer gathering plaudits for his sally, well-pleased with himself for having raised a laugh.

Kimble began making sawing motions above the book.

'Good,' said the judge. 'That's enough. Now hold up the knife so that we, and the jury in particular, can note the position of your grip . . . Good. Now put it down, pick it up again and pretend to be stabbing someone you are facing with a thrust upwards towards an imaginary heart.' Turning to Gregg he said, 'Would you care to volunteer to act as recipient of the thrust, Mr Gregg?'

A riffle of laughter ran through the public gallery. To me, the scene was bizarre, a jet-black farce.

'I beg to decline the offer, your lordship,' said Gregg. 'I'm not sure that my insurance policy covers accidental wounding by a Crown witness.'

More general amusement as though this was a cross-talk act between two popular comedians.

Kimble duly went through stabbing motions at the end of which, and after showing his grip to judge and jury, he agreed with Gregg that he'd held the knife in a slightly different way.

'I have no further questions,' said Gregg, and he sat down.

Spendlove was instantly on his feet. 'Would you say conclusively, without a shadow of doubt, that in your opinion the grip in the first part of the experiment would leave traces in quite a different place from the grip in the second part, or would you describe the difference as marginal, even non-existent?'

It was Gregg's turn to jump to his feet.

'The witness may only give an expert opinion on the subject of fingerprinting, your lordship, not on the way he personally would cut bread or a body.'

'Quite so. It's all quite unscientific but I would remind you that the experiment was your idea.'

'Indeed it was and I think it has shown that there is a difference in grips and, that being so, one might expect to see more than one set of prints on the knife-handle.'

I don't know about the jury, but I was becoming confused. Perhaps it was Gregg's objective to get everyone so muddled that the fingerprint evidence was dismissed.

'Have you any further questions, Mr Spendlove?' the judge asked.

'Not at present, your lordship, but I shall raise the matter again with my next witness.'

Kimble left the witness box, the book was returned to the judge, and the next witness was called. He turned out to be a forensic pathologist called Dr King. He had a round, rubicund face which

103

reminded me of a Toby Jug and looked as though he would be more at home swapping jokes in a pub than cutting up cadavers in a mortuary.

His responses to Spendlove's questions amounted to an account of being called to Fran's Pantry late Saturday night, of examining the corpse, and of a subsequent fuller examination when he conducted an autopsy. The stab wound was consistent with one which had been made by a knife having a serrated edge. The deceased had been wearing a thin summer dress and the knife had easily pierced the fabric and the blade had been driven with such force that the blade had entered the abdomen and penetrated to the heart.

Up to this juncture the evidence had been unexceptional but then Spendlove said, 'I believe you have had considerable experience of injuries caused by knives, both incised wounds and stab wounds.'

'That is correct.'

'And in some cases the knife has been grabbed from, say, a flat surface and almost instantly used to inflict a wound?'

'I have had cases of that sort.'

'Would the knife be held in a way calculated to give maximum grip or might it be held in the way the assailant would customarily use it? I have in mind that if a man uses a certain type of knife for one purpose, and one purpose only, and uses it daily for cutting a number of slices of bread, might he not in extreme emotional arousal grip the handle in the manner to which he is accustomed rather than in a way which, on measured consideration, might be more effective for his purpose?'

Dr King nodded his head vigorously. He was, after all, a prosecution witness and he didn't want to spoil their case. 'I certainly wouldn't argue with that proposition,' he said.

'Thank you . . . Your witness,' he said to Gregg.

Behind me, in a voice very *sotto*, Warder Fluck murmured, 'Your brief's got a lousy case. I don't envy him.'

Gregg stood up slowly, hitched his gown which, like his wig, seemed shabby and faded. They might both have been hand-downs from some eminent advocate, a sort of professional inheritance.

'Dr King,' he began, 'we have listened with interest to the

stretched conjectures of my learned friend, but can you in all honesty say that anyone intent on murder with a bread-knife would attempt to commit that murder as though he were slicing bread?'

'I'd think not, but I can't be positive.'

'I welcome your honesty, Dr King, as I'm sure members of the jury will. In other words, if someone has murderous intent he, or she – we mustn't neglect the sex who have had their fair share of murderers – is as likely, probably more likely, to hold the knife in a stabbing rather than a carving, or slicing, way?'

Dr King looked discomfited. 'I really can't say. As I mentioned earlier, there are no hard and fast rules.'

'But I understood you had considerable experience of injuries caused by knives. Or so we were led to understand. Nevertheless, there are no hard and fast rules. So, let us assume that the accused picked up a bread-knife as though about to resume his job as preparer of sandwiches, no matter that it was late at night and there'd be no customers to eat the sandwiches, and then struck the fatal blow. Was it an upward thrust?'

'It was.'

'You are sure of that?'

'Perfectly certain.'

'You were following hard and fast rules about the angle of impact of the knife, were you?'

Dr King no longer looked like a cheerful Toby Jug. 'Yes,' he snapped.

'It's good to know that there are some hard and fast rules in your profession,' said Gregg condescendingly. 'Can you let the court know from your examination of the deceased what height she was?'

'About 1.635 metres.'

'For those of us who still think in feet and inches could you please convert that measure?'

'About five feet four inches.'

'Do you know the height of the accused?'

'No.'

'I'll tell you. He is almost a foot taller than the deceased. To strike the fatal blow, would such a differential in height have meant him being obliged to stoop slightly, or slightly bend his knees?'

Dr King gave the question some thought. During the pause a distant ambulance siren could be heard.

'I'll bet that poor sod's predicament's no worse than yours,' muttered Warder Fluck, ever ready to undermine my morale.

'He would probably have bent slightly,' said Dr King at length.

'The wound could more easily have been inflicted by a smaller person?'

'Probably.'

'So now we have someone who picks up a bread-knife as though proposing to begin his kitchen duties, albeit there will be no customers. He then buckles at the knees before administering a fatal blow. One wonders what the deceased was doing during this somewhat inept performance. Did you find any injuries on her hands, any cuts or abrasions to indicate resistance?'

'No.'

'So she placidly stood by while her assailant picked up a bread-knife, buckled at the knees, and made a stabbing motion while holding the knife as though about to make himself a late-night sandwich. Did she simply allow this to happen, or were there signs, by cuts or otherwise, that she tried to protect herself?'

'I found no indications of self-defence.'

'It could be said, and probably will be said by the prosecution, that this passivity on her part could be interpreted as trust that whoever held the knife would not use it against her because he, or she, was well-known to her; a friend perhaps. In your experience would this be a reasonable assumption?'

'I think so. Yes.'

'This would certainly broaden the spectrum of possible suspects. But I must not ask you to comment on other possible suspects, Dr King. I doubt if his lordship, or my learned friend Mr Spendlove, would be happy if I adopted such a line. However, I should like to know whether, apart from there being no marks on the hands, or other indications of self-defence, there was anything else which, in any way at all, you found unusual. Anything external or internal. Anything at all. And please don't hurry your answer. Think about it.'

The courtroom seemed vacuumed of sound during the pause before Dr King spoke.

Somewhat hesitantly he said, 'There was, er, a slight contusion, or bruise, er, at the back of the neck.'

'A slight contusion? What could have caused this?'

'I have no idea, except . . .'

'Except what?'

'I once had a case in which the deceased practised sexual deviations. A similar mark had been made. It had been caused by a piece of thin wire which had been used to make the deceased crawl forward on hands and knees.'

A shock-wave ran through the courtroom. Press bench notebooks looked like a flock of seagulls taking wing.

A court official shouted, 'Silence!', and when the hubbub subsided Gregg said, 'We won't pursue the question of what might or might not be the deceased's sexual preferences . . .'

I was appalled. The thought that a mark on the back of Eve's neck could have been made by her being dragged around like some animal was not only deeply offensive, it was an impossibility. If there was a bruise, it must have resulted from something while I was living with her and, since we had spent nearly all our time together, whether at work or leisure, I knew there must be another explanation. Because I was absorbed in thinking what could have caused the bruise I missed Gregg's next questions but I believe he returned to the issue of handling the knife, and angle of attack, before Dr King was allowed to leave the witness-box.

The judge examined his watch as though it were a birthday present which he'd just strapped on his wrist and was admiring for the first time. 'I think that's enough for today,' he said. 'The court is adjourned.'

A disembodied voice called, 'Everybody stand!'

Everyone stood while the judge with his egg-cosy wig and red-robed trappings left the courtroom.

'Come on, Charlie,' said Warder Fluck. 'Back to your hutch.' As we descended the stairs to my cell he went on, 'If you ask me, this will be an open and shut case. I wouldn't be in your shoes for all the beer in a brewery.'

2

Now that the first day's session was over I paced the cell waiting for Mr Frobisher's arrival. Like most prison cells it contained a minimum of necessary furniture and a stark lack of any softening amenity. However, it was clean, well-lighted, and provided toilet facilities. As such places go, it was probably one of the best, but there was something about the cell's atmosphere which put me on edge, something oppressive, an intangible unease, which seemed to dwell here. No one, not even the most cheerful and well-balanced visitor, would care to linger here. I was very glad when Mr Frobisher was ushered in. Even though he looked unwell he brought an air of comforting normality.

'How are you bearing up?' he asked, taking a seat at a bare table.

'I'm all right.'

'I thought it went well,' he said. 'Gregg was good. He's got the prosecution rattled. Did you see the look our friend Clench gave him when he left the witness-box?'

'Yes, I did see.'

'And he threw Dr King.'

'You think I've got a good chance then?'

'I do indeed. But there's one thing we need to know, and perhaps you can help us. Gregg mentioned it to me when the court adjourned. He attaches importance to the contusion at the back of Eve's neck.' Mr Frobisher's eyes loomed larger with enquiry. 'Gregg would like to know whether . . . in the privacy of the bedroom . . . how shall I put it . . .'

I put an end to his dithering. 'We never played sado-masochistic games,' I said.

'Ah. Then I wonder how she got the marks.'

It flitted through my mind that Eve had sometimes seemed strangely under Moira's domination, but the thought that they could have indulged in aberrant practices was quickly squashed. I knew Eve. She could never have been a sexual submissive.

'Gregg thought it an unusual sort of bruising,' Mr Frobisher went on, 'it isn't something which would occur in everyday life. It's not like a bruise one can get from bumping into furniture when one's spectacles have been mislaid.' He gave a dry chuckle. 'That's happened to me a few times, I can tell you.'

I didn't care about his ocular misadventures; I'd had an inspired thought. A lightning association of ideas – Moira, sexual deviations, witchcraft, protection against evil – brought a blindingly certain conclusion.

'I've got the answer! It must have been the necklace. Eve wore it all the time. A crucifix suspended on a gold chain. She was wearing it that night. Usually it was covered by a sweater but on that night she was wearing a dress with a low neckline.'

'Necklace? Yes, that could be, but—'

'Moira,' I interrupted. 'It must have been Moira. I'll bet she saw the crucifix and tried to tear it off Eve's neck. And at the same time she grabbed the bread-knife and stabbed!'

A certain weariness clouded Mr Frobisher's face. 'This obsession with Mrs Makepeace . . .'

'Eve thought she was a witch. I know it sounds ridiculous, but she did. She had reasons. She wore the necklace with crucifix to counteract any evil influences. Moira would have seen it and in the heat of an argument tried to wrench it from her. Eve might have tried to hold on to the necklace and that's why her hands weren't in a position to stop the knife. It could all have happened in a second.'

Mr Frobisher thought a long time before speaking. At last he said, 'I doubt if there's any mileage in the witchcraft angle but I'll certainly inform Gregg. It seems to me that if your hypothesis is correct, by pulling on the necklace the assailant would have drawn Eve forward and, if at the same time a thrust had been made with the knife, the knife would have penetrated deeper than if Eve had been backing away. Yes, we might have something there. I wonder where the necklace is.'

'Where are the clothes she was wearing?'

The question discomfited Mr Frobisher. If he could have retreated behind his voluminous moustache he would have run for cover.

'It's an upsetting subject, I know,' he said, 'but the clothes will be bagged-up at the mortuary. Any rings and personal jewellery will be in safe keeping.'

He needn't have been sensitive about the matter. I am a realist. I don't expect reverence or special treatment for the dead from mortuary employees. I could well believe that Eve's clothes would be bundled into a bag, tagged, and slung into a locker.

'Wouldn't it be worth seeing if the necklace is among her effects?' I asked.

Mr Frobisher brightened. 'Well worth it,' he replied.

'And if it isn't among her effects – where is it?'

'That is the question. And a good question it is. Find the necklace and, unless it was thrown away, we could have found the murderer.' Mr Frobisher stood up. 'I must contact Gregg about this development. He may wish to recall Dr King. I'll see you tomorrow. In the mean while, keep your chin up and if you have any complaints about your treatment, however slight, let me know. Unless and until proved guilty you are an innocent man and must be treated as such.'

The evening dragged but was tolerable thanks to a transistor radio I was allowed to have. I tuned into my favourite station and found that a long programme was being devoted to the works of Leoncavello including a full performance of *Pagliacci*.

I didn't expect to sleep well and it must have been three in the morning before I drifted into slumber. It was a dream-filled sleep, and one dream, or nightmare, possibly germinated by the betrayal of the clown in *Pagliacci*, was particularly vivid.

Some years ago I had gone on my own to a performance of *Wozzeck*, Berg's opera about a simple-minded soldier who is bullied by a sergeant who humiliates him further by seducing Wozzeck's woman, Marie. The climax of the opera comes when Wozzeck murders Marie and then drowns when he goes to recover the murder weapon, a knife.

I'd obtained two tickets for the opera but at the last minute Eve had developed a splitting headache. She had begged me to go on my own.

110

I returned after the performance to find the bedclothes rumpled but no sign of Eve. She arrived half an hour later and said that after I'd left she had gone to bed but had been woken by the telephone. A friend had asked her to go round to discuss arrangements for a party at the local tennis club; feeling much better, she had agreed. I believed this story, although Eve's change of demeanour was remarkable: from being a disconsolate woman clutching at her head she had become vivacious and shiny-eyed. I have since sometimes wondered whether she really visited her friend or had spent three or four hours with Saul Harris, a suspicion reinforced by the fact that, although the hour was late, she had wanted to have a bath and I knew she'd had a bath during the late afternoon shortly before the headache developed.

The opera, *Wozzeck*, and Eve's night out became the constituents of a nightmare in which I was a conscripted soldier. I was queueing for a meal in an army canteen when Moira appeared and began to taunt me about Eve who, she said, was deceiving me with Harry Feldman, who had managed to avoid conscription and was continuing his career in accountancy. The scene changed and Moira and I were standing by a river bank and when I said I couldn't believe that Eve would take Feldman as a lover Moira said, 'You've got it wrong. It's not him, it's Saul. She's running around with Saul Harris while you're on sentry duty!' A sentry-box, resembling an upended coffin, suddenly appeared at my side. A rifle with bayonet attached was propped against the sentry-box which, I observed, had a cross carved on its lid. I seized the rifle and thrust the bayonet at Moira. Blood spurted from her chest and I saw it wasn't Moira I'd stabbed, but Eve.

I woke from the nightmare in a sweat and for a while was haunted by the recollection of terrible images trawled from the deeps of my mind. The memory had faded by the time the court was reconvened but I still felt a free-floating anxiety which wasn't entirely connected with the proceedings which lay ahead.

The public gallery was again packed to capacity with morbidly curious spectators and the press bench was occupied by a bevy of reporters. The judge took his place beneath the royal coat of arms and with a shuffling and rustling everyone except Gregg sat down. As soon as a hush fell he requested that the previous witness be recalled as further evidence had come to light which could have considerable bearing on the case. The matter had been discussed with Mr Spendlove who had no objection as, like himself, Mr Spendlove was concerned that no hindrance be put in the way of a proper defence.

'Very well,' rejoined the judge rather irritably, 'recall the last witness.'

After reminding Dr King that he was still on oath Gregg asked, 'You will recall mention of a slight contusion at the back of the deceased's neck. Could this have been caused at or around the time of death?'

Dr King thought. 'It could,' he said.

'And could it have been caused by a thin gold necklace being violently wrenched by someone, someone standing in front of the deceased?'

'It's possible.'

'If I informed you that the deceased was wearing such a necklace, and was seen to be wearing it not only by the accused but by a waitress who had served them at a hotel earlier in the evening, would it seem probable, rather than just possible, that the bruise was caused by the necklace being tugged?'

'Yes, probable.'

'And if at the same time that the necklace was tugged the assailant struck with the knife could the forward propulsion of the deceased's body have caused the knife to go deeper than it otherwise might?'

'Yes.'

'And conceivably the deceased might have raised her hands to protect her necklace which would account for the fact that there are no gashes on her hands, no signs of resistance?'

'Conceivably, yes.'

'I understand that a small gold crucifix hung from the chain. I appreciate that religious symbolism, and the hatred of the Christian symbols by those who practise the occult, are not within the scope of expert evidence you are allowed to give, but in the course of your career in forensic medicine have you had first-hand experience of a case where a religious symbol has been the precipitating factor in a murderous attack?'

'No, I haven't.'

'Thank you, Dr King, that is all,' said Gregg smoothly.

The public gallery buzzed with whispers and reporters scribbled notes. Gregg had cleverly insinuated the occult into our case. Tomorrow's popular press would no doubt seize on this. Any news of the occult or black magic in a murder case was good for circulation figures.

'Any further questions?' the judge asked Spendlove.

'None, your lordship.'

'I have one,' said the judge and from under heavy eyebrows he regarded Gregg sternly. 'Are you intending to produce this necklace as an exhibit? If so, I propose to adjourn proceedings and have a recess so that you and Mr Spendlove can argue before me legal points as to circumstantial evidence.'

Gregg rose to his feet. 'No, my lord. I have to tell you that enquiries have been made of the mortuary superintendent and there is no necklace among the deceased's effects. It has completely disappeared. This is a matter I may have cause to refer to when later witnesses are called.'

'I see . . . Dr King, you may stand down.'

The next witness was called and the public gallery hummed with whispers. Interest had been whetted by Gregg's reference to the occult and now, stalking towards the witness-box, was the thin, gangling figure of Mrs Andrews. She was dressed entirely in black and a small black conical hat was perched on her head. Only a broomstick was needed to complete the ensemble. Someone at the back of the gallery smothered a laugh.

After she had been sworn in, Spendlove put his first question. It was an innocuous enquiry about the length of time she had lived in Aldeburgh.

'All my life, sir,' she replied.

Answers to further questions showed that here was a poor widow working to make ends meet, an honourable member of local society, and a woman of strong moral principles whose testimony would be unimpeachable.

'And now,' said Spendlove, 'I should like you to tell the court about your time at Fran's Pantry. How long were you employed and in what capacity?'

'I cooked. I was there about four and a half months.'

'And then you left. Tell us about that.'

Mrs Andrews craned forward. 'Pardon?'

'Were there any events leading up to your decision to leave the employment of Mrs Harris?'

'Oh, yes, sir.'

'Could you tell the court what these were?'

'The atmosphere.'

'Can you be a little more explicit? What do you mean by "atmosphere"?'

Mrs Andrews looked directly at me. 'It was him and her,' she said.

'You are referring to the accused and Mrs Harris?'

'Yes, sir.'

The judge intervened. 'Mrs Andrews, what I and the jury wish to know is how what you call an "atmosphere" was created. Can you give examples of what constituted "atmosphere"?'

Before she could reply Spendlove had inserted a quick, sycophantic, 'I'm much obliged, my lord,' as though the judge had by a stroke of brilliance simplified a complex issue.

'The words that passed between them,' Mrs Andrews said.

'What sort of words?' asked the judge, who seemed to be taking over Spendlove's job.

'Well, sir, there was the time when Mrs Harris, who had been out front, came into the kitchen and said, "What do you think you're doing? I don't provide bed and board for you to sit there trying to solve today's cryptic." He'd been doing a crossword puzzle, you see, when there were dishes in the sink waiting to be washed. He said, "Don't nag me. I'll do them in a minute." She said something about doing them now, and he'd better watch his step. He replied she was the one who should watch her step or she might take a very nasty tumble when they went out for a walk after work.'

'You had the impression that by this the accused was threatening to cause injury to Mrs Harris?' Spendlove asked.

'Don't lead,' said Gregg loudly.

'I am not leading,' snapped Spendlove angrily.

'Mr Spendlove,' the judge intervened, 'perhaps you could rephrase your question.'

'Certainly, my lord . . . Mrs Andrews, can you tell me how you interpreted this exchange of words?'

'They were quarreling. That's what I mean by "atmosphere".'

'You took what the accused said seriously?'

'Of course I did. Wouldn't anyone? He was as good as saying he'd do her a mischief if she ticked him off about not washing up. He gave her a really spiteful look, I can tell you.'

'Thank you for your very clear account of what took place on one occasion. But one occasion doesn't make an atmosphere any more than one swallow makes a summer. Were there other occasions when the atmosphere distressed you to the point of feeling you must hand in your notice?'

'Oh, yes, sir. There was the time he broke a cup. Mrs Harris was naturally annoyed. She accused him of being clumsy, which he was. I nearly had a heart attack when he went at her as though he was going to strangle her. I think if I hadn't been there he would have done her serious harm. That's my guess.' She darted a glance in my direction before adding, 'And it's my guess he had murder in his heart.'

Gregg was instantly on his feet. It was the first time I had seen him move so fast. 'My lord, must we have such prejudiced speculations?'

'No, Mr Gregg, we cannot . . . Mrs Andrews, please confine yourself to facts. Keep your guesses out of this.'

'I'm sorry, sir, but I speak as I find. There was an atmosphere.'

The judge turned to Spendlove. 'Please continue.'

'Mrs Andrews, you were unhappy at Fran's Pantry?'

'I was, sir.'

'People get unhappy with their jobs for various reasons. These might be poor pay, unsociable hours, personality differences, and so on. For one reason or another you were unhappy and you left the employ of Mrs Harris even though, as a widow on a meagre pension, you needed the income.'

'That's right, sir.'

'Some people would swallow their principles if their source of income was threatened. You must have felt very strongly about this "atmosphere".'

'I did, sir.'

'Was the atmosphere the sole reason why you decided to leave or were there other reasons?'

'Other reasons, sir.'

115

'Tell us about these other reasons.'

'It wasn't just the atmosphere in the kitchen. And that was bad enough. Even when Mrs Harris wasn't around I caught him watching me, trying to catch me out, trying to show I couldn't do my job properly, and I didn't like that. I think he'd have liked me out of the way too, if you take my meaning.'

Before Gregg could make another protest the judge said, 'Apart from kitchen differences, was there anything else which made you unhappy?'

'Yes, sir.'

'Then tell us.'

'In one way I didn't blame him for having nasty ideas. He must have known what everyone knew.' Mrs Andrews had never looked more malevolent as she continued, 'She was no saint. The opposite. I didn't know this when I took the job, or I never would have. But my boy told me one day just after I'd started that she'd go into a pub on her own and brazenly—'

Gregg was on his feet. He didn't have to speak. The judge spoke for him.

'Mrs Andrews,' he said in a kindly voice, 'I can understand your outrage at what you might have heard, but what you hear from others is what we call "hearsay" and is not admissible evidence. We don't want to know what your son may have told you about Mrs Harris's conduct in a public house but whether you witnessed such conduct. Did you?'

Mrs Andrews recoiled as though she'd been slapped in the face. 'I never visit such worldly places,' she said indignantly. 'I don't like my boy going there but he's a man and I can't stop him.'

The judge turned to Spendlove. 'Do you wish to pursue this line?' he asked.

'Not with this witness, my lord . . . Mrs Andrews, you have told us about an atmosphere caused by friction between the accused and Mrs Harris, and how this disturbed you, but was anything ever said to you by either party to indicate what might be the basis for such friction?'

Mrs Andrews frowned. 'If you mean, "Why did I think he tried to get at her?" I think it was plain jealousy.'

'And what makes you think that?'

From the moment the direction of questioning had focused on

Eve's pub visits I had sensed a sort of prurient eagerness sweep through the public gallery and press bench. The scent of enjoyable dirt was in the air; I was fearful of what slanders Mrs Andrews might now utter.

'What makes me think it was plain jealousy? I'll tell you. It was because one day he said to me, "Eve is too attractive for her own good." '

I could vaguely remember having said something similar, but it had been a throwaway line in an amusing context.

'Why should he say something like that to you?' Spendlove asked. 'You and he weren't exactly bosom friends who might exchange confidences, were you?'

'I should say not,' replied Mrs Andrews, the epitome of righteous indignation. 'The very thought,' she added.

'Then why make such a statement to you of all people?'

'I don't know why, sir, but I do know what made him say what he did.'

'What was that?'

'One day Beryl, that's the waitress, came in laughing. She said Danny had just come in and asked Mrs Harris to marry him. Of course I knew Danny was eleven-pence half-penny in the shilling, but Mr Markby didn't, and that's what must have made him say what he did.'

'Eleven-pence half-penny in the shilling,' interjected the judge, rolling the words around in his mouth. 'What does that mean? Or am I committing a judicial solecism, like "Who is Marilyn Monroe or Frank Sinatra?" '

'It means someone who is mentally sub-normal, my lord,' explained Spendlove in his most ingratiatingly servile manner.

The egg-face cracked slightly. 'I see. It must be a pre-decimalization term.'

Spendlove laughed obsequiously. 'Quite so, my lord.'

An usher handed me a note from Mr Frobisher. It said: 'Did you have any arguments with Eve in front of Mrs Andrews?'

At the foot of the note I wrote: 'It was friendly banter. We were joking. Mrs A. had no sense of humour.'

The usher took the note to Mr Frobisher.

Spendlove asked if there were any other evidences of jealousy on my part.

'Not that I can put my finger on, sir. But I wouldn't really have blamed him. She always struck me as the flighty sort.'

'Thank you, Mrs Andrews. That's all."

Spendlove sat down having concluded his examination in chief.

'Can I go, sir?' Mrs Andrews asked the judge.

'Just a moment.' The judge turned to Gregg who was deep in conference with Mr Frobisher. 'We are waiting, Mr Gregg. Do you wish to cross-examine?'

Gregg stood up. 'I'm sorry, my lord. A minor point needed clarification.' He hitched up his gown and faced Mrs Andrews. Subdued talk from the gallery died down.

'Mrs Andrews,' Gregg began, 'is it true to say that in the last ten years you have had as many as fourteen jobs either as a cook or a home-help or doing unskilled work in no fewer than three small industrial businesses in the vicinity of Saxmundham?'

'It may be. I don't keep a count.'

'I can assure you it is. And in all of these you have handed in your notice usually because of some affront, real or imagined?'

Mrs Andrews gave a venomous look. 'I have strong principles, moral principles, unlike some I could name.'

'Then let us examine these principles,' said Gregg smoothly. 'You are a regular worshipper at church, are you not?'

'Not church!' Mrs Andrews spat out. 'I go to a *meeting* house.'

'I am so sorry. A *meeting* house. Every Sunday?'

'Every Lord's Day.'

'Ah, yes. The sect to which you belong might properly be described as very low church, might it not?'

'That's your description, not mine.'

'Members of your sect believe that they are chosen by God and on the Last Day you will be called to heaven and everyone else condemned to eternal damnation. Is that correct?'

Mrs Andrews hesitated. 'I suppose so. I know what I believe. I'm not entitled to speak for anyone else.'

'But you believe in what I've just said about heaven and eternal damnation?'

Mrs Andrews cleared her throat but her words came out hoarsely. 'Yes, I do.'

'And in your view both the accused and Mrs Harris are damned as worthless sinners?'

Mrs Andrews turned to the judge. In a croaky voice she said, 'Can I have a glass of water, your worship?'

'Certainly. And you may sit while giving evidence, if you wish.'

While water was being fetched Mr Frobisher came over to me. 'Tell me more about this friendly banter with Eve,' he said.

3

Explaining domestic in-talk to an outsider is difficult. In the early years of our marriage Eve and I, when making love, would sometimes use a sort of baby-talk, and sometimes when things were going really well we would pretend to be annoyed with each other, even playfully insult each other, always taking care not to transgress known boundaries of sensitivity. These exchanges often included excruciating puns and would end in laughter or going to bed. Later in our marriage, when I grew more work-obsessed and Eve became increasingly bored, the baby talk and silly insults, sometimes accompanied by shows of mock anger, all dried up. Indeed, all forms of communication began to shrivel and wither.

But after a week or two at Fran's Pantry we began, tentatively at first, to swap occasional verbal threats. In an odd way, almost impossible to explain, such conduct was a measure of the security we felt with each other. I tried to convey this to Mr Frobisher while an usher took a carafe of water and a glass tumbler to the witness-box.

'I see. Yes, I understand,' he said, but I was sure he didn't understand. His magnified eyes had a slightly glazed look. 'This interruption is a nuisance,' he said. 'No counsel likes breaks when he is getting into his stride.'

'I didn't know Mrs Andrews had had so many jobs. How did you find out about that?'

'We've been busy. Our enquiry agent's been busy. We've made good use of the time you've been on remand.'

He left me to return to his seat just behind Gregg. The two men conferred while Mrs Andrews swallowed water in sips, managing to hold the tumbler with little finger crooked in what she probably imagined was genteel elegance.

'Bet you wish it was poison,' muttered Warder Fluck. 'She's doing you no good at all.'

At last Mrs Andrews put down the tumbler. 'Thank you,' she said in a clear voice. 'That's better.'

The judge nodded at Gregg who stood up and recommenced his cross-examination.

'I was asking, Mrs Andrews, whether you considered the accused and Mrs Harris both to be worthless sinners.'

'It's not for me to say, sir. Our Lord said, "Judge not, that ye be not judged." '

'And that dictum, taken if I remember rightly from the Sermon on the Mount, is one of these principles of yours – not to judge others?'

'Yes.'

'It seems to me difficult to reconcile such exemplary Christianity with some remarks made earlier in your testimony.' Gregg rifled through papers and then read out. ' "He gave her a really spiteful look." . . . "She accused him of being clumsy, *which he was*." . . . "She was no saint. The opposite." . . . "I think it was plain jealousy." . . . "Danny was eleven-pence half-penny in the shilling." ' Gregg put down the papers. 'Those are all judgemental comments, are they not, Mrs Andrews?'

Mrs Andrews looked as though she'd just sucked a bitter lemon. 'If you say so, sir.'

'I do say so, and most emphatically. However, you are, nevertheless, a woman of strong moral principles. You have said so yourself, so let us examine these principles further. Do you have many friends, Mrs Andrews?'

'I do, among the Brethren.'

'But not with those outside this tight-knit sect?'

'No, sir.'

'It is part of your principles not to be friendly with those outside your flock?'

Mrs Andrews licked thin lips as though about to make a declamation. In a strong, clear voice she said, 'St Paul has instructed, "Be ye not unequally yoked together with unbelievers: for what fellowship hath righteousness with unrighteousness?" '

I couldn't tell whether Gregg was thrown by this text but he seemed a little off balance because he asked, 'Would you mind repeating the first part of what you've just said?'

121

A grim smile flitted across Mrs Andrews's lips; she seemed to be enjoying the chance to throw scriptural quotation at Gregg.

' "Be ye not unequally yoked with unbelievers",' she said.

Gregg repeated the line as though testing a length of verbal cloth for size. After a long pause he went on, 'I think whoever translated from earlier versions of the New Testament to give us what is sometimes called the King James Bible has committed the sin of a double negative and "not unequally" could be understood to mean "equally".'

The judge, who had become visibly impatient, said, 'We are not in a theological seminar, Mr Gregg. Please come to the point.'

'With the greatest respect, my lord, I was endeavouring to understand the exact meaning of a phrase upon which some of the witness's moral principles are based, but I confess myself defeated. She must be a woman of profound intellect.' So heavy was the sarcasm that someone in the public gallery tittered and a few of the reporters grinned openly. Before the judge could issue a reproof Gregg hurriedly went on, 'Do you watch television, Mrs Andrews?'

'I do not."

'Why not?'

Spendlove jumped to his feet. 'I must protest, your lordship. The witness's leisure-time occupations are neither here nor there.'

The judge nodded. 'I'm inclined to agree. What is the object of your question, Mr Gregg?'

'I am anxious to discover whether there are any comedy shows which appeal to Mrs Andrews. I want to ascertain whether she has a sense of humour and, if so, in what direction. It is, I assure your lordship, an important factor in this line of questioning.'

The judge turned to Mrs Andrews. 'Do you have a sense of humour?' he asked.

'I think so, your worship.'

'There you are, Mr Gregg. There's your answer. Simple.' The judge's voice was resonant with self-satisfaction. 'You don't have to go round the houses with questions about comedy shows on television most of which I have seen strike me as being singularly tasteless and unfunny.'

'I am much obliged for your lordship's opinions on contemporary television comedy,' responded Gregg equably, 'but the witness's answer doesn't go quite far enough . . . Mrs Andrews, do you understand what I mean by "playful banter"?'

'Playful banter?'

'Let me explain. In many a family there is playful banter which to anyone outside the family circle might sound thoroughly insulting, or even threatening. Things said aren't intended to be taken literally. Husband and wife, two lovers, children – especially siblings – can all indulge in this word-play. It appeals to their sense of humour. It is nothing more than playful banter. Does that explanation help?'

Mrs Andrews shook her head. 'It's not my idea of fun,' she said.

'What is your idea of fun?'

A few seconds elapsed before the question was answered.

'When I was younger we used to play Consequences sometimes.'

'At Christmas and other festive occasions?' Gregg asked.

Every inch a statue of black-clad unyielding morality, Mrs Andrews replied, 'For the Brethren Christmas is nothing more than an excuse for worldly excess.'

'I won't argue with that. Instead, I must put it to you that you were mistaken in thinking that instances which contributed to "atmosphere" in the café kitchen, instances when the accused and Mrs Harris exchanged insults and threats, were in any way meaningful. I put it to you that this so-called atmosphere was the result of nothing more than playful banter.'

'I don't think so.'

'And you don't think so because it is quite clear that such verbal games are outside the range of your experience and they would probably be against your strong principles, would they not?'

'Our tongues should be used for the word of the Lord.'

'And do you use your tongue for the word of the Lord?'

'I try, sir, but sometimes I fail.'

'Indeed! Indeed! You have totally failed to understand that what you heard pass between the accused and Mrs Harris was nothing more than playful banter.' Once more Gregg looked down and rustled through his papers, allowing the jury to dwell on his last remark. Then he continued, 'I understand the reason you gave Mrs Harris for leaving was that you felt the accused was spying on you. Why should he want to spy on you?'

'To catch me out. Trying to make out I couldn't do my job.'

'For what purpose?'

'So he could get me out of the way and he could get a cook who was more worldly, more his sort.'

'Could you give the court an example of how he tried to show you couldn't do your job properly?'

Mrs Andrews gazed upwards as though seeking heavenly help. None was forthcoming. Her silence became protracted.

'You must answer the question,' said the judge gently.

'I can't give an exact example. I didn't give him the chance. But he was always giving me looks, following me with his eyes in whatever I did, hoping I'd do something wrong.'

'Have you heard of paranoia, Mrs Andrews? It is a condition which sometimes manifests itself in the sufferer believing he or she is being spied upon, even persecuted?'

'I think so,' Mrs Andrews replied doubtfully.

'Wouldn't you agree that you were being paranoiac?'

'No, sir. I'm telling the truth.'

Gregg gave an audible sigh. It was an indication that he didn't expect to get anywhere with the paranoia argument. But he persisted.

'I suggest that it was a figment of your imagination that made you think you were being spied upon.'

'No, sir.'

'But if you were, it would amount to persecution, would it not?'

The judge's black brows contracted as he stared hard at Gregg as if trying to penetrate his mind and its devious processes. I too wondered what was to be gained by this line of argument.

'A sort of persecution,' replied Mrs Andrews, again in a doubtful tone of voice.

'And instead of resenting this you should surely as a practising Christian have blessed him.'

Mrs Andrews leaned forward in her chair. 'Sorry?'

'You should have blessed him,' repeated Gregg loudly.

'Bless him? Why?'

'Does it not say in the Scriptures, under the imprimatur of St Paul, no less – "Bless them that persecute you; bless, and curse not." '

'Really, Mr Gregg,' the judge exclaimed. 'I've already told you this is not a theological seminar, nor is it a forum for a battle of biblical quotations. You will kindly refrain from treating Holy Writ as a sort of point-scorer in a quiz contest. I am a Christian myself, and I don't like Holy Writ taken in vain.'

'Quite right,' Mrs Andrews chimed in.

The judge turned sharply and I thought he was about to reprimand her, but his quelling look was enough to make her sit back.

'I apologize for any offence given to your lordship's sensibilities,' said Gregg urbanely, 'but I'm endeavouring to show that the witness is a muddled thinker, someone who flaunts her principles but doesn't abide by them. Nevertheless, bearing in mind your lordship's strictures, I will try to avoid reference to Holy Writ and I trust the witness will do the same . . . Now then, Mrs Andrews, I would like you to tell the court how you felt when you heard of Mrs Harris's death. Were you upset?'

'Not exactly, sir. I wasn't really surprised.'

'Not surprised? Why not?'

'Well, him and her, living together in sin; anything can happen to people living in a state of wickedness. It was a judgement on her.'

'A judgement by the Almighty?'

'Maybe. I don't know. I guessed from the start it would be that man.' She shot a quick glance at me. 'I never liked the look of him and furthermore I can't abide a man in my kitchen.'

'I see,' Gregg mused. 'You are suggesting that the accused was the object of divine wrath?'

'It may be.'

'And the Almighty, knowing of your views on sinful behaviour, and of your dislike of a man in your kitchen, decided that the accused should suffer the punishment of your testimony against him in this court?'

The judge, who had been tapping the bench surface with a ballpoint pen as if warning Gregg not to go too far with remarks about the Almighty, said, 'You need not answer that question, Mrs Andrews.'

Unflurried, Gregg continued, 'You have made it clear that in your opinion, for what that is worth, you have strong moral principles and a strong Christian belief. It is the over-riding precept of that belief that one should love one's neighbour, is it not?'

'Yes.' Mrs Andrews aimed the affirmative at Gregg as though it were a dart.

'A love untarnished by prejudice and bigotry?'

Mrs Andrews said nothing.

'Is that intended as a question, Mr Gregg?' the judge asked.

'It was somewhat rhetorical, your lordship. I have no doubt that when your lordship comes to sum up you will give due weight to the manner in which this witness's evidence has been heavily coloured by religious bigotry and blind pride, and so I have no further questions to ask.'

The judge, who had stopped tapping with his pen, momentarily pointed it at Gregg. 'I shall sum up as I think fit and proper and I need no advice from you, Mr Gregg . . . Mr Spendlove?'

'No further questions, my lord.'

'You may stand down, Mrs Andrews.'

Clutching her black handbag like a talisman Mrs Andrews stepped down from the witness-box and, head lowered, hurried to the rear of the court.

The judge glanced at his watch before saying, 'Are you proposing to call many more witnesses, Mr Spendlove?'

'Two, my lord.'

'Then I think this would be an appropriate time for an adjournment for lunch.'

When the judge had left the courtroom, no doubt for a repast of fine food and wine, I was taken down to my cell and offered the choice of fish, chips and peas or meat pie, chips and peas.

'They are both equally horrible,' advised Warder Fluck.

I opted for the fish course which was followed by apple pie and custard accompanied by a mug of strong tea.

'Better get used to this sort of grub,' said Warder Fluck.

It wasn't a cheering forecast and I was glad when Mr Frobisher arrived after having lunched at a nearby hotel.

'It's going well,' he said confidently. 'I could tell the jury didn't care much for Mrs Andrews. Gregg made her seem a thoroughly unreliable witness. If he can deal with the other witnesses as effectively I'm sure we'll have more than a sporting chance.' He paused. 'That damn knife is a nuisance. If only Mrs Makepeace or someone had pulled it out and mixed their prints with yours . . .'

I asked a question which had been at the top of my mind. 'Can

126

you call Beryl, the waitress, as a witness when it's our turn?'

'Why?'

'Well, she was in and out of the kitchen and I can remember her being there when Eve and I were having a bit of banter and Beryl laughed. She saw the humour. In fact, she joined in.'

Mr Frobisher was shaking his head before I'd finished speaking. 'No, Mark. I'll put it to Gregg but I'm sure he'll agree with me. You see, if we call Beryl the prosecution will be entitled to have the last word when it comes to the closing addresses, but if you are the only witness, or if we call no witness, then the defence can have the last word, and the last word is influential. It can stick in the minds of the jury.' Mr Frobisher's lips parted in a smile beneath their luxuriant overgrowth. 'The prosecution haven't been able to establish *mens rea*, or intention to kill, on your part, and they are scratching around for a motive. The best they can do is to imply that you were jealous and this resulted in a murderous attack – but where is the evidence of jealousy? There isn't any.'

He stood up. 'Time I went back. Keep your chin up.'

As he walked out of the cell he staggered slightly, as though a little drunk, but he regained his balance. I hadn't smelled alcohol on his breath and he hadn't seemed inebriated. From having dined with him on previous occasions I knew he was a modest drinker and his staggering gait worried me. He was like a lifeline to a drowning man and, at this period, he was the most important person in my life. It would be a catastrophe if he became ill again. All I would have to sustain me would be an implacable determination to find out who had murdered Eve.

4

When the trial resumed the first witness to be called was a youth who walked with such a jerky, self-conscious gait that it looked as though he was being manipulated from above by a puppeteer. He was tall and lanky and had a narrow, bony face. His long fair hair was tied in a pigtail, or queue. I recognized him as someone I'd seen at Aldeburgh and was certain that on at least one occasion he'd been a customer at Fran's Pantry.

He took the oath in an inaudible mumble.

'Speak up,' said the judge sharply. 'We aren't lip-readers.'

The youth seemed to bend like a sapling hit by a storm blast. 'Sorry,' he said.

'Take the oath again,' the judge ordered. And then, 'That's better. Kindly proceed, Mr Spendlove.'

The prosecuting counsel gave a slight bow before turning to peer at the youth over his half-moon spectacles.

'Your name is Barry Hunt?'

'Yes, sir.'

'And you reside at number fourteen Kingsmill Court, Aldeburgh?'

'That's right.'

'And you are unemployed?'

'Yes, sir.'

'How old are you, Mr Hunt?'

'Nineteen. Nearly twenty.'

'I believe you frequent a public house known as the Three Tuns near the old railway station . . . That is a question, Mr Hunt.'

The youth swallowed. 'Yes.'

'Some time ago, on a Saturday evening in April, something happened at the Three Tuns. Can you tell the court what this was? And please speak up.'

Hunt cleared his throat. 'I was drinking with my mates when Danny came in. He tried to join us like, but we didn't want nothing to do with him. I mean, he's a bit loopy, isn't he? Anyway, someone told him to get lost. But he didn't go. So we ragged him a bit. But he still didn't go. And then Jack gave him a shove and it was then Mrs Harris stepped in and . . .'

'Just a moment,' the judge interrupted. 'Is this Danny the same pre-decimalization Danny to whom reference was made by the previous witness?'

'I believe so, my lord,' said Spendlove.

'I see. Please continue.'

Spendlove turned to Hunt. 'What was Mrs Harris doing at the Three Tuns?'

'She was having a drink.'

'On her own?'

'She was that night. Usually she meets a mate of hers there, a woman who drives over from Leiston, but tonight her mate hadn't turned up. That's what she told me later.'

'Yes, yes. We'll come to what occurred later in due course. Tell the court what happened after someone gave Danny a shove.'

'Well, she stepped in to protect him, didn't she?'

Before Spendlove could open his mouth the judge snapped, 'It isn't for you to ask questions, Mr Hunt.'

With an unexpected show of spirit Hunt replied, 'I wasn't asking no questions, sir, my lord.'

For a moment I thought the egg would burst and yolk be scattered all over the courtroom but the judge contained himself. 'Please proceed, Mr Spendlove, and endeavour to prevent your witness from employing the vulgar mode of speech by which every answer he gives terminates in a pointless question.'

'I will do my best, my lord . . . Mr Hunt, how did Mrs Harris protect this person called Danny?'

'She got hold of his arm and led him outside.'

'And then?'

'I followed them, didn't I?'

Before the judge could explode Spendlove said, 'Don't answer all my questions with a question. Just stick to the facts. What occurred when you followed Mrs Harris and Danny?'

'I told her I was sorry for what had happened, and I'd take Danny home to where he lives. She thanked me and said she'd come too. She said her mate hadn't turned up and she could do with a breath of fresh air. We all went down to Slaughden where Danny lives and left him with his Mum and Dad.'

'And then?'

'Mrs Harris said it was a lovely night. A full moon. She thought she'd carry on walking along the sea-wall. I said I wouldn't mind doing the same if it was all right with her. She said it was.'

'You and Mrs Harris walked along the sea-wall. Were there any others taking a night stroll?'

'No, sir.'

'And then?'

'After a bit she said she'd like to go back along the beach but it's quite a drop from the wall, I was surprised. But she got on her knees, lowered herself, and dropped down and I did the same like. And then it happened.'

'What happened?' asked Spendlove in a patient voice.

'Well, she put her arm through mine, didn't she? And in next to no time we were kissing like.'

'Were you surprised to find yourself kissing with Mrs Harris?'

Hunt had everyone's attention and relished the limelight. Even his pigtail seemed to stiffen with pride at this moment of fame.

'I was surprised, sir.'

'And then what happened?'

'We did it like.'

'Did what, Mr Hunt?'

'Screwed, sir.'

I was horrified, appalled. I managed to keep my face stonily straight but it was an effort. I felt like screaming, 'He's lying! Eve wouldn't do that!'

Spendlove paused a moment before saying, 'By "screwed" I take it you mean you had full sexual intercourse with Mrs Harris. Is that correct?'

'Yes, sir. It was great. Magic. I'd always fancied her.'

Spendlove said something but I hardly heard him. I was bottling up fury, using a maximum of self-control. I tuned in again as Hunt was saying, 'She told me it had been a sight better than serving up coffee and cakes but we should separate now and go to our own homes.'

He looked around the court as though expecting a round of

applause. He got none from Spendlove who, probably irritated that the point he was trying to make had been by-passed, said, 'Just a minute. Wasn't there something else she said about this experience she'd had with you?'

'Something else?'

'Did Mrs Harris make any comment about having sexual intercourse with someone to whom she was not married?'

Hunt thought. 'Oh, yes,' he said at length. 'She told me she was glad she wasn't going home to a jealous husband.'

'Anything else?'

'Something about jealousy being a terrible thing and when men got jealous they could be very violent, even when they had no right, not being married like.'

'This remark about jealousy – was it spoken in a lighthearted manner, or did you get the impression she was being serious?'

'She was dead serious, sir.'

'Thank you, Mr Hunt. That is all.' He turned to Gregg. 'Your witness.'

When Gregg was first introduced to me he had seemed a fat, arrogant bully who was contemptuous of my story and indifferent to my plight. But as the trial progressed these early opinions had been replaced by a growing faith in his ability to defend me and in his skills as an advocate. And now, as he rose to cross-examine Hunt, I felt like shouting, 'Flatten the lying bastard!' as though he was a boxer entering the ring and I was behind his corner. I wanted him to demolish and destroy the youth who had made Eve seem like a cheap pick-up.

After hitching up his gown in what had become a familiar mannerism Gregg asked, 'Mr Hunt, I don't wish to seem insulting, but do you understand what is meant by being on oath, as you are now?'

'Yeah. Why?'

Without raising his voice, and speaking in a most temperate way, Gregg said, 'Any falsehood, any lie, could result in you being sent to prison for perjury, and I wouldn't want that to happen, and I'm sure neither would you. You understand me?'

'Sure.'

Hunt was no longer the subdued and mumbling youth who had entered the witness-box; he was cocky.

'I'm glad you realize the vital importance of being absolutely truthful,' said Gregg, and then, his voice hardening, 'I'd like to take you through the last part of your evidence. I have no question to ask on the first part. I can well understand that Mrs Harris, a compassionate woman, should come to the aid of the unfortunate Danny, and I can understand that you should have followed her out of the Three Tuns to apologize. That was entirely commendable. I can understand that you should both walk home with Danny and that you and Mrs Harris should enjoy a short further stroll. Although late April it was presumably not a cold night, and although the sea-wall has no lighting no doubt the full moon gave sufficient light. Anyone can understand that you and she should walk together, particularly as you'd struck up an accord over the unfortunate Danny.'

Gregg paused and I could see the judge was becoming impatient with this extended repetition of uncontested evidence. But the atmosphere in the court was one of increasing tension. It was as if everyone was waiting for Gregg to pounce.

'I can also understand,' he continued, 'that a walk along the beach would be a pleasant way of returning to town but there is one thing that puzzles me and I would be grateful for your assistance on this.' He looked directly at Hunt. 'During what was a fairly long walk together, to say nothing of the time spent in the public house, did you notice what Mrs Harris was wearing?'

'Her clothes, you mean?'

'I mean her clothes.'

'Well, she was wearing a sort of pink dress, wasn't she, with a red jacket on top.'

'And how was she shod?'

'Shod?'

'I assume she was wearing shoes, or was she bare-footed?'

'No, she had shoes. Red shoes.'

'Flat-heeled red shoes?'

'No. They had heels. Quite high heels like.'

'You are sure of that?'

'Yeah, I'm sure. She had a nice pair of pins and high heels made them look good.'

Gregg nodded.'That is what I'd thought. And I'm glad your recollection is so clear. Most helpful. And when she lowered herself from the sea-wall, was she still wearing these shoes?'

'Yes, she was. Why should she take them off?'

'Quite. So she was wearing high-heeled shoes and walking on a shingle beach. I put it to you that the only reason she took your arm was to keep her balance. Wasn't that so?'

Too late Hunt realized that a trap had been laid. He looked less cocky as he answered, 'Maybe.'

'And I further put it to you that you mistook her action in taking your arm, and you thought she was indicating a willingness to enjoy closer contact with you.'

'I didn't think anything.'

'You didn't think anything when an attractive woman – a woman who you have publicly admitted you fancied – took your arm on a deserted beach? I put it to you that you were sexually aroused.'

'She was giving me a come-on.'

'You thought that she was; you wanted to think she was. I am suggesting it was nothing of the sort, and I'm further suggesting that you took advantage of the situation – the lonely beach, the allure of a full moon, the closeness of the woman you fancied – to increase the physical contact.' Gregg raised his voice. 'In short, I'm suggesting you raped her!'

A collective gasp went up from the public gallery.

Hunt went pale and he gripped the edge of the witness-box. 'No, I never. I never did.'

'Speak up, Mr Hunt,' said Gregg in an acid voice. 'I want your denial to be clearly heard.'

'I didn't rape her. She was asking for it.'

'Oh, come now. You expect us to believe that a mature woman, a woman old enough to be your mother, a woman of substance who had a comfortable bedroom in her own property less than a mile away, couldn't wait to have sexual intercourse with you on a stony beach, a place accessible to anyone else who cared to take an evening walk. Why should she want to do a thing like that?'

Hunt swallowed and opened his mouth, closed it, opened it again and said, 'I've told the truth.'

'You are saying that Mrs Harris, a woman of experience and sophistication, was so madly attracted to you that she couldn't wait to get you into a comfortable bed but lay down on a stony, damp beach, so that you could gratify your lust. Is that what you are saying?'

'I didn't rape her.'

'I put it to you in the most forcible way I can that you did. You took advantage of the situation and raped Mrs Harris.'

'No!'

'Did she thank you for what you'd done and ask to see you again? And remember you are on oath.'

A sheen of sweat covered Hunt's forehead and his pigtail had wilted. 'Not exactly,' he said.

'Precisely. She didn't want to see you again after being raped. Did you see her again? And' – Gregg wagged a finger at the youth – 'I would advise you most strongly to speak the truth. Did you see her again?'

'I may have done.'

'In the Three Tuns?'

'No.'

'Where?'

Hunt delayed his reply for so long I wondered whether he was going to speak but at last he said, 'I think I might have gone for a coffee at the place she ran.'

'And she welcomed you with open arms?'

Hunt winced. 'No.'

'I should think not. She probably told you to get out. I'm glad that, at least, you've spoken the truth in this respect. It avoids the necessity of my having to call a witness to say you had been to the café at least twice in May. Mrs Harris did tell you to go, didn't she?'

Hunt hesitated before replying. 'Sort of,' he said, 'but she wasn't unfriendly. She said things had changed and to forget what had happened.'

'I should imagine she would want to forget having been raped,' remarked Gregg. 'I have no more questions to ask you.'

He sat down and, like two figures in a Swiss clock, the moment one barrister sat down the other would rise.

Spendlove stood. 'Mr Hunt, to your knowledge was this sexual congress between you and Mrs Harris reported to the police?'

'Not to my knowledge, sir.'

'The event happened some months ago – you have not been summoned for indecent assault or rape?'

'No, sir.'

'Thank you.'

Spendlove sat down and Hunt was given permission to leave the witness-box. A murmur of talk and a swivelling of eyes followed him as with his curiously disjointed gait he made for the exit at the rear of the courtroom.

I could have jumped into the ring and hugged Gregg. He had won convincingly on points, if not by a knock-out. It was now clear to me why Eve had acquired a somewhat unsavoury reputation in certain quarters. Hunt had boasted about his 'conquest' to his friends and, by Eve not reporting the offence, his boasts had gone unchallenged.

Why hadn't Eve gone to the police? Why don't a lot of raped women go to the police? Mostly, I imagine, because they hate the publicity which can follow and the attempts by defence counsel to besmear and degrade them by alleging that they were willing participants. Trials for rape in open court can seem, for the woman, like being soiled twice over, first physically and then mentally. Knowing Eve as I did, I could believe she'd try to put the episode behind her. I didn't blame her for not telling me about it; she might have thought such a disclosure would blight the delicate bloom of our new-flowering love.

I felt such a surge of anger against Hunt that had he appeared beside me in the dock I'd have flattened his face with my fist. The desire to revenge myself on him was almost as strong as the desire to discover who had murdered Eve. Perhaps I wasn't as open-minded and reasonable as I liked to think, or perhaps the strain of waiting for the trial, and the trial itself, was having a profound effect on my nature and my self-image.

And then it occurred to me that maybe it was Hunt, not Moira, who was responsible for Eve's death. Had he followed her into the café after she'd waved me goodbye, and then stabbed her when she refused his demands for sex?

This was a question to be considered later, when I was alone in my cell, because Moira had just walked into the courtroom and I needed all my faculties to concentrate on her evidence as a prosecution witness.

5

I hardly recognized her. Instead of sloppy sweater and baggy trousers she was wearing a pale mauve blouse under an elegant dark purple two-piece. The skirt was knee length and in the brief glimpse I had as she mounted steps to the witness-box I saw she had legs to match Eve's for shapeliness. But even more startling, she'd had her hair coiffed to give her a gamin look and her face was a patina of skilfully applied cosmetics. Earrings of filigree gold studded with tiny amethysts hung from the lobes of her ears and a matching gold brooch with a large amethyst in its centre decorated one lapel of her costume. She looked feminine, and the vague likeness to Eve which had struck me when I'd first seen her was accentuated. She was no longer the ugly sister.

She read the oath in a clear voice which seemed in a higher register than I remembered.

Spendlove opened with questions which established Moira as a single woman who travelled widely and was keen on motor cars. She enjoyed the theatre and was a supporter of various animal charities. She was presented as a capable and self-reliant woman with a positive outlook on life. Spendlove then moved on to the friendship with Eve and established their bond as school friends (although no mention was made of cats) and then to the time when they had lost touch with each other.

'Why was that?' Spendlove asked.

'Quite simply I fell in love with a marvellous man in Canada and married him. I think Eve rather resented this, or perhaps she was envious, and decided to get married herself. She found someone and, for want of anyone better, she married him. I never met him.'

'And who was the man she married?'

Moira looked towards me. Her face was expressionless. 'Him,' she said, 'the accused.'

This was completely at variance with what Eve had told me. Eve's version was that events had happened the other way around; Moira had married the Canadian in a pique when she'd heard that Eve had married me.

'You lost touch,' said Spendlove, 'but many years afterwards you met again?'

'Yes.'

'Tell the court about this meeting.'

'Eve had managed to get in touch with me again. My husband had died and I came to England to live at Leiston. I went to the south of France on holiday and met up with Eve who was living there with a man called Saul Harris. She'd taken his name by deed poll but unhappily he died. She was bereft. She had loved him dearly. He was the opposite of the man she'd married and been divorced from. He was generous with time and money, and he wasn't possessive.'

'And then what happened?'

For the next few minutes Moira painted a picture of a grief-stricken and penniless Eve and how she, Moira, had decided to help. She had encouraged Eve to buy Fran's Pantry in Aldeburgh and had loaned her money for this purpose as well as making an extra loan to finance necessary alterations to the premises.

It was during this monologue and while I was sourly regarding Moira's new look, so different from her usual scruffy gear, that a thunderbolt of inspiration hit me. I hastily scribbled a note about the apparel she'd been wearing when I first met her and had the note passed to Mr Frobisher. He read it and went into a huddled whisper with Gregg and Fiona James.

I picked up the threads of Spendlove's continuing examination-in-chief. He was saying, 'I understand you and Mrs Harris had differences and you decided to call in these loans.'

'We had differences, yes. But I never intended to call in the loans.'

'Can you tell the court something of the background to these events?'

'Certainly. As I've said, I had never seen Mark but he had come back into her life. She introduced him to me as a former

137

neighbour who had come to Aldeburgh and, by the strangest chance, had walked into her café one day.'

'The strangest chance? What do you mean by that?'

Moira tilted her head back almost as though she was defying in advance any contradiction of what she was about to say, and the movement of her head caused the tiny gemstones in her earrings to wink across the well of the court.

'What do I mean by the strangest chance? Simply, I'm sure he knew he'd find her there. He is an obsessive sort of man and I have no doubt that after the divorce he managed to keep track of her and—'

Gregg was on his feet. 'My lord, these are pure conjectures and unless substantiated should be dismissed as such.'

'I agree. The jury will disregard what has just been said . . . Mrs Makepeace, you mustn't air unsupportable suppositions. Can you produce evidence that the accused kept track of his ex-wife's movements?'

'No, my lord.' Moira bowed her head and the earrings danced. 'I'm sorry, my lord.'

Spendlove continued, 'And so, for a while, you were deceived into thinking that a man who was, in fact, an ex-husband was nothing more than an old friend, a neighbour who had once lived in the same road as Mrs Harris?'

'That's right.'

'Why should Mrs Harris practise a deceit like that?'

Moira raised pencilled eyebrows. 'I know I mustn't make suggestions I can't support but from something she told me later I think she was ashamed of herself for entertaining someone who hadn't exactly been the best husband in the world.'

Spendlove took a sip from a glass of water, put the glass down, and said, 'What I am about to ask is crucial, so please think very carefully before you reply . . . In what way did you discover that matters were not as you thought?'

Moira, quite unflurried by his warning, answered, 'I discovered it after Eve and I had been to see a production of *Hedda Gabler* in Ipswich. On the way back she confessed that Mark wasn't a friendly neighbour; he was her ex-husband.'

'What followed then?'

'I was shocked. In the south of France she'd told me how insensitive he'd been to her needs, how he had cramped her individuality, almost destroyed her self-esteem. I told her she was mad to allow him back into her life.' At this point Moira's voice lowered and became the voice I recognized. 'We had an argument about it and I'm sorry to say the evening ended badly. But I loved Eve. I cared about her. And I didn't want her to make the same mistake twice. I didn't want her to contemplate remarriage.'

'But you called in the loans you had made to her. That was hardly the action of an old friend.'

'I'm glad you raised that,' said Moira. 'Yes, I called in the loans, but not out of vindictiveness or malice. I did it to try and make her see sense. I hoped that the threat would be enough to make her drop any idea of continuing her relationship with Mark.'

'But you changed your mind?'

'I knew Eve would be suffering and I couldn't bear that. I decided that if she really wanted to go back to him, even though I thought he was a walking disaster area, I mustn't interfere. And so I decided to let her know that my threats to call in the loans would be stopped.'

'And what action did you take?'

'I decided on impulse to go and see her, to tell her what I hoped would be good news. I telephoned but there was no reply. Again on impulse I decided to drive over to the café. I wrote a note to drop through the letter-box if she hadn't come in.'

'And so you drove to Aldeburgh, to Fran's Pantry, and what did you find?'

'After parking my car I went to the front door. To my surprise – well, not exactly to my surprise because Eve was very slack about locking up – I found that I had only to push the door and it opened. I assumed she was out somewhere and I decided to go in and leave my note on the kitchen table.'

'Yes, and then?'

Tension in the courtroom tightened. This was to be the revelation of the discovery of Eve's body. I could hardly stomach looking at Moira standing in the witness-box, so poised, so confident, so *alive*!

'I called out her name. I called out, "Eve, are you there?" She didn't answer. I walked into the kitchen and saw her. On the floor by the fridge, with the handle of a knife sticking out, and bloodstains all over her dress.'

'What did you do?' Spendlove asked in a voice which had

become slightly muted as though out of respect both for the dead and for the living bereaved. 'What action did you take?'

'I rushed over to her and felt for her pulse but she was obviously dead. There was nothing I could do for her and I knew I mustn't disturb the body' – Moira took a deep breath – 'and so I phoned the police, and I waited, and I wondered who could have done such a terrible thing to such a lovely person.'

'Quite so. And the police arrived fairly soon, I believe, and took charge of the matter.'

'Yes. They were very good. Of course they asked me a lot of questions. I explained that I was Eve's best friend, best woman friend, and that she'd been living with a man recently. They asked where he was, and I said I didn't know, but I was surprised he wasn't around because he always seemed to stick pretty close to Eve.' Moira paused and for a moment I thought she was going to play the part of best friend being overcome by emotion at the memory of the fateful night. But after a sigh she gallantly continued, 'The police asked if I knew of any address where he might be. I said he had a flat in London. I knew Eve kept an address book and where it was. I got it and showed it to the detective and said there might be a note of Mr Markby's address in it. Sure enough, there was. Written in pencil by Eve. Then the detective asked me about next-of-kin and I told him about a cousin of Eve's I'd met a couple of times. Eve didn't have any close family.'

'And then what happened?' asked Spendlove, his voice still respectfully muted.

'Nothing much. I was feeling terrible knowing that Eve must have died still thinking I was annoyed with her and meaning to call in the loans.'

And then Moira actually played the part of being overcome by emotion. She lowered her head and sniffed. It seemed she was about to burst into tears. A sympathetic hush at the sight of a grieving friend was broken by the judge.

'Are you feeling all right, Mrs Makepeace?'

Moira raised her head and said, 'This isn't like me. I can usually cope. I'm sorry. But yes, I'm all right, my lord.'

I had to admire her acting ability. She was playing the part of brave little woman to perfection.

Spendlove continued, 'Can you tell the court what happened

after the police had arrived and you had helped with addresses?'

'When I saw there was nothing more I could do, and Eve's body had been decently covered, I went home.'

'You went home, presumably to be alone with your thoughts and to try to come to terms with your grief.'

'I couldn't get over what had happened. Eve didn't have an enemy in the world. Or I thought she hadn't, but I didn't know everything about her private life.'

Spendlove took so long before asking the next question I wondered if he had finished. But at last he asked, 'Are you a Christian?'

'Yes. I don't go regularly to church but I try to follow Christ's teaching.'

'There are many like you, if I may say so. We have heard in evidence that Mrs Harris wore a crucifix on a gold chain. Had you ever seen this?'

'Oh, yes. A number of times.'

'Such an ornament can be worn for religious beliefs or simply as a fashion accessory. This necklace has been referred to earlier in these proceedings and I'm wondering if you can throw any light on its provenance.'

Moira shook her head. 'I don't know when Eve got it. It may have been a gift from someone. I doubt if Eve wore it for any reason other than she liked it.'

'Apparently this necklace hasn't been found among Mrs Harris's effects. As a close friend do you have any idea where it might be?'

Moira shook her head again and her earrings bobbed and twinkled. 'I've no idea. Maybe it was stolen by whoever killed her.'

'And yet, so I understand, nothing else was stolen.'

'I'm afraid I can't help,' said Moira with a disarming show of frankness which implied a willingness to help if only she could.

'Thank you, Mrs Makepeace.'

Spendlove sat down.

As Gregg rose to cross-examine, my pulse rate increased. Would he take advantage of the information I'd conveyed to Mr Frobisher in my note?

His opening question startled everyone, including me. 'Mrs Makepeace,' he said, 'the court has heard your very lucid version of events as you saw them but what I should like to know is whether you agree with me, and others, that love and hate are but two sides of the same coin. Do you agree with that proposition?'

'I suppose so,' replied Moira guardedly.

'Yes or no, Mrs Makepeace?'

'Yes, in general.'

'I see. In general, yes.'

At this point Gregg seemed to have lost his way. He fumbled with papers in front of him. Was he looking for my note, I wondered. Then, turning to face Moira fully, he said, 'Mrs Makepeace, you are on record as saying that you loved Mrs Harris. Could you please amplify this statement?'

For the first time Moira looked less than self-possessed. After a pause she said, 'I meant I cared about her.'

'I care about a lot of people, Mrs Makepeace, but that doesn't mean I love them. You have said you loved Mrs Harris. If that is so, by the same coin of love, which has hate on its obverse, you must have been capable of hating her.'

'I never hated Eve.'

'No? But from what we have heard you seem to have had very ambivalent feelings towards her. One minute you appeared to be old and close friends and the next you are calling in loans which could wreck Mrs Harris's business venture.'

A faint flush added colour to the make-up on Moira's face. 'I have already explained,' she replied coldly, 'it was an attempt, however misguided, to make Eve see sense. Not to get herself trapped by a man who had made her so unhappy earlier in her life. I thought if he learned that Eve was in debt and might lose the café he might quickly disappear.'

'You seem to have disliked him.'

'I didn't like him.'

'You hated him?'

'No.'

Gregg hitched up his gown before saying, 'You present yourself as a caring person. I should like, for a moment, to dwell on your caring activities. It was mentioned earlier that you supported animal charities. Can you tell the court the names of these charities?'

'The Cats' Refuge in Wickham Market and the Cats' Sanctuary at Colchester.'

'Any others?'

'The World Wildlife Fund.'

'Any others?'

'If a collection comes round for the RSPCA, I would give.'

'But cats are your main interest?'

'Yes. They can't speak for themselves and have no one to defend their interests. They can't afford the services of highly-paid barristers.'

A gust of amusement at this crack swept through the back of the courtroom and Spendlove ducked his head to conceal a smirk.

Unperturbed, Gregg went on, 'I understand that as a term of endearment you would call Mrs Harris "Sister Cat". Is that correct?'

Moira hesitated before replying, 'Yes.'

'Are you interested in the occult, Mrs Makepeace?'

Moira's face became so hard that her make-up was in danger of crazing. 'No, I am not!'

'In folklore, cats are regarded as the familiars of witches and I am . . .'

Spendlove jumped up so fast he might have been launched by a rocket. 'My lord, I object most strenuously to this line of questioning.'

'And so do I,' responded the judge. 'Mr Gregg, you had better justify this line of argument or drop it altogether. This is a trial for murder in a court of justice, not a discussion group on the occult, or witches, or things paranormal.'

'I will bear that in mind, my lord,' replied Gregg politely. 'Most helpful. I am truly grateful.'

'Don't try to be sarcastic with me, Mr Gregg,' said the judge angrily.

'My lord, I wouldn't dream of it . . . Mrs Makepeace, would you not agree it was a remarkable coincidence that, on the very night Mrs Harris was killed by someone unknown, you should at that exact time decide to lift your threat of calling in the loans to Mrs Harris?'

Moira thought at length before replying. 'I don't think it remarkable. Eve and I had always been very close and I think I had a foreboding about her. I knew I must tell her not to worry about the loans. It may seem odd to you, but we were on a wavelength and sometimes there was a sort of telepathy between us.'

'A sort of telepathy,' repeated Gregg in a ruminative voice. 'In deference to his lordship I will not enter into a discussion about the paranormal. We'll leave it that this extraordinary coincidence of your being first to arrive on the scene of a murder was partly because you had telepathic misgivings about your friend. So, following these misgivings, and prompted by a desire to make amends for a quarrel, you telephoned Mrs Harris, got no reply, and decided to drive to Aldeburgh to see her and, if she wasn't at home, to leave a note.'

'That's right.'

'Tell me, how were you dressed?'

This was it! At last Gregg was going to use the information I'd sent to Mr Frobisher.

'Dressed? How do you mean?' Moira asked in surprise.

'Were you smartly dressed as you are now?'

'No. I was probably in old slacks and a sweater.'

'And you didn't change to go out?'

'No. I went as I was.'

'In your car? The Aston-Martin?'

'Yes.'

'We've heard what happened when you arrived. You found Mrs Harris's body, you rushed over to her and felt her pulse, and you realized she was dead. Is that correct?'

'Absolutely.'

'By what method did you feel for the pulse?'

Moira frowned, gave a short, nervous laugh, and said, 'With my fingers, of course. How else?'

I could hardly breathe as I waited for Gregg to spring the trap. He did so by remarking, almost as an aside, 'You must have first taken off your gloves.'

For a moment or two Moira lost her composure. She looked frightened and vulnerable. Recovering her poise she said, 'I wasn't wearing gloves.'

'You possess a pair of string-backed driving gloves?'

'Yes.'

'My information is that you invariably wear these gloves when driving your car, an open tourer. Why didn't you wear them on that night?'

A pervading stillness and silence, broken only by the ticking of the courtroom clock, became so acute it was almost intolerable. Moira seemed paralysed. She stood motionless; a figure frozen by guilt uncovered. It was obvious to me, and I prayed it was clear to the jury too, that she had been wearing gloves and therefore could have plunged the bread-knife into Eve without leaving fingerprints.

At last her lips moved. Speaking slowly she said, 'I was in such a hurry. I was anxious about Eve. I must have forgotten them.'

'In a hurry even though you anticipated that you might not find Mrs Harris at home?'

'Yes. I wasn't myself that night. I desperately wanted to heal the rift with Eve.'

'It is so important that I must ask you again – are you absolutely sure you weren't wearing gloves that night?'

'I'm sure. I know I would have remembered taking them off to feel Eve's wrist for a pulsebeat.'

'But you do agree that normally you always wear gloves when driving?'

Moira's 'Yes' was little more than a whisper.

'Thank you. I have no further questions.'

Spendlove was immediately on his feet.

'Mrs Makepeace, to clear up this red herring about gloves trailed by my learned friend can you tell the court where you normally keep these gloves? Do you keep them indoors or in your car?'

'There's no special place.'

'Then you must occasionally mislay them, forget where you've put them?'

'I remember now what happened,' replied Moira in the clear voice of conviction. 'I'd washed them that very day. They were still damp and I'd left them in the airing cupboard.'

'A very reasonable explanation,' commented Spendlove as he sat down.

Moira left the witness-box.

The prosecution case was closed.

Act One in the grim play was over. It was now my turn to go on stage.

6

Having once been a key witness in a major fraud trial I shouldn't have felt so nervous now. It wasn't as though I hadn't once dealt with a rigorous cross-examination and emerged successfully. But perhaps because I was the target, and not a piece of ammunition in a prosecution case, I had to struggle to keep a tremor out of my voice as I read the oath.

Gregg rose to his feet. I was aware that his junior, Fiona James, was looking at me intently. As our eyes met, she smiled. Her smile was an encouragement, something I badly needed.

'Mr Markby,' Gregg began, 'would you describe yourself as a jealous man?'

I realized at once that he was going to make 'motive' an important issue. If the prosecution had a weakness, it was the matter of motive. My nervousness vanished.

'No, I'm not a jealous man.'

'In other words, you are the complaisant sort, the sort who if married to someone wouldn't object to your wife taking lovers?'

This was a tough question. 'I don't think I'd be complaisant,' I said, 'but neither would I be aggressive about the situation. I'd try to behave in a civilized manner and try to find out why things had got to the stage where my wife needed another man.'

'Mrs Harris was formerly your wife. You divorced her, did you not?'

'Yes.'

'On what grounds?'

'She'd gone off with another man and it seemed pointless for us to remain married.'

'But didn't you try to find out why things had got to the stage where she needed the attentions of another man?'

146

'I didn't have the opportunity. She left me before I realized there was another man.'

'And you weren't jealous of this other man who had stolen your wife?'

'I was hurt. I'd thought he was a friend. He was a client who'd dined at our house. I didn't know he was coveting my wife. I was completely deceived.'

'You were deceived, but weren't you also jealous once you knew the facts?'

'No.'

'When you met your ex-wife again, at the beginning of May, you extended your holiday to help her run the café known as Fran's Pantry. At any time during the period between meeting her and her death were jealous emotions aroused in you?'

'No. There was nothing to be jealous about. We had rediscovered happiness together.'

'I must now put it to you directly – did you murder your ex-wife as a result of jealousy or from any other motive?'

I was completely calm as I answered, 'No, I did not. I have never at any time in my life contemplated murdering her or anyone else.'

Gregg then switched from unproven jealousy to my proven honesty. In an extended preamble to a question he mentioned my role in the fraud trial and he was so fulsome in his praise of my conduct, my sense of honour and integrity, that I wondered whether he had forgotten saying he couldn't make out if I was a truly honourable man or simply an honest fool. In different circumstances I would have found his eulogy extremely embarrassing. As it was, I was fairly glad when he concluded it with, 'Complete honesty in all your relationships, and dealings with others, means a great deal to you, I would think.'

'Yes, it does.'

'Even when complete honesty is to your disadvantage.'

'Yes.'

'I wonder if it has occurred to you, as it has to me, that you wouldn't be in the position you now find yourself if you had been less than honest.'

Everyone's eyes were on me. Even the judge had turned to give me judicial attention.

'If I'd been guilty of the crime which I've been accused of, I could certainly have concocted a more plausible explanation for going to London. But why should I do such a thing? I'm not guilty, and I've told the truth.'

Gregg nodded. 'Exactly. You've told the truth. You had the opportunity to manufacture a more convincing explanation for returning to London than vandalism of your flat when there was no vandalism. But you told the truth even though the truth was met with scepticism and disbelief. Now will you tell the court how you came to meet your ex-wife again and what ensued, but first, to nail a mischievous imputation made by a previous witness – had you been tracking your ex-wife's movements since she left you and were you aware you'd find her at Aldeburgh?'

'No, I was not, and I had no idea of her movements.'

'Thank you. Now, in your own words and taking your time, tell the court about meeting your ex-wife.'

I went through the whole saga starting with the booking at a hotel and concluding with my parting from Eve, the discovery that my flat hadn't been vandalized, and Clench's arrival when I was about to return to Aldeburgh. Fortunately I am blessed with an excellent memory and could narrate the whole story without pause or self-correction, and I flatter myself that it was detailed and accurate. When I'd finished Fiona James gave a nod of approval. Gregg too seemed satisfied although, once or twice, I'd noticed him shifting around, altering his stance like someone who has been waiting too long in a queue and is tired of standing.

Given the opportunity to speak once more he asked, 'With hindsight would you have behaved any differently?'

'No. I'm glad I extended my holiday. I loved Eve. My only regret, and it is an enormous regret, is that she should have been killed and the killer still be at large.'

'You loved her and were completely happy with her?'

'I did, and I was.'

'It must have come as a dreadful shock to you when you learned of her death.'

'It did. It was terrible. I don't think I shall ever get over it.'

'Thank you, Mr Markby.' Gregg glanced sideways. 'Your witness,' he said.

Spendlove rose and looked at me over the rim of his spectacles.

'Why did you choose Aldeburgh for your holiday?' he asked.

'I like the place. I've had many holidays there.'

'Many holidays with the late Mrs Harris when she was your wife?'

'Yes.'

'How many?'

This stumped me. 'I can't say the exact number. Possibly fifteen. Maybe more if you count day visits.'

'You both enjoyed it there?'

'Yes.'

'Because your ex-wife had enjoyed it so much it must have been a sentimental journey to go once more to Aldeburgh.'

'In a way I suppose it was.'

'And perhaps to see her there.'

'How could I? The last I knew of her she was in the south of France.'

'Is that so? I put it to you that after you moved to London you felt lonely and, never having really lost touch with her, you knew of the death of the man with whom she'd been living and eventually you decided you must see her again. You knew where to find her and, the very day after your arrival, you made contact.'

'That is just not true.'

'If it isn't true then you must admit that it was quite remarkable you should meet again by sheer chance. The odds against it must be millions to one.'

His scepticism, tinged with mockery, annoyed me but I could only say, and it sounded feeble, 'Such things do happen.'

'Do they? Mostly in romantic novelettes, I imagine. Not only do I put it to you that you knew where to find your ex-wife but you were willing to undertake the most menial of tasks to ingratiate yourself with her. You couldn't wait to wash up dirty dishes which had been used by strangers. Did you scrub the kitchen floor too?'

I gritted my teeth and said, 'Yes. Twice when Eve was under the weather and very busy I did clean and polish the floor.'

A murmur of surprise came from the public gallery.

Spendlove's voice was edged with contempt as he asked, 'And were you paid for being a servant, or should I say, for being servile?'

I knew I mustn't lose my temper. I mustn't allow Spendlove's baiting to get under my skin.

'I wasn't paid.'

'No? Then perhaps your reward was to be permitted to move into the mistress's bedroom.'

I said nothing.

'That is a question, Mr Markby.'

'Is it? I thought it was an impertinent assumption.'

The moment I spoke I regretted the words. I had lost my cool. Gregg's head, which had been bowed, lifted sharply and a look of dismay crossed Fiona James's face.

'Will you answer my question, Mr Markby, without indulging in personal abuse. Was your reward to be permitted to move into the mistress's bedroom?'

'The question of a reward didn't enter into it. We were in love.'

'Ah, you were in love,' Spendlove cooed in a sugary, sentimental voice. 'How touching!' He paused and his drained, ascetic face feigned an expression of perplexity. 'But,' he went on, 'surely as a man of honour, and that is how you have so painstakingly been presented, as a man of honour shouldn't you first have remarried the lady before moving into her bedroom?'

'We were intending to get married,' I replied, almost without thinking.

'You were? In that case I expect you bought her an engagement ring. Did you?'

I had to reply, 'No.'

'Perhaps *you* were hoping to remarry but Mrs Harris didn't share your enthusiasm for wedlock. After all, she had found the previous marriage so tedious that she left you for another. I suggest that you proposed marriage and were rejected.'

'That isn't true.'

'And I further suggest that rejection of your proposal caused you to feel resentful and your resentment was ignited to fury when you discovered Mrs Harris wasn't averse to granting favours elsewhere.'

I was aware of my team – Gregg, Fiona James, and Mr Frobisher – all gazing anxiously at me, willing me to keep calm.

'That isn't true,' I said again.

'But you knew of the rumours connected with her, you must

have done. Let me refresh your memory.' Spendlove glanced down at his notes. 'In your evidence, when speaking of the time you spent in Aldeburgh, you mentioned that when this alleged telephone call was made from a Mrs da Costa you and Mrs Harris thought, before you answered the call, that it might be another communication from a man who had been making obscene calls.'

'That's right.'

'How many of these calls had there been?'

I had to think hard, and at the same time be prepared to explain why the calls hadn't been reported.

'There were two or three,' I said.

'And who took the calls? You or Mrs Harris?'

'I took the first . . . Eve took one . . . No, two.'

'And what did the caller say?'

I wished I'd never referred to obscene calls earlier.

'Well, Mr Markby, we are waiting – what did this caller say?'

'I don't know what he said to Eve. I don't think she told me.'

'What did he say to you?'

I took a deep breath. 'He called her a whore.'

'He called her a whore,' repeated Spendlove with evident relish. 'How did you react to that?'

'I didn't believe it.'

'You didn't have the faintest suspicion it might be true?'

'No. The man was obviously a pervert with a warped mind.'

In a wondering voice Spendlove said, 'What a remarkable person you are. By a freakish chance you meet your ex-wife whom you have divorced following her adultery and, instead of running a mile to get away from her, you can't wait to show your servitude by washing up dishes and cleaning the kitchen floor, and then, when someone makes an anonymous telephone call stating that she is a whore you are not in the least suspicious that she might be capable of further infidelities.'

He looked at me above the half-moon spectacles as though expecting some comment. I made none.

'Quite remarkable,' he continued. 'I might almost say, quite unnatural. It makes me wonder if you are quite so honest as you have been painted. Indeed, more than wonder. I put it to you that, on top of resentment at being refused when you proposed marriage, you were angry at what you heard about your ex-wife.

And I also put it to you that there was no call from a Mrs da Costa – who, incidentally, seems to have vanished into thin air – but yet another obscene call. Isn't that the case?'

'No. It was Mrs da Costa on the line.'

'Was it? Where is she now, then? Why isn't she here to give evidence on your behalf?'

'She and her family left on a flight to the West Indies after making the call. I've no idea where she might be now.'

'She told you your flat had been vandalized, which it hadn't, and then dashed off to disappear in the West Indies?'

'Yes. I know it may sound strange, but it's the truth.'

'Sound strange!' Spendlove exclaimed. 'It's the most bizarre and unbelievable tale I've ever heard. Come now, Mr Markby. Let us have the real truth. The call wasn't from Mrs da Costa but was another call from the man who described your ex-wife as a whore. As a result of this call, and his allegations, you had a violent argument with Mrs Harris which finally ended when, in a fit of rage, you grabbed a knife with fatal results.'

I was so choked by his accusation that I could hardly speak but, when I did, it was to shout, 'No!'

'But you admit, you have no alternative but to admit, your fingerprints, and yours alone, were on the lethal weapon.'

'Yes, I had been slicing bread for sandwiches earlier in the day and before using the knife I had washed it because jam had got on it.'

'Washing up dishes, cleaning floors, slicing bread for sandwiches . . . You were certainly trying to win back your faithless ex-wife. How galling it must have been to find that the leopard, or the she-leopard in this case, hadn't changed her spots.'

His disgusting imputations about Eve infuriated me so much I was consumed with hatred for Spendlove. How dare he say such things! It was only when Gregg surreptitiously raised a cautioning finger that I managed to hang on to the tatters of self-control.

In a falsely polite voice I said, 'I'm sorry, but was that a question or was it an observation intended to make me look a fool and to tarnish the memory of the woman I loved?'

'It was a perfectly legitimate comment,' replied Spendlove drily. 'I put it to you most forcibly that, contrary to what you say, you were jealous and in a fit of uncontrollable rage you killed your ex-wife.'

'No.'

'You are persisting in your denial of murder even though the facts are glaringly against you?'

'Yes.'

'I would remind you that you are on oath.'

This was too much. 'And I would remind you,' I said, 'that I don't have to be on oath to tell the truth.'

The judge turned to me. 'I didn't warn you about using intemperate language to Queen's Counsel a minute or so ago, but I am warning you now that it can only have an adverse effect on your case.'

I did the right thing. I hadn't been servile to Eve but I was servile now. I bowed my head slightly and said, 'Very well, my lord. I understand your warning.'

'Good . . . Mr Spendlove, please continue.'

I braced myself for Spendlove's next question. It was unexpectedly anodyne.

'Tell me, Mr Markby, how did you spend your days before you met your ex-wife again – purely by chance?'

'I am a music lover. I went to concerts, played tapes, listened to compact discs.'

'Yes, but what human contacts did you have?'

'I might exchange a few words with occupants of neighbouring apartments. Mrs da Costa came regularly for various domestic duties. I would shop for my own needs. I kept in touch with a few former clients and prepared their accounts.'

'And?'

'And nothing,' I said.

'What an eventful life. No wonder you enjoyed working in a busy café and how distressed you must have been when you realized your ex-wife didn't want to share your exciting existence . . .' He paused, and then quite abruptly said, 'I have no more questions.'

Gregg now rose to his feet, as he was entitled to, for re-examination.

'As a lover of music,' he said, 'and particularly of music in the form of opera, do you have difficulty in comprehending the emotions portrayed as, for example, in Verdi's *Otello*, or Rossini's *Otello*, or even Debussy's *Pelléas and Melisande*?'

'No, none at all. And I think Verdi's *Otello* is his supreme work.'

'And so you can understand the emotion of jealousy?'

'Yes.'

'But you were not jealous of your ex-wife?'

'No. Jealousy hasn't personally affected me although I can understand it in others.'

Gregg said, 'Thank you,' and sat down.

The judged glanced towards the clock. 'I think we've heard enough for today,' he said. 'The court will adjourn.'

As his red-robed figure topped by an elaborate egg-cosy left the courtroom everyone stood as though an unseen orchestra was playing the National Anthem.

'It's tough being a judge,' muttered Warder Fluck. 'What a hard life, sitting on a throne all day. The poor old chap must be quite worn out.'

154

7

When Mr Frobisher came to the cell his eyes seemed to loom larger than usual, giving the impression that he was a moustached marmoset.

'You did well,' he said.

'He got me rattled once or twice. I hate these slurs on Eve. She wasn't like that at all.'

'No. Of course not. But when it suits their purpose prosecuting counsel are no respecters of *de mortuis nil nisi bonum*. Don't let it get you down. Keep your end up. You'll be all right. The closing speeches come tomorrow and you can be sure Mr Gregg will make the most of having the last whack. But don't expect a verdict tomorrow. The judge is sure to want the evening to prepare his summing up.'

'You think there's a good chance of acquittal?'

'I do. They haven't really got anywhere with motive and although the bread-knife is a difficulty it could have been held in someone's gloved hand.'

'Moira Makepeace's,' I said.

'We don't know that, Mark. But Gregg will certainly mention gloves.'

'She had to think quickly to come up with that story about having washed the gloves.'

'Yes. Quick thinking.' Then, like the white rabbit in *Alice* rather than a marmoset, he reached inside his coat and took out a gold hunter watch. 'My goodness,' he said, 'look at the time. I must rush. I've got a Law Society dinner tonight. I'll see you tomorrow, Mark, and remember – chin up.'

Once the cell door had been closed and locked I settled down to record the events of the day, reconstructing as best I could the exchanges between various players in the drama.

When Shakespeare wrote of one man in his time playing many parts he was giving a broad outline of a lifespan. He could have added that in each of the seven ages a man, or a woman, plays a number of parts. Moira had demonstrated her versatility in part-playing during a single age. How cunningly she had lied about seeing the necklace many times, how brilliantly she enacted the role of grieving friend, how cleverly she'd pretended to have fallen in love with a rich Canadian! She was a mistress of deceit.

By the time I'd written about the day's events and eaten my supper I was ready for bed. The cell's window lacked curtains and light from outside threw a barred shadow on one of the walls. Even at night I couldn't escape from the knowledge that I was a prisoner, and sleep – that boon which becomes most elusive when most needed – evaded capture for a long, long while. Dawn was breaking when finally I drifted into slumber only to be woken moments later, or so it seemed, by Warder Fluck bringing my breakfast.

'You must be on over-time,' I remarked.

'And thank God for it,' he replied. 'Toffs like you don't know what it's like to be working class and hard up.'

It was the first time I'd ever been called a toff and I didn't know whether to be flattered or insulted.

'It's a pity they've done away with capital punishment for murder,' Fluck continued. 'I always liked it when they reported that the condemned man ate a hearty breakfast. I'll bet it was more than your cornflakes and boiled egg.'

Oddly, I felt no animosity towards Fluck. 'The traditional is always reassuring,' I said. 'I can see your point.'

To my surprise he replied, 'I hand it to you. You're not the common run.'

When Mr Frobisher arrived he looked as though, like me, he'd had a bad night. Since his illness his moustache had lost some of its vitality and it was now sagging like the whiskers of a tired sea-lion. He enquired how I was.

He looked so dejected that, to buck him up, I said, 'Fine.'

'Good. Today is the day for final addresses and I'll wager Mr Gregg will come out on top.'

'I hope so.'

'He will. Mark my words. Keep smiling.'

156

I hadn't been smiling but I said, 'I'll keep smiling,' with a ton of irony.

'Good man . . . anything else?'

'Anything else?'

'Anything you want to say. Last minute thoughts?'

What was he driving at, I wondered. 'No,' I said.

'Right. I'd better be going. Gregg doesn't like it if his instructing solicitor isn't available. I'll see you in court.'

Eternity, like infinity or God, is an unverifiable concept, but it seemed an eternity, such is the difference between psychological and chronological time, before I was escorted to the courtroom.

My previous life – early childhood in a Cotswold village, boarding school, studying to be a chartered accountant, meeting and marrying Eve, a house in Ash Close, Finchley, the birth of Joanna, more accountancy, Joanna growing up and developing into a beautiful young woman, the fraud trial, Joanna's untimely death, Eve's desertion, life as a single man in a London flat – all these seemed illusory. My entire life had been spent in a cell or in this courtroom. This was either eternal life or eternal death. I would forever be cabin'd, cribb'd, confin'd.

The endless drama restarted as Spendlove rose to address the jury. Speaking in a dry monotone he repeated his theory that I must have known I'd find Eve at Aldeburgh and, aware that she was an unattached woman, I had set out to woo her again. To this end I had been willing to be a drudge, a lowly servant. And then I had wormed my way into her bedroom. I had thought I had won her and was possessive of what I'd won. In denying that I was a jealous man I had protested too much and the more strenuously I denied the charge of jealousy the more evident it had become that I was, in fact, extremely jealous. No one would ever know what argument preceded the fatal stabbing. I had alleged there had been a call from an untraceable Mrs da Costa but it could well have been another obscene call and this had provoked a violent confrontation. It was probable I had been brooding on Eve's wayward nature for some time, nursing dark suspicions, and had even planned a confrontation when a pretext presented itself.

And so Spendlove went on, weaving permutations of what might have been, but only able with authority to say exactly what

157

had happened – Eve had been stabbed with a knife bearing my fingerprints. I began to wonder if he would ever stop his fanciful talk about jealousy, about the long arm of coincidence – 'extended beyond belief' – which had precipitated me into Fran's Pantry one morning in May, about the non-vandalizing of my flat, and about Eve's willingness to copulate with Hunt on the beach. 'If it had been rape,' Spendlove said, 'would she not have screamed, and would she not have been heard? She was a fit and healthy woman doing a demanding everyday job, she was a woman of the world, she could easily have fought off an attack from the youth who had given evidence, a youth, who it must be said, was anything but an ideal specimen of male physique.'

It went on and on. I thought he would never stop but eventually he wound up his address by asking that the jury bring in a verdict of murder as charged.

Gregg stood up and began his speech in my defence. It was the jury's duty to weigh up whether I was guilty of the crime as charged beyond all reasonable doubt. It was certainly clear beyond reasonable doubt that I was an exceptionally honest man whose account of events both to the police and in court had been a model of consistency.

What a fragile case, what a frail house of cards, the prosecution had built, he said. Apart from police evidence which was routine and partly concerned with forensic matters the witnesses produced by the prosecution were as weird an assortment of characters as anyone could imagine. There was a paranoiac religious bigot who couldn't abide men in the kitchen, and a youth who boasted about 'screwing' a woman old enough to be his mother. 'Raping' would have been more apt. The jury shouldn't be deceived by appearances. The youth was thin and wiry, and with the strength which comes from unbridled lust – a lust he freely admitted – could easily have overpowered a middle-aged woman who was off balance and fatigued after a hard day's work. And, apart from the sexual episode, it had been necessary for prosecuting counsel to prompt the youth into saying something about jealous husbands in an effort to bolster up a feeble and unsubstantiated motive for murder.

The only other prosecution witness had been an elegantly dressed lady – elegantly dressed for the occasion – who reckoned to be in telepathic communication with the murdered woman who was called 'Sister Cat'. In response to a mysterious foreboding this witness had jumped into her car and dashed off to Aldeburgh late at night. Although normally she wore gloves when driving she explained – and her explanation was extremely tardy – that on this occasion gloves hadn't been worn because they had, by peculiar chance, been washed that very day. And so it cannot be suggested that her gloved hand held the fatal weapon. But the hand of someone else, almost certainly gloved, must have.

On top of all this, and quite without evidence to back it, was the hypothesis that I, the accused, knew my ex-wife was living at Aldeburgh. Nothing to support this theory had been advanced.

The evidence adduced by the prosecution witnesses, said Gregg, was entirely circumstantial. It was a rag-bag of vindictive opinion, boastful lies, uncertainties, and amazing premonitions. The only hard and fast fact were that my fingerprints, and mine alone, were on the bread-knife.

'Let us consider the bread-knife,' he said. 'Let us consider the only piece of evidence which in any way links the accused with the charge of murder. His fingerprints were in a place on the handle appropriate for slicing bread but not for stabbing. He would have been obliged to bend at the knees to insert the blade at the angle at which it was thrust. But, and this is the most important factor of all, and I beg you, members of the jury, to weigh it and consider it most carefully . . . Why on earth should the accused have left the knife bearing his fingerprints in the body?'

Gregg waited for a murmur from the public gallery to subside before going on, 'The accused is an intelligent man. He is highly articulate and you have seen him to be a clear thinker under the pressure of probing cross-examination. Is a man of this calibre likely to leave the murder weapon in the body? You, men and women of the jury, are all men and women of the world, the real world, the world in which horrible crimes occur, and you must have read in your newspapers, or seen on television, cases of reported murder in which the police have to search for the murder weapon whether it be a knife, a gun, or a club. They who murder with a weapon invariably try to dispose of that weapon. They don't leave it lying around; that is, not unless *they wish to frame some innocent person*. And so I ask again – why should the accused have left the bread-knife bearing his fingerprints in the dead woman's body? Why didn't he pull it out and dispose of it? Why let go of the handle and walk away? Such conduct doesn't make sense. And if you agree it doesn't make sense the whole of the prosecution case, with its shaky infrastructure of questionable circumstantial evidence, falls to the ground. I therefore ask you in the name of reason, in the name of common sense, but above all, in the name of justice, to find the accused not guilty.'

Gregg sat down. I felt like applauding. He'd done a fine job. Mr Frobisher smiled at me, and so did Miss James. Gregg simply gazed down at his papers. He looked exhausted.

The judge said he would give his summing up the following morning.

8

From my cell it was impossible to see whether the sky was a prisoner's tent of blue but from interlaced light and shadow I surmised it was a fine day in the world of the free. This seemed a good omen.

Warder Fluck was almost cheerful. 'We've been running a book on you,' he said. 'We always run a book on the good cases. The betting is odds on you'll get off.'

'I hope you put a fiver on that,' I responded good-humouredly.

'I've put a tenner on you getting sent down,' he said. 'If it comes off, I stand to make fifty quid and that's all I need for a down-payment on a satellite dish.'

'I hope you lose,' I said, but not ungraciously.

'Don't be selfish,' he replied with the grimmest of smiles.

The judge was late in arriving. Had he overslept? Had he been caught in a traffic jam? Whatever the reason, there were no apologies for keeping everybody waiting. Reading from a thick sheaf of notes he began the summing up.

It went on a long time, nearly two hours, but I must say that mostly it was a fair and balanced review of what had been said. But I didn't like it when he told the jury that Gregg's suggestion that no murderer would walk away leaving the murder weapon embedded in the dead body was pure hypothesis. Even the most intelligent of men occasionally did stupid things. Pure intelligence wasn't necessarily an ingredient of the instinct of survival. To be cunning and street-wise was more of an asset in this respect.

On the question of motive, the jury had heard uncorroborated evidence that the accused possessed a jealous disposition, but the defence strenuously denied this. There was no direct evidence that as a result of jealousy a life had been taken either as a result of careful planning or through extreme provocation. In defence it had been suggested, no more, that the accused might have been framed. No explanation had been given as to why this should be. However, this was a matter the jury should consider in addition to asking themselves whether the motive of jealousy had been sufficiently established.

The judge continued to pose questions carefully balancing pros and cons. Would a man who had coolly and calculatedly murdered someone come out with an extraordinary story about his property having been vandalized when clearly it wasn't? To make the story realistic one might have expected him to wreck the place himself. Surely he could have thought of a better reason if guilty for having left the scene of the crime.

As the summing up continued I felt there was a bias in my favour. But for the wretched bread-knife, I would have been home and dry. 'However,' the judge went on, 'the defence has been categoric in stating that the accused is not guilty of murder and therefore has not attempted to raise the issue of manslaughter which is a lesser crime. I can only direct you, the jury, on the facts as presented and say that you may come to the conclusion that, although manslaughter has not been raised as a defence during the trial, nevertheless if on the facts you consider that the accused did not deliberately plan murder but killed the deceased in a moment of passion, possibly inflamed by jealousy of a woman who was not a model of fidelity when married to the accused, then you may consider whether a verdict of manslaughter would be appropriate. But, and I stress this most emphatically, before arriving at such a conclusion you must be satisfied beyond reasonable doubt that the accused did kill his ex-wife.'

Shortly after delivering this piece of guidance the judge concluded his summing up and the jury was instructed to retire to consider its verdict. I was taken back to my cell.

'I reckon they'll be out a long time,' said Warder Fluck gloomily. 'I'll have to wait quite a while before I know whether I'm going to enjoy satellite TV.'

'I feel sorry for you,' I responded with transparent insincerity.

It wasn't transparent enough for him. 'You take the cake,' he said, 'feeling sorry for me. You should be feeling sorry for yourself. You're the one who's going to be banged up for life.'

When Mr Frobisher came to see me he looked worried.

'It wasn't a bad summing up,' he began, 'but I wish the judge hadn't waved a manslaughter verdict under the jury's noses. Mr Gregg was very annoyed, I can tell you.'

'Was the judge out of order?' I asked.

'Not exactly out of order, but it muddies the waters.'

As always, before he left he told me to keep my chin up, but this well-meaning advice only irritated me and I was glad when he'd gone.

Waiting for the jury to return a verdict which could mean life imprisonment or freedom is not an everyday experience of ordinary folk. It can best be described as being like waiting to be seen by a dentist knowing that possibly a tooth extraction lies ahead, and having a terrible dread of dental treatment. If this can be imagined, and multiplied a hundredfold, then the awful apprehension of having to await a jury's verdict might be dimly imagined.

The hours passed with the speed of sleepy centipedes. Having been glad to see the back of Mr Frobisher I would have welcomed his return but when a visitor eventually did arrive it was Miss James with the news that the jury hadn't been able to reach a decision and were being taken to a hotel for the night, protected from any intrusion, until they were able to resume their deliberations the next day.

'I'm sorry to be the bearer of such tidings,' she said. 'It looks as though it might be a close-run thing.'

'What do you think?' I asked.

She pulled a face. Her mouth stretched and her nose wrinkled. 'I don't know,' she said at length. 'I don't know what to think. It was naughty of the judge to throw in that bit about manslaughter but he's well known as a bit of a maverick. Most judges don't like their cases to go to appeal but he doesn't seem to mind.'

'If things go against me, will there be an appeal?'

'That's for Mr Gregg to advise,' she said primly, and then with a softening smile, 'but we shan't let you down. Be sure of that.' Her expression changed once more – she had the sort of face which telegraphs emotions – and she looked very serious. 'There's something else I've got to tell you.'

'What's that?'

163

'It's why I'm here, and not Mr Frobisher. Not long after he left you he complained of pains in his chest and he's been taken to hospital.'

Deeply dismayed by this news I asked if his condition was serious.

'We don't know yet,' Miss James replied, 'but he went white as a sheet and had to be taken away on a stretcher.' Then, to my astonishment, this woman who looked young enough to have been my daughter reached across the table and rested her hand on mine. 'Try not to fret,' she said, 'I know it must be hell but you're not alone.' She slowly removed her hand. 'If you think you might find sleep difficult, ask to see the police surgeon. I'm sure he'll let you have a sleeping pill.'

'Thanks for the thought, but I'm against sleeping pills and tranquillizers, Miss James.'

'So am I,' she said, 'and please call me Fiona.' She stood up. 'I'll go now. I've got to get home but I'll come again in the morning.'

As she moved away I said, 'Fiona?'

She turned swiftly. 'Yes?'

'Do you think I'm guilty?'

She gave a sweet smile. 'No. I don't think you're guilty. I think . . . I think you're just a very unlucky man.'

The cell door closed behind her but I felt better than before her visit although I felt worried about Mr Frobisher, who had been such a loyal friend.

During the evening I found myself thinking of Fiona James who seemed, for a while at least, to have replaced Mr Frobisher as a sort of lifeline between me and the grinding mills of blind justice. When she had rested her hand on mine a solitaire diamond ring had shimmered on the third finger of her left hand and for a reason I can't explain I wasn't altogether glad to realize she was probably engaged to be married. This may sound absurd in view of the pressure I was under, and the anxiety about Mr Frobisher's health, but perhaps I needed an escape or outlet from more oppressive thoughts. It certainly wasn't due to sexual attraction or what is commonly known as falling in love. Eve was the only woman who had ever affected me in this way and I was as determined as ever, whatever the jury should decide, one day to root out and punish the person who had killed her.

That night I slept reasonably well. Possibly one becomes used to being, in Fiona's words, 'a very unlucky man', and there comes a stage when you think you might as well accept Fate and live out your predestined role as one of Life's losers and desist from trying to buck the inevitable.

But this somewhat fatalistic view of my lot didn't spread to, or infect, a consuming desire to avenge Eve's death. Moira was a prime suspect but although she could have bribed Verity da Costa to make the phone call from Heathrow, waited until I was clear of the house, and then entered to confront Eve, it was difficult to understand her motive unless she had intended to have an argument, possibly about me, and the quarrel had got out of hand.

More and more I began to suspect Hunt. It seemed likely that by force – I couldn't believe it was by consent – he'd had sex with Eve, and it was evident he'd visited Fran's Pantry subsequently. Was it beyond the bounds of possibility that he'd been lurking around on that Saturday evening, had seen me leave, and gone into the house? This scenario presupposed that he would be wearing gloves which seemed unlikely. Nevertheless Hunt couldn't be ruled out.

There is a small building, one room up and one room down, which before the 1939–45 war had been used as a storage depot for Wall's ice cream. After the war it had been converted into a tiny cottage. This building, isolated in a small car-parking area, was close to Fran's Pantry and could have been used for concealment. Hunt could have hidden behind it until I'd driven away. . . . But surely it was beyond his competence to bribe Verity to make the phone call.

When Fiona arrived the following day I refrained from mentioning these thoughts partly because there seemed no useful purpose and partly because I didn't want to seem an obsessive bore. What is vitally important to one person can be an enormous yawn to someone else.

Her face was flushed when she arrived and for the first time I saw her without her barrister's wig. 'Sorry I'm late,' she said, 'the blasted car wouldn't start. How are you?'

'Fine. Any news of Mr Frobisher?'

Solemnity clouded her features. 'It's not good. He's in intensive care. He had a pretty bad coronary.' The cloud passed. 'You look well. No problems with sleep?'

'None.'

'Great.' She smiled, and then she lifted a black bag she was carrying. 'The trappings of my profession. I must go and get robed. Can't be late. But I'll come and see you and report when there is anything to report.'

More waiting, and as each leaden minute passed I became increasingly anxious. The jury were evidently having difficulty in reaching a verdict.

Fiona returned to tell me that the judge had just informed the jury he was prepared to accept a majority verdict.

She stayed for a few minutes and we talked about music, the novels of Jane Austen, the law relating to drunk-driving, about anything except my trial and its possible outcome. Shortly before she left I admired the ring on her finger and asked if it was an engagement ring.

She lifted her hand, splayed her fingers so that they stood out stiffly, and gazed at them almost as though they didn't belong to her and she was looking at the ring for the first time.

'Yes, it is,' she said.

'Who's the lucky man?' I ventured, using the phrase which through popular usage has long since lost the lustre of genuine gallantry but still retains a faint sheen of socially acceptable flattery.

'I'm not sure he thinks he's lucky,' she replied with a smile. 'I've been terribly busy lately and had to cancel a couple of dates. But he's a lawyer too and should understand.'

'A barrister?'

'No, solicitor.' She lowered her hand and closed the fingers. 'I think I'd better get back. I hope you won't have to wait much longer.'

I thanked her for coming to see me.

Another hour passed and then, just as I was thinking there'd be no news before lunch, I was summoned to return to the dock. The jury had arrived at a verdict.

Warder Fluck told me that one could always tell which way the verdict would fall by studying the jury as it assembled. If members looked at the prisoner, he would be not guilty; but if they avoided looking in his direction he would be found guilty.

My heart sank as twelve men and women, good and true, filed into their places. Not one so much as glanced at me.

The clerk of the court stood up and asked, 'Members of the jury, are you all agreed upon your verdict?'

The jury foreman, a dapper individual who wore a red carnation in his buttonhole, replied, 'We are.'

'How say you then: do you find the prisoner, Mark Markby, guilty or not guilty of the murder of Eve Elaine Harris?'

I shall never forget the foreman, standing very erect, his head held back, as he uttered the single word, 'Guilty.'

A shocked gasp ran through the courtroom. I suddenly felt very weak at the knees and missed the next words spoken by the clerk but managed to pull myself together when he was asking, 'Prisoner at the bar, have you anything to say why the court should not give you judgement according to the law?'

'Yes,' I said, and my brain went into overdrive. 'I am not guilty! *Not* guilty! There's been a gross miscarriage of justice and, however long it takes, I will find out who is responsible for the murder of the human being who was most dear to me. I shall never rest until he or she is standing where I stand now, an innocent man wrongly convicted.'

A moment of taut silence followed as the judge waited to see if I'd finished. Briefly our eyes met and, I may be mistaken, but I thought I detected compassion in his.

'Mark Markby,' he said, 'you have been found guilty by a jury of your fellow countrymen of the murder of Eve Elaine Harris. On that verdict I offer no comment. I am constrained by law, as it at present stands, to sentence you to life imprisonment which I hereby do.'

As I was escorted down to the cell Warder Fluck murmured, 'Hard cheese, mate,' which showed that he too had an ounce of compassion.

'Good viewing,' I replied.

I was still in a daze when Gregg followed by Fiona came into the cell. I was aware that, in the absence of Mr Frobisher, Smithers was with them, but my whole attention was riveted on Gregg who said, 'We'll appeal, of course. It's outrageous. The judge indicated quite clearly at the end of the summing up that at the worst it was manslaughter, not murder.'

All of a sudden the judge was a good guy! I almost laughed. First, he shouldn't have waved manslaughter under the jury's noses and now it was a plank on which an appeal might be based!

'The verdict,' Gregg fumed, 'went against all reason. I have never heard such a perverse verdict.'

I don't know why, but perhaps the sheer ghastliness of the situation made me crack a joke. Maybe I was determined, in Mr Frobisher's cliché, to keep my chin up.

I said, 'Maybe they didn't like the food at the hotel where they were billeted and thought they were passing a verdict on the chef's cooking.'

Gregg looked at me unbelievingly but Fiona said, 'That's the stuff. Don't give in.'

On impulse I asked, 'Will you visit me in prison?'

She nodded her head. 'Yes. I'll visit you. Don't lose heart. We've got a fighting chance.'

I was kept in the cell for another day while a place was found for me in a prison. At that time there was a problem with overcrowding and many prison officers were working to rule. A vacancy was found for me in a prison in north London and, handcuffed, I was taken there.

PART III

1

As a common convict I was photographed – full face and profile – stripped of my clothes and given regulation blue prison garb to wear, and allocated a number.

The prison had open floors which could be surveyed by the guards and was a place where the only sounds were of voices and struck metal – iron staircases, aluminium trays for food, metal piss-pots. I was given a cell to share with Colin Whittaker, a coloured Barbadian, pimp and thief. The cell walls were decorated with pin-ups, all of women who had obviously contributed much to the revenue of silicon-implant surgeons. Their breasts looked like balloons about to burst.

Whittaker was listening to a Walkman radio when I was introduced to him. We shook hands and the screws – how easy it is to adopt prison slang – left us to get acquainted. Amazingly, and this was a stroke of luck, I discovered he had been listening to a concert on Radio Three. He was a great admirer of Leonard Bernstein and knew a surprising amount about this great American composer and conductor. The scores of *West Side Story* and *Candide* were among his favourites.

I can't stress how important it is to have a cell-mate with an interest in common and I hand it to the prison authorities, if it was a considered decision on their part, that they paired me with Whittaker.

I didn't share his sexual interests, however. After we'd established rapport over musical taste he asked, 'Do you like tail?'

I said I was not all that interested.

'You not gay?' he asked with a worried look.

'No,' I said, 'I'm not gay.'

'We got some here. Bird makes some guys that way . . . I hope you won't find objection to my gallery.'

I said I didn't but noticed there was a preponderance of females with huge bosoms.

He laughed. 'I like that. Preponderance. You sound like a scholar. Yeah, I like big tits, but you notice nothing else?'

'No. What else?'

'They all white tits, man.'

'So they are.'

He grinned and, like most black people, displayed a set of perfect teeth. 'I'm not racist. I'm not prejudiced against the white majority.'

'I'm glad.'

'You prejudiced?'

I thought of Verity and how she'd let me down and for once I was slightly less honest. I said, 'Colour isn't important. It's what's up here' – and I tapped my head – 'that's important.'

'Right along,' he agreed.

And so the friendship with Whittaker began.

He advised me about my position in the convict's hierarchy. He said, 'Everyone here knows who's who, and who's been done for what. Even before you got here you were reckoned a killer. That's good. You didn't kill a kid but a free-flying bitch. No one's going to mess with you.'

In prison one looks forward to letters and visits. They are gold. My first visitor was the agent of the landlord of my Kensington flat. He did his best to pressurize me into selling my leasehold interest but I didn't want to lose the only tangible security I possessed. At the end of a long and sometimes acrimonious conversation he agreed to employ someone to check on the flat, keep it in running order as it were, and also to maintain my car lying idle in an underground car-park.

'It'll cost,' he said.

'I'll pay,' I replied.

And that clinched the arrangement. I knew I would be rooked, charged excessively for services of no actual benefit to me, but at least I would be preserving a base to which I could eventually return.

I received few letters but one visitor was Colonel Bamber, whose loyalty to the flag was impressive; another visitor was Fiona.

It was as we looked at each other through a glass partition that

Fiona said, 'I'm sure we'll do well on appeal, but don't just pin your hopes on that. I'm going to make some enquiries of my own. And I'm pressing for your transfer to a Category C prison which will be much more open.'

'Won't that be difficult? I'm supposed to be a killer.'

'Difficult, but not impossible.'

It was on her second visit that she gave me two pieces of news. The first was that the appeal against my conviction should be at some time in November or December. The other news was that she'd found out what Hunt had been doing on the night of the murder.

He had been taking part in a darts match as a member of the Three Tuns team and playing in a pub some fifteen miles from Aldeburgh. There were many who could vouch for this. It was an unbreakable alibi. Hunt could be ruled out as a suspect.

'And anyway,' Fiona said, 'I think we agree he isn't capable of arranging decoy phone calls from Heathrow.'

I told her how grateful I was for her support.

'That's all right,' she said, 'I don't like to see an innocent man condemned and I'll do my best to discover anything to add to our appeal.'

'I don't care what it costs,' I said. 'I'll pay. It's not enough to clear me. I want Eve's killer found and punished, and if the law can't punish him or her, I will.'

She gave a troubled frown and looked away. For a short while neither of us spoke.

The subdued murmur of urgent whisperings filled the visiting room. The sound was composed of agonized uncertainties, pathetic bravado, and raw despair. Here wives, mothers, children, and friends could communicate with identically dressed inmates who, seated in line, looked like a row of railway station booking clerks dealing with travellers seeking tickets as they spoke through grilles in glass panelling.

Fiona turned back towards me. The frown lines had gone but the trouble had settled in her eyes.

'What's the matter?' I asked, and my lowered voice was part of the desperation permeating the room. It would be hard to bear if for some reason this young woman, whom I hardly knew, decided she'd had enough of fighting for my cause.

'What's the matter, Fiona?'

173

'I don't like it when you talk the way you did.'

'Like what?'

'This talk of punishment. It sounds so vindictive, so vengeful, and these are self-destructive emotions.'

'But can't you see how I feel?'

'I can. But keep it in proportion.'

'Sorry.' I felt genuinely contrite but no less vengeful. In future I'd keep this emotion under wraps.

She was smiling now and for me it was as if the grey North Sea was suddenly sparkling under a shaft of sunlight.

'It's part of my make-up,' I said. 'Ever since I can remember I've felt that if you've done anything wrong you should be punished, and if others do wrong they should be punished. That's one reason I gave evidence at the fraud trial. But I'm not beyond redemption, I hope.'

'Good. Now let's talk of other things.'

The remainder of her allotted time flew by.

'You'll come again?' I asked anxiously as she rose to leave.

'Of course I will, silly!'

It is absurd but I treasured that 'silly'. It was a signal that we were on slightly more intimate terms than legal representative and client.

It was on Fiona's third visit that she brought the sad news of Mr Frobisher's death. Two days after leaving the hospital following a successful heart by-pass operation he had been knocked down by a car driver who had ignored the lights at a pelican crossing.

'That's the sort of thing that makes me want lawbreakers to be punished,' I said.

'I shan't argue with you about this particular instance,' she replied.

On her next visit I knew the moment I saw her she had some interesting news. Her expressive face was animated and, sure enough, as soon as I sat down she told me that the private detective, at some risk to himself, had discovered that Verity da Costa's husband had been dealing in drugs and had pulled off a coup which had provided enough money for him and his family to return to their homeland.

'And so,' Fiona concluded, 'nobody bribed him and Verity to make that call.'

'Then why did she?'

'I can't answer that. Maybe it was their idea of a joke. Maybe Verity thought she couldn't tell you the real reason why they could afford to leave England but felt you ought to know that your flat wouldn't be looked after and wanted you to go back there. Honestly, Mark, I don't know. But you can rule out bribery by Mrs Makepeace.'

'But if Hunt is out of the picture, and she is too . . . who?'

She shook her head. 'I don't know. Maybe it was an unknown intruder who tried to get hold of her necklace while threatening her with the knife and then something went horribly wrong and he fled in panic. If he'd been on the prowl for a likely robbery or burglary he could have been wearing gloves.'

It was while she was speaking I noticed the ring was missing from her left hand. I didn't make any comment at the time but as the visit was about to end I asked, 'Has something happened to your engagement ring?'

'Yes. I've given it back.'

'May I ask why?'

'You may. Our meetings grew less and less. Mostly it was because we each got tied up with our work but then I found out that partly it was because he was sleeping with someone else.' She looked me straight in the eyes. 'I'm not a sharer, Mark.'

'Neither am I. All or nothing.'

The moment the words had left my mouth I realized from the curious expression on her face that she was mentally trying to square what I'd said with a different impression. Visiting time was already over and people were leaving, some tearful, some relieved to be returned to a normal world, but Fiona delayed her departure.

'I thought you were more liberal about such things,' she said. 'You were very reasonable about your ex-wife.'

'What do you mean?'

'Well, she wasn't exactly . . . And yet . . .'

A screw intervened. 'Come along, madam. Time's up.'

'I don't understand you,' I said to her.

'Time's up,' the screw repeated.

'Tell you next time,' she said.

There can be an awful anti-climax after a visit if, in the dying

175

moments, an uncertainty has been sown. Why had Fiona thought I'd been very reasonable about Eve, and what would she tell me on her next visit? I felt low in spirits and Whittaker did nothing to dispel depression by reminiscing about women he had known. During his randy and boastful monologue he informed me that he'd discovered the ideal cure for insomnia.

'You tell me you don't sleep well, man,' he said, 'next time you want your friendly sandman to call on you just try remembering and counting all the women you ever had, and I'll guarantee you'll be asleep before the end. I tell you, it beats counting sheep.'

As (apart from a single episode in my youth of which I'm not very proud), the only woman I'd ever had was Eve, his tip was useless.

One advantage of sleeplessness was that I could use the piss-pot without embarrassment. Whittaker always slept soundly. However, on the night after Fiona's visit I had a nightmare and was woken by him shaking me.

'What gives, man? Why the shouting?'

'Was I shouting?'

'Sure were.'

'I had a bad dream.'

'Must have. You woke me.'

'Sorry.'

He returned to his bunk and was soon snoring but I deliberately stayed awake for fear of continuing the nightmare. It was similar to the *Wozzeck* dream, only this time Eve had a hag-like appearance and seemed bathed in a greenish aura. She had climbed out of a coffin to poke a skeletal finger at me. 'It's all your fault I did it,' she accused, and then jumped on top of me. We struggled and I felt a great weight press down on me and I shouted for help. It was then that Whittaker awakened me.

By this time I had adapted to the rigid prison routine in which time for refreshment and recreation are precious oases in an endless desert, and the notion of time almost assumes the omnipotence of the notion of God. Prisoners become slaves of time as they count and tick off the days on wall calendars. Whittaker was no exception. Each night he would strike out a numeral on his calendar and count up the time to his release. Without a firm date fixed for the appeal hearing I wasn't in such a clearly defined situation. I existed in time's no-man's-land.

176

Rule 6 of the *Prison Rules* states that the purposes 'of the training and treatment of convicted prisoners shall be to establish in them the will to lead a good and useful life on discharge and fit them to do so'. To me this seemed a piece of idealistic claptrap. I was wrongly being detained but it didn't alter my opinion that the primary purpose of imprisonment is to punish so severely that the miscreant is deterred from further antisocial behaviour. My own purpose was clear as crystal and hard as steel. It was to survive the present ordeal, and my survival aids would be music on the radio, books from the prison library, and writing, before dedicating myself to hounding down whoever had killed Eve.

As the minutes and hours dragged heels to the next visiting day I became more hopeful and optimistic and, when the day arrived, I felt the excitement of a young man awaiting the arrival of his sweetheart, which was extraordinary because I wasn't in love with Fiona.

When one's visitor arrives one is summoned from the cell and escorted to the visiting room. Whittaker, who seldom had a visitor, was in luck. Someone had applied to see him. He left the cell with a banana-like grin stuck on his face. I awaited my turn with mounting impatience. Gradually it seeped into my mind that perhaps Fiona might not come. Had she forsaken me? When the visiting time had expired and Whittaker rejoined me I felt a bitterness which grew when he triumphantly flourished a glossy photograph of the top-half of a woman whose torso seemed to consist of two jumbo-sized breasts.

'Get a load of them Bristols, man,' said Whittaker. As he fixed the photo to a rare blank space on his side of the cell he informed me that his visitor had been the owner of the mammary monsters. 'I'm over the moon,' he shouted. 'She wants me to go back to her.'

I hardly heard Whittaker as he gabbled about the women he had known and pimped for. What had happened to Fiona? Had her car let her down again? Had she been involved in an accident? Or – unbearable thought – had she decided I wasn't worth visiting any more?

When finally Whittaker finished giggling, chuckling and whinnying at his good fortune he enquired, 'Your chick not come today?'

'No, and she isn't my chick.'

'Don't sweat it, man. Take it easy. No chick's worth the grieving.' With this advice he turned to admire once more the latest acquisition to his gallery of pin-ups. 'What headlights!' he marvelled.

Two days later a letter arrived from Fiona.

She explained that she had been laid low by a vicious bug but was recovering and looking forward to seeing me next week. 'All news then,' the letter concluded, 'with love, Fiona.'

With love!

'You heard from your chick?' Whittaker asked.

'Yes.'

'Thank Christ for that. You been looking like you were pining for a pine drape.'

I think if she hadn't appeared on the next visiting day I would have been desolated, but she did come.

'How are you?' she asked as I sat down opposite her.

'Fine. Much better for seeing you.'

'I'm sorry about last time.'

'How are *you*?'

'OK. But I was in bed for two days.'

'I missed seeing you.'

'I missed seeing you,' she replied.

In prison one can lose the skill of obliquely directing a conversation towards a desired topic. One comes bluntly to the point, and it was without finesse or subtlety that I plunged directly into a subject which had been on my mind.

'What was it you were going to say about Eve when you had to leave on your last visit? You said, "Tell you next time." '

Her face fell. 'Oh, yes. That. I rather wish I hadn't said anything.'

'But you did. Tell me now.'

'If you insist.'

'I'm not insisting, but I'd like you to.'

Looking me full in the face she said, 'Eve wasn't what you thought she was. Are you sure you want to know?'

2

From the smiling face of greeting Fiona's expressive features were now etched with concern. I was filled with an oppressive sense that the rock of my belief had changed to quicksand. Had I been a disciple of Jesus Christ it would have been the equivalent of fearing that he was about to be exposed as a charlatan. Nor is this a wildly inflated analogy because in a curious way there was an element of worship in my feelings towards Eve which, far from dissipating at her death, had intensified. I venerated her memory. And so, did I want to hear that she hadn't been what I thought she was?

'Tell me,' I said.

'You won't like it, Mark.'

'All right, you've warned me . . . Go on.'

'I'm afraid there's substance in what some of the witnesses implied at the trial.'

She spoke so quietly I had to lean right forward to catch her words.

'You mean she wasn't raped by Hunt,' I asked. 'She consented?'

'I don't know about that. What I do know, or rather, what our enquiry agent has discovered, is that there were others.'

'What? In Aldeburgh? I can't believe it.'

'Yes, in Aldeburgh, and also possibly someone in London.'

I was angry. 'How the hell does this agent know?'

'He interviewed certain people and carried a concealed tape-recorder. I've seen the transcriptions.'

I felt as though I'd been hit in the stomach. Fiona waited for me to recover. At last I said, 'Who is this someone in London?'

'It's hearsay but one of the men interviewed said she'd told him of a man, someone who'd just been released on parole, who she was going to visit. She said this man had a mews flat in Mayfair.'

'Feldman! Harry Feldman!'

'Possibly.' She too was leaning forward and we were as close as we could be. 'Look, Mark, I wish to God I'd never said what I did. I shouldn't have left you to brood about it.'

'I knew Feldman had always fancied Eve but she told me she found him repulsive. I still can't believe . . .'

'Mark, try to put it behind you. You've got your life to live. Don't cling to the past.'

'My life to live! That's rich!' And then I had an insight, a flash of thought which would scotch talk of Eve's alleged promiscuity. 'What about Moira?' I asked. 'What about Moira Makepeace? She and Eve were close friends. I even suspected lesbian tendencies at one stage. Moira would never have entertained a friendship with Eve if what you've told me was true.'

'Mrs Makepeace is a very complex woman,' replied Fiona. 'I've been making some enquiries of my own about her. When she said she supported charities and mentioned animal charities, she was only saying the half. Quietly, unostentatiously, she does other good works.'

I nearly laughed. The idea of Moira doing good works was absurd. 'What good works?' I asked.

'She helps people who, for one reason or another, are disadvantaged. There's a recluse she visits and goes shopping for. There's an old man, a widower aged ninety, who won't have home helps, meals on wheels, or any sort of social service. Mrs Makepeace takes him a hot dinner every Sunday without fail. And there's a blind couple who live in Saxmundham. Mrs Makepeace visits them regularly and reads any mail that's come through the post and answers some of the letters on their behalf. And, of course, there was your ex-wife. Mrs Makepeace did support her and—'

'And served notice that she was calling in the loans,' I interrupted.

'And testified that it was because she was trying to make your ex-wife "see sense".'

I could scarcely believe what I was hearing.

'Moira Makepeace seems to have fooled you just like she fooled the court,' I said. 'She isn't like that at all. She's an evil and dangerous woman.'

'Why do you say that?' Fiona asked quietly.

'Eve told me she suspected Moira of being a witch. And there were other things she said about her.'

'And you believed all you were told?'

I was lost for words.

'Mark, I'm sorry. I truly am. But perhaps it's for the best that you should know that Mrs Harris – Eve, that is – wasn't always truthful. You must face it, and come to terms with the fact that she wasn't quite the woman you thought she was, and neither is Mrs Makepeace.'

'I can't believe what I'm hearing.'

'Do you want me to leave?'

'No!' I reached out to hold her and hit plate glass.

She responded by reaching back and touching the glass. For a few moments I was so overwhelmed by emotion I was unable to speak and then, pulling myself together, I said, 'I still want to find out who killed Eve.'

'Of course you do.'

'But not to punish. At least, not by me. Let the law take that on.'

She smiled. 'That's better. Now let's talk of something else. I have some good news.'

'You have? I could use some good news.'

'I'd have told you earlier but you had to . . .'

'I had to blunder in with questions about Eve.'

'They were on your mind. But let's forget all that. Mr Gregg has been really putting on the pressure and he's managed to get a date for the appeal hearing. Next month. It's been promised.'

'How did he manage that?'

'Influence,' she replied enigmatically.

I asked her the date of the hearing and what would be involved.

'It'll be on the fifteenth, all being well. Mr Gregg will appear before three judges. They can dismiss the appeal, quash the conviction, or substitute a conviction for another offence, or alter the sentence.'

'What about a retrial? It was a crazy verdict.'

Fiona shook her head. 'No chance. A retrial can't be ordered unless the appeal succeeds on the ground of fresh evidence, and we have no fresh evidence to offer.' She looked earnestly at me.

'I believe in you and I'm spending a lot of my spare time conducting my own line of enquiry. I'm spending most weekends in Aldeburgh.'

I was intrigued. 'What's the line of enquiry?'

She gave a little smile and for a moment I glimpsed what she must have been like as a mischievous child. 'That's a secret,' she said.

Then by mutual consent we dropped talk about the case and spoke about ourselves, learning about each other's lives and interests. All too soon it was time for her to leave.

That night, while lying awake, I thought about what Fiona had told me about Eve. If correct, Eve had not only been sexually indiscriminate in her choice of partners but she had lied to me. It was ironic that I, who set so much store by honesty, should have been so closely involved for so long with a liar. Dredging memory I recalled incidents during our married life when I had suspected a lie but had dismissed the suspicion as unworthy. Apart from the occasion when she'd avoided going with me to a concert by pleading a headache, there had been other excuses and evasions or outright denials as when, in my presence, one of our friends had asked her what she was doing in Richmond on a Thursday afternoon. Eve flatly denied having been anywhere but at home all day. 'It must have been my double,' she had said.

In one way my growing doubts about her were of benefit. They lessened my intent to hunt down and punish her killer. More and more I was coming round to Fiona's view that vengeful emotions were self-destructive. But if the idea of punishment had weakened I was still driven by a need to find out who had murdered Eve. No mystery, except the riddle of the universe, is insoluble; and for my own peace of mind, and for a sense of purpose, I had to know the solution to the puzzle. My life having been imbued with an accountancy mystique – if there is such a thing – I not only like problems to be solved but I want the books to be balanced.

Once more I ran through the short-list of suspects. Hunt had been ruled out but there was still Moira. I wasn't to be taken in by stories of her philanthropy. She had a vicious side to her nature.

Who else? A complete stranger?

What about Harry Feldman? It had been a shock to hear that

Eve may have visited him in London, presumably before I arrived on the scene. I remembered the anonymous letter I'd received after the fraud trial. It had said, 'He who uses the knife will have the knife used on him.' This threat, with its reference to a knife, now had an early prophetic ring. A knife had been used to bring me down. Was this the fulfilment of a menacing prediction or simply a spooky coincidence?

Disappointments, like sorrows, come not as single spies but in battalions. Fiona didn't visit me during the following three weeks. She wrote to say her mother was very ill and being nursed in a Frankfurt clinic and she had to go to her. I knew, from what I'd been told on one of Fiona's visits, that her father had died five years earlier and, a year later, her mother had married a German industrialist.

In due time I was taken to the Court of Appeal under guard. Fiona came to my cell. She had returned from Frankfurt the previous evening. Her mother's condition had improved and a full recovery from a mystery virus was expected. Gregg and Smithers were also present and so we didn't have a chance to speak privately.

The appeal was brilliantly presented by Gregg. It would be a work of supererogation to reproduce all he said. In brief, he summarized in scathing terms the evidence of prosecution witnesses. The Crown Prosecutor – not Mr Spendlove – didn't attempt to rebut any of Gregg's points and I had the impression that tacitly he agreed with Gregg.

The judges retired to consider the appeal and I was taken back to prison.

Two days later, with an officious rattle of keys – how warders love their belted ring of keys! – the cell door was opened.

'It's for you, Markby,' said the warder. 'The dep gov wants to see you.'

I put down a well-thumbed edition of *The Day of the Jackal* and said, 'Why?'

'Don't ask me. Come along then. Look smart.'

'Look smart? In this gear?' I enquired.

My cell-mate laughed. He approved of anything resembling truculence and was, I think, agreeably surprised at my attitude.

'Don't give me lip, Markby. Let's be having you.'

I went with him and was taken to a room where, in the presence of the deputy governor, the warder, Smithers, and Fiona, I was informed that the sentence of murder had been quashed and a sentence of manslaughter substituted in its place. The term of imprisonment had been reduced from life to four years. Everyone seemed pleased. I didn't know what to feel. Obviously I was glad of the reduced sentence which, with remission for good conduct, could mean that I'd be out on parole within maybe two or three years, but I was still technically guilty of killing Eve, and this was a terrible miscarriage of justice.

While I was absorbing the news I was told that I would shortly be transferred to a more open prison in Worcester. Here again, everyone seemed to think I should jump for joy. I could only say, 'Thank you.'

An awkward silence fell. Clearly something more had been expected. Perhaps I should have given a shout of jubilation.

The deputy governor seized the hiatus by its throat and shook it out. 'I won't say we'll be sorry to be losing you, Markby' – ha! ha! – 'but I'm sure you'll find more facilities, more outlets, than we're able to provide.'

This time I didn't meekly say, 'Thank you', I said, 'I never killed Eve. One day, if it takes the rest of my life, I'll find her murderer and bring him or her to justice.'

This small outburst was greeted with a look of total indifference by the deputy governor; Fiona's eyes were downcast.

The deputy governor stood up. 'Well, that's all. If I don't see you again, and, don't misunderstand me, I hope I shan't see you again, good luck.'

This time I managed a polite, 'Thank you.'

As the deputy governor moved away Fiona spoke. 'Excuse me, but may I have a private word with Mr Markby?'

He looked like a man who has been put on the spot. 'Oh, all right,' he said, as though granting a begrudged favour, 'but the officer must stay by the door. I can't allow total privacy.'

Fiona gave a nod of assent and, turning to Smithers, said, 'I'll see you outside.'

When we were alone except for a stony-faced warder standing by the door Fiona said, 'I'm still with you, Mark. I'll come and visit, but Worcester won't be easy, especially as I want to pick up the threads at Aldeburgh.'

'What are the threads? I'd love to know.'

She placed a finger on her lips and gave her mischievous-child smile. 'All in good time. Have patience.'

'Give me a clue.'

'A clue? . . . It involves night work.'

I said, 'You're a tease.'

'Am I? But I wouldn't tease you, Mark. Not unless you wanted me to.'

With this cryptic remark she picked up her handbag. 'Goodbye for now,' she said and she brushed my cheek with a kiss. Then, with a nod to the warder, she left the room.

'The exit is first right and second left, miss,' he called out.

A 'Thanks' floated in from the corridor.

The warder turned to me. 'Why is it, I ask myself, that cons always get the best-looking birds.'

3

The Worcester prison, a building constructed in the 1920s, was set in rolling countryside. Although each man had a cell and toilet of his own – no more degrading slopping out – the building had the narrow enclosed corridors of a Victorian institution unlike the open-floored prison I'd left behind. Nevertheless, there was more scope for freedom of movement and leisure-time activity. It was possible to go for walks in the spacious grounds and, as it was now autumn, the season of preparing for winter's onslaught and next year's spring, I spent a lot of spare time in the well-maintained gardens, digging, pruning, and planting bulbs. This was the way, I became convinced, that all but the most hardened criminals could retain self-respect while in custody.

Visiting hours were generous. My first visitor gave his name as Green. I couldn't think who this was and when I was shown into the visiting room I didn't recognize the man who advanced to shake my hand.

'Don't you remember me?' he asked.

I looked at the bald-headed man with a leathery lined face and gradually in a memory photofit I perceived a youngster at school.

'Brian Green!' I exclaimed.

'The same. I've been abroad, mostly in the Far East, since leaving school and got back to the UK earlier this year. I've been following your case in the papers, and thought I'd come to see you. I never really thanked you for what you did.'

I was baffled. 'Thanked me?'

'Don't you remember? Mr Rogers came into the refectory, saw me with a bread roll in my hand, spotted another that had been thrown, and jumped to the conclusion that I'd been chucking bread around. Told me to report to my housemaster for a whacking. You stood up and said you'd thrown the first roll and I hadn't done a thing. I've always admired the way you did that. You could have got away with it, but you didn't. And you got the whack.'

Green stayed about an hour and we sat at a table and chatted over cups of tea. He said he'd read in a tabloid that I was something of a loner and he'd wondered if there was anything he could do to help. He believed I was innocent as did others who had read reports of the trial. 'I know how straight you were as a boy,' he said, 'and people don't change.'

I thanked him for his concern but said that everything was under control. I would be all right. He left me with his address and a promise that if I needed anything he'd do his best to provide it. I didn't see him again but his visit reaffirmed my belief (a belief which had been damaged by events) that in the long run, and sometimes in strange ways, there is a reward for the good one has done.

Fiona visited me and we got to know each other better. She had no further information but said her researches were progressing well. More than that she wouldn't say. She took a childish pleasure in being secretive. By now I realized I was close to falling in love, natural enough in the circumstances, but foolish considering our age difference. But our embraces on meeting and parting became warmer and I sensed that I meant more to her than being a convicted criminal on whose side she had fought.

It was on her fourth visit that I knew instantly something was wrong. We embraced but she pulled quickly away and there was sadness on her expressive face.

After fetching cups of tea from a counter at the far end of the room, and some slightly stilted talk about her journey and the weather, I asked if she'd made any progress with her enquiries.

'Yes. Yes, I have.'

I knew something was disturbing her. Whatever progress she had made was lying heavy on her mind. She seemed to be carrying an unwelcome burden and unsure where to deposit it.

Like someone offering to lend a hand with the carrying of a weighty suitcase I said, 'Tell me about it.'

'I don't know how to say this . . .'

'Take a deep breath,' I said.

She gazed at me with eyes so troubled that I wondered if the appeal verdict had been reversed and the life sentence reinstated.

'What's happened, Fiona? Tell me.'

Her gaze didn't waver as she shed the burden on her mind.

'I'm sorry to have to ask you this, Mark, but are you absolutely sure you didn't do it?'

'Do what? I don't understand.'

'Kill her.' Hurriedly she added, 'Perhaps by accident.'

I'd told her to take a deep breath but my own breath was taken away. When I could speak it was to utter, 'You can't be serious.'

'I am serious, Mark. Are you sure?'

'Am I sure? Of course I'm sure! Kill Eve? Who's put that crazy idea into your head?'

Heads turned at the next table and I realized I must lower my voice. In a more subdued tone I asked, 'What's all this about?'

'I've been spending a lot of time at Aldeburgh.'

'Yes, I know. Go on.'

'Going out late at night.'

'So what?' I began to be annoyed. 'Come to the point, Fiona.'

'I met Mrs Makepeace's friend, Dorothy, the woman she shops for and who will only go out at night.'

I was bewildered. 'What about it?'

'It wasn't easy. I had to meet her a number of times before she trusted me. At first we exchanged "Goodnights" and then, gradually, a little more, and in the end I was walking with her.'

Taking care not to speak too loudly I said, 'I wish you'd come to the point. What are you trying to say?'

It was she who raised her voice slightly. 'Let me tell it in my own way.'

'Tell whatever you've got to tell, but don't take all day about it.'

I wished I hadn't said that. She looked as though I'd slapped her across the face and in that moment I realized I had fallen in love with her.

'I'm sorry,' I apologized. 'I didn't mean it to sound like that.'

'It doesn't matter. What was I saying? Oh yes, I joined Dorothy on her nightly walks. By degrees I won her confidence. She didn't know who I was. She didn't know I was involved in your case. I pretended I was just a visitor who liked Aldeburgh and was think-

188

ing of buying a holiday cottage.' She paused. 'I hated the deception.'

'But why?' I asked. 'What was the point? I don't get it.'

'I'm sorry I'm taking so long. But it's important that I put events in the right sequence. My legal training. I should explain that all along I'd felt that, if there was a key, Mrs Makepeace held it, but I knew I'd get nowhere with her. For one thing, she'd seen me in court and would know I had a special interest. But it occurred to me that she might have confided something to somebody and it could be the recluse she went shopping for. A recluse isn't likely to gossip or reveal secrets. And so I set out to get to Mrs Makepeace through Dorothy. Naturally I didn't talk directly about the murder case. I had to wait until she said something which would make my questioning seem natural. My chance came last weekend. It was about ten o'clock and we were walking along the Crag Path. As we drew near Fran's Pantry which, incidentally, has an estate agent's "Sold" notice board outside, Dorothy asked if I'd read about Mrs Harris's murder. I said I thought I had, but would she refresh my memory.'

Fiona gave a wry smile. 'It was devious of me.' And then she added, 'I hope you don't think that's my usual style. It isn't. I was trying to find out something which might pin the murder on Mrs Makepeace and clear you completely.'

'And I appreciate it. But go on. What did this weird recluse say?'

Fiona tensed and sat very upright in her chair as though bracing herself against some invisible shock-wave. 'Dorothy said she saw you leave and come back,' she said.

I was aghast. 'She couldn't. I didn't.'

'That's what she said.'

'She must be dreaming or inventing. I never went back.'

'She said you did,' Fiona persisted.

'She doesn't know me.'

'She does. By sight. Twice, at night, she'd seen you and Eve together.'

'And I suppose she saw me stick a bread-knife into Eve,' I asked sarcastically.

'No. It wasn't like that.'

'What was it like?'

189

'She said you were in such a hurry you'd left your car engine running. She was curious. She hung around. About a minute, or two minutes at most, after you'd gone in you came out and drove away. Very fast.'

'This is rubbish. A fantasy. But go on.'

'Because she'd met Eve once, and Eve had said she could call in at any time, she decided to go and see her. I think it was because she sensed there might be something titillating. As a recluse I imagine she's starved of excitement. I don't know, but that's my guess.'

'And she just walked in?'

'According to her you had just walked in. Eve must have left the door unlocked, and according to her you left in such a hurry you didn't bother to close the door behind you.'

It was a grim scenario but I had to laugh. 'That is not me,' I said. 'I'm very careful to close doors properly. Always have been. I'd never have left without making sure the door was properly fastened behind me. It must have been someone else.'

'She's positive it was you, and I'm only telling you what she said.'

'Carry on, then.'

'She went to the door, which wasn't properly closed, and knocked. There was no reply. So, being inquisitive, she went inside. She had, after all, been invited to drop in any time.'

'Some dropping in!'

'According to her she called out, "Mrs Harris," and then went through to the kitchen. The first thing she saw was the telephone dangling by its cord. Dorothy went over and picked it up. "I'm a tidy sort of person," she explained to me. As she was about to replace it she heard a man's voice on the line. He was audible, possibly because his voice was raised. He said, "What the hell's going on?" Dorothy put the phone back in its cradle on the wall, turned and saw the body on the floor. She panicked.'

'This is unbelievable,' I said.

'Do you want me to go on?'

'Please do. I can't believe what I'm hearing. It's black comedy.'

Fiona hesitated. 'I had doubts about coming here. If you're going to treat . . .'

'No, carry on. I won't interrupt again.'

'Well, as I said, according to her she panicked. She went outside, walked about a bit, and then phoned Mrs Makepeace from a public booth. Mrs Makepeace told her to wait near the Moot Hall and that she'd be over straight away. She arrived within a few minutes. Together they went into Fran's Pantry. Moira felt for a pulse but Eve was dead. I'm not sure exactly what happened next but, according to Dorothy, she pleaded with Mrs Makepeace to keep her out of the picture. She couldn't bear the idea of being questioned by the police. Mrs Makepeace agreed and said she'd cook up a reason for being there and nobody need know that it was Dorothy who had discovered the body. And that's what I heard last weekend. Dorothy thanked me for listening and said it had been on her conscience and she'd needed to tell someone. She begged me not to let it go any further.'

I'd been shaking my head during the last part of Fiona's tale and I continued shaking it after she'd finished.

'No way is that true,' I said. 'It's a complete fabrication. Either Dorothy was hallucinating, or she's mad, or it's a notion Moira Makepeace has planted in her mind.'

'Why should Mrs Makepeace do a thing like that? What has she to gain?'

I didn't know, but the question was irrelevant compared to the most urgent of all questions. 'You don't believe I did it, do you, Fiona?'

I've seldom seen anyone look more unhappy than when she replied, 'What can I believe?'

'I don't know Dorothy's motive for telling such a story but it simply isn't true. Why should I turn round and go back just after having left?'

'Perhaps you realized you'd forgotten something.'

'I didn't forget anything. I said goodbye to Eve and drove straight to London.'

A silence fell between us.

'I've been agonizing about this ever since the weekend,' she said at last. Then, using her hands in a helpless, appealing gesture, she asked, 'Do you think it's possible, just possible, that you might have blotted the whole thing out of your mind?'

I could hear the edge of bitterness in my voice as I said, 'So you really think I killed the woman I loved.'

'I don't know what to think, but . . .'

'But my fingerprints were on the knife, mine and no one else's. And you've found a deluded lady with a vivid imagination who's constructed a fairy tale around the event.'

'I'm sorry, Mark, but I happen to think Dorothy is perfectly sane. Almost pathologically shy, perhaps, but not a fantasist. In some ways she's very down to earth. She's *au fait* with what's going on in the national and international scenes. She knows the price of household goods down to the nearest penny. She isn't in any way out of touch with reality.'

As easily as a meteorologist can read changing cloud patterns in the sky I could read the expressions on Fiona's face and now I could see she was convinced that Dorothy really had seen me return. In the signalling system of facial semaphore I can be the opposite. Eve once told me I'd make a good poker player; nobody would know what sort of cards I held. But if I reveal little outwardly there may be a spinning carousel of emotion within, and during the past few minutes I'd felt anger, disbelief, bitterness, and now, scorn at Fiona's credulity.

'You've been completely taken in by this cock-and-bull story,' I said. 'I expect you've got some theory about the man who was supposedly calling Eve on the telephone and said, "What the hell's going on?" '

'As a matter of fact, I have.'

'Let's hear it, then.'

'I've thought about it a lot.'

'I'm sure you have. Let's hear it.'

'And it struck me that you might have walked in, having come back for something you'd forgotten, and heard Eve speaking on the phone. You listened and realized she was speaking to a man.' She stopped. 'Is this necessary?'

'Go on. I want to hear your theory.'

'It's only a conjecture. An explanation of why you could have become extremely violent.'

'I'm listening.'

The tension between us was so acute we were no longer in a prison visiting room. We might have been alone on another planet.

'Supposing, just supposing, you heard her saying something

192

like, "He's gone. He won't be back tonight. Let's meet." '

'Is that it? Is that the end of your suppositions?'

'Not quite. Supposing she had used his name. Supposing she had said, "Harry" or even "Harry, darling".'

She waited for my comment but the shock of her theory made me dumb.

'Harry Feldman,' she went on, 'the man she was reputedly seeing before you arrived in Aldeburgh, the man who, not to put too fine a point on it, you shopped. Supposing that is what happened. You could have seen red, rushed in, and in fury grabbed the knife.'

I recovered the use of my voice. 'If that's what you think happened, you'd better go.'

'It could have happened like that.'

'You obviously think I killed Eve. You'd better go.'

She stood up. 'All right. I will.' As she moved away she turned and said, 'I was only trying to help you. Strange as it may seem, I do care about you.'

And then she left and, not for the first time in my life, I knew the meaning of heartbreak.

4

One of the screws who had been discreetly observing us came across and said, 'You all right, mate?'

'Yes, thanks.'

'You don't look so good. Better go back and lie down. I'll take you.'

I was aware of curious glances following us as he escorted me from the room, an arm slipped through mine and keys gripped in his free hand.

Back in my cell I lay on the bed and tried desperately hard to reconstruct my movements on that fatal Saturday night. I could easily recall Eve's slender figure as she stood waving me off. I had wound down the car window and stuck out my arm to wave back until I turned the corner at the end of the street. I could vaguely remember driving down the High Street, or maybe I was confusing the scene with other times I'd driven down this street at night. My next clear memory was at the junction with the A12, some six miles from Aldeburgh. I'd been forced to brake suddenly and a car following too closely behind had bumped into the rear of my car. The other driver and I got out of our vehicles to inspect for damage but there was none. We had wished each other 'good-night' and gone on our ways. I could remember little else until I drove into the underground car-park beneath my block of flats. I had gone upstairs to my flat and, wondering what disorder and vandalism I would find, had entered to discover everything just as I had left it many weeks before.

Over and over again I went through the process of leaving Eve and arrival at my flat, twisting and torturing my brain to come up with something new. It was impossible. Try as I might, I couldn't recollect having returned to Fran's Pantry, nor could I think of what I might have returned for.

194

That evening before going to supper I went to the prison library to see if it contained any medical reference books. I didn't believe I'd suffered, or was suffering from, amnesia, but I wanted more precise knowledge of this condition. Apart from an ancient dog-eared edition of *Black's Medical Dictionary* which had nothing to offer on the subject there was a home medical encyclopaedia entitled *Your Family Doctor*. From this volume I learned that amnesia can follow after something terrible has occurred and the patient can't deal with the memory. Forgotten memories can sometimes be recalled when the patient feels secure or is under the care of a psychiatrist.

This didn't help much but it passed my mind that if – intolerable though the idea was – I had blotted out a dreadful memory, I could have driven from Aldeburgh to the A12 junction in a zombie-like state and only been shaken out of it when the minor accident took place.

That night, after lights out, I deliberately tried to imagine a sequence of events which would fit Fiona's theory. I pretended I'd left my shaving kit behind. Even though I had a duplicate kit at the flat, nevertheless I wanted to return to collect the kit I'd left at Fran's Pantry. Next, I imagined leaving the car with its engine running. No point in switching it off; I'd only be a few moments. I hurry to the front door and find it unlocked. I hurry through the restaurant area to the kitchen. Hearing Eve's voice I pause at the kitchen door. She is speaking on the phone and her back is to me. I hear her saying, 'It's all clear, Harry darling, he's gone away and won't be back until some time tomorrow. Can you come over for the night? I know it's late but . . .' I call out her name. She drops the phone and turns in horror. I rush towards her and grab the bread-knife . . .

It was no use. Not only did this feat of imagination ring no bells, strike no chords, or otherwise attune itself to my memory cells, it was downright nonsense. I would never have behaved like that. I dare say I'm not totally immune from feelings of jealousy but I know myself well enough to be sure that I would have smothered or otherwise kept under control such an emotion. I would either have waited until the phone call ended and then asked for an explanation or, just as likely, I would have made a quiet exit, driven to London and when there, telephoned Eve to say I'd overheard her conversation and wouldn't be returning to

195

Aldeburgh. She could pack up my belongings and send them by carrier, cash on delivery.

But this certainty about my behaviour didn't appease my restless mind. Could it be remotely possible, I wondered, that I was duping myself with a massive self-deception, and Fiona's theory was on the right lines?

For someone proud of his honesty such massive self-deceit was almost unthinkable. Deceit. There had been so much deceit, but it was always the deceit of others. During marriage there had been deceit – deceit forgiven, I might add – by Eve. Then there was the deceit of my partners, the deceit of fraud. And, since arrival at Aldeburgh, there had been an avalanche of deceits.

First, there was Eve's stupid deceit in pretending I was a former neighbour and not her ex-husband. This was a deceit which had directly led to the quarrel with Moira. There was Verity da Costa's deceit that my flat had been vandalized. Fiona had been deceived by her fiancé and had broken her engagement, but she, in turn, had deceived Dorothy by pretending she was looking for a holiday home. And, to be honest, hadn't I been guilty of self-deceit by telling myself for quite a long while that I wasn't in love with Fiona?

Were there any limits to deceit? In all human affairs it seemed to be measureless and uncontainable, and it was dangerous, never more so than when it was self-deceit. And yet, even after reaching this damning conclusion, I was utterly convinced I hadn't killed Eve, and this wasn't self-deceit. It was now more imperative than ever that I found out who actually had murdered her. My sense of purpose was restored and honed to a sharp cutting edge. If it took the rest of my life and all my money I'd hunt, corner, and in my present mood, kill.

Mentally exhausted, I fell into a deep sleep.

The days and weeks passed. I was visited by loyal to the flag Colonel Bamber and, after a space of nearly a month, by Fiona. I had written to her shortly after her visit, apologizing for any bad behaviour on my part and pleading with her to visit me again. I suggested that as she believed Dorothy's version of events, and I was equally certain I was guiltless, we should avoid the topic. It was time to move forward and draw a veil over the past.

Day after day I awaited a reply. It came twenty-three days after

196

her visit, a brief letter to say she'd been recalled to Frankfurt as her mother had suffered a massive stroke and in spite of life-support systems had died. She would visit me on her return to England.

She arrived on a day when windows were blurred with rain and every visitor carried a dripping umbrella. Fiona too carried an umbrella; it was as black as the topcoat and costume she was wearing. The meeting wasn't easy; we were both nervous and conversation limped. But it was wonderful to see her again. It was less wonderful for her, I think, because when it was time for her to leave she said, 'Mark, before I came here I made up my mind that I wouldn't abandon you but, on the other hand, I wouldn't come here very often.'

'How often?' I asked and my future trembled on the brink of her answer.

'Once a quarter,' she said.

'Then I shan't see you again until after Christmas, until the new year.'

'That's right.'

'Will you write to me?'

She considered the request, and she had what I thought of as her 'legal look'; the barrister weighing up the merits of a case.

'Do you want me to?' she asked at length.

'Of course I do!'

'Very well, I'll write but don't expect more than one letter a month, and it may be fairly short.' Her voice softened slightly. 'You must remember, I'm a busy woman, Mark.'

'I know.'

'And I do have a social life.'

'Once a month, then,' I said, clinging to her promise.

'Once a month.'

She offered her cheek for a kiss as we parted. This time I didn't need to be assisted back to my cell, although I was escorted. It was the same screw who remembered the previous occasion.

'You've got a nice little lady there,' he remarked, 'but she'd look better wearing something brighter. Black doesn't do a prisoner's morale no good.'

Over the next three years my morale fluctuated. It rose and dipped with Fiona's visits and departures. Her letters which

197

arrived on roughly the first of each month were treasured, read and reread. They were scanned for any scrap of increasing affection but there was little reward on this count. Mostly she spoke of cases in which she was involved with driblets of news about social life. All concluded, 'With love – Fiona.'

It was in a letter two months before I was due to be released on parole that she mentioned someone called Tristram. They had been to a fancy-dress ball together. She had gone as a French maid and he had been a Red Indian chief. The only comfort I extracted from this was that they had been incompatibly attired. Red Indians aren't noted for having romantic liaisons with French maids. Was I jealous? A little perhaps, and I wished she'd chosen something more conservative to wear.

It was on her very last visit, a week before my release, that I noticed she was wearing a band of gold on her finger.

When I'd brought her a cup of tea I asked, 'Have you been married, Fiona?'

'I guessed you'd notice it. Tristram and I were married a fortnight ago. We got back from the honeymoon yesterday.'

The bottom dropped out of my world. In an effort to be casual I said, 'You didn't tell me, but then, why should you?'

'I did think about it. I thought a lot. But in the end I decided it would be better if you knew when we met.'

I said it, something I should have said more often to Eve during our marriage. I said, 'You know I love you.'

She nodded her head. 'Yes, I do, and I'm flattered. If it's any consolation, Mark, for a while I think I was in love with you.'

'But what Dorothy said . . .'

'We won't go into that. What's important is that I do love Tristram and I do care about you, but not in the same way.'

I summoned up the guts to say, 'Is that it? Is this the end?'

'You'll be out next week, Mark. You'll be free, subject only to regular reporting and a clean sheet. My role as your visitor is over.'

'You mean – I shan't see you again?'

'I think it better not.'

I held on to self-respect by saying, 'In that case, thanks for all you've done, for your letters and visits. I shall never forget you.'

'And I shan't forget you,' she said. She glanced at her watch.

'I know I've only just arrived but after this I think it would be difficult, awkward, don't you? I'll stay if you like but maybe . . .'

'It would be better if you went?'

'Yes.'

She reached out and took my hand. For a couple of seconds we held hands. To my surprise I saw tears in her eyes. She withdrew her hand and stood up. 'Good luck, Mark,' she said, and she was on her way. I watched her. She didn't turn round even when the door was unlocked for her.

I returned to my cell. The future had almost arrived and it would be a future in which I would strive to clear my name.

There is little else to say except that my flat was in good order when I returned to it. I wondered whether my car would start, but it did. The battery had been kept charged.

I kept a tyre-pressure gauge in the glove-pocket on the dashboard and decided to check that the pressures were correct. I opened the pocket to get the gauge and the first thing I saw was a gold necklace with a crucifix attached.